1

The Little Colonel's Christmas Vacation

by Annie F. Johnston

Copyright © 8/13/2015
Jefferson Publication

ISBN-13: 978-1516888726

Printed in the United States of America

Contents

CHAPTER I..3
 WARWICK HALL 3
CHAPTER II..11
 "THE OLD GIRLS' WELCOME TO THE NEW" 11
CHAPTER III...21
 AN EXCURSION 21
CHAPTER IV...31
 "KEEP TRYST" 31
CHAPTER V...40
 A MEMORY-BOOK AND A SOUVENIR SPOON...............................40
CHAPTER VI..50
 CHRISTMAS CAROLS 50
CHAPTER VII...57
 HOMEWARD BOUND...57
CHAPTER VIII..65
 A PICNIC IN THE SNOW...65
CHAPTER IX...72
 A PROGRESSIVE CHRISTMAS PARTY 72
CHAPTER X..81
 THE DUNGEON OF DISAPPOINTMENT...81
CHAPTER XI...88
 IN THE ATTIC...88
CHAPTER XII..96
 HUMDRUM DAYS...96
CHAPTER XIII...104
 IN THE FOOTSTEPS OF AMANTHIS..104
CHAPTER XIV...111
 "CINDERELLA" 111
CHAPTER XV..118
 A HARD-EARNED PEARL..118
CHAPTER XVI...127
 "SWEET SIXTEEN" 127
 THE END...135

CHAPTER I.

WARWICK HALL

Warwick Hall looked more like an old English castle than a modern boarding-school for girls. Gazing at its high towers and massive portal, one almost expected to see some velvet-clad page or lady-in-waiting come down the many flights of marble steps leading between stately terraces to the river. Even a knight with a gerfalcon on his wrist would not have seemed out of place, and if a slow-going barge had trailed by between the willow-fringed banks of the Potomac, it would have seemed more in keeping with the scene than the steamboats puffing past to Mount Vernon, with crowds of excursionists on deck.

The gorgeous peacocks strutting along the terraces in the sun were partly responsible for this impression of mediæval grandeur. It was for that very purpose that Madam Chartley, the head of the school, kept the peacocks. That was one reason, also, that she proudly retained the coat of arms in the great stained glass window over the stairs, when circumstances obliged her to turn her ancestral home into a boarding-school. She thought a sense of mediæval grandeur was good for girls, especially young American girls, who are apt to be brought up without proper respect for age, either of individuals or institutions.

In the dining-room, two long lines of portraits looked down from opposite walls. One was headed by a grim old earl, and the other by an equally grim old Pilgrim father of *Mayflower* fame. The two lines joined over the fireplace in the portraits of Madam Chartley's great-grandparents. It was for this great-grandmother, a daughter of the Pilgrims and a beautiful Washington belle, that Warwick Hall had been built; for she refused to give up her native land entirely, even for the son of an earl.

At his death, when the title and the English estates were inherited by a distant cousin, the only male heir, this place on the Potomac was all that was left to her and her daughter. It had been closed for two generations. Now it had come down at last to Madam Chartley. Although it found her too poor to keep up such an establishment, it also found her too proud to let her heritage go to strangers, and practical enough to find some way by which she might retain it comfortably. That way was to turn it into a first-class boarding-school. She was a graduate of one of the best American colleges. The patrician standards inherited from her old world ancestors, combined with the energy and common sense of the new, made her an ideal woman to undertake the education of young girls, and Warwick Hall was an ideal place in which to carry out her wise theories.

The Potomac was red with the glow of the sunset one September evening, when four girls, on their way back to Washington after a day's sightseeing, hurried to the upper deck of the steamboat. Some one had called out that Warwick Hall was in sight. In their haste to reach the railing, they scarcely noticed a tall girl in blue, already standing there, who obligingly moved along to make room for them.

She scrutinized them closely, however, for she had seen them in the cabin a little while before, and their conversation had been so amusing that she longed to make their acquaintance. Her face brightened expectantly at their approach, and, as they leaned over the railing, she studied them with growing interest. The oldest one was near her own age, she decided after a careful survey, about seventeen; and they were all particular about the little things that count so much with fastidious schoolgirls. She approved of each one of them from their broad silk shoe-laces to the pink tips of their carefully manicured finger-nails.

As the boat swung around a bend in the river, bringing the castle-like building into full view, a chorus of delighted exclamations broke out all along the deck. The four girls hung over the railing with eager faces.

"Look, Lloyd, look!" cried one of them, excitedly. "Peacocks on the terraces! It's the finishing touch to the picture. We'll feel like Lady Clare walking down those marble steps. There surely must be a milk-white doe somewhere in the background."

"Oh, Betty, Betty!" was the laughing answer. "You'll do nothing now but quote Tennyson and write poetry from mawning till night."

"They're from Kentucky," thought the girl in blue. "I'm sure of it from the way they talk."

As the boat glided slowly along, Lloyd threw her arm around the girl beside her, with an impulsive squeeze.

"Kitty Walton," she exclaimed, "aren't you *glad* that the old Lloydsboro Seminary burned down? If it hadn't, we wouldn't be on ouah way now to that heavenly-looking boahding-school!"

The sudden hug loosened Kitty's hat, held insecurely by one pin, and in another instant the strong breeze would have carried it over into the river had not the girl in blue caught it as it swept past her. She handed it back with a friendly smile, glad of an opportunity to speak.

"You are new pupils for Warwick Hall, aren't you?" she asked, when Kitty had laughingly thanked her. "I hope so, for I'm one of the old girls. This will be my third year."

"How perfectly lovely!" exclaimed Kitty. "We've been fairly crazy to meet some one from there. Do tell us if it is as fine as it looks, and as the catalogue says."

"It is the very nicest place in the world," was the enthusiastic reply. "There are hardly any rules, and none of them are the kind that rub you up the wrong way. We don't have to wear uniforms, and we're not marched out to walk in wholesale lots like prisoners in a chain-gang."

"That's what I used to despise at the Seminary," interrupted Lloyd. "I always felt like pah't of a circus parade, or an inmate of some asylum, out for an airing. Keeping in step and keeping in line with a lot of othahs made a punishment out of the walk, when it would have been such a pleasuah if we could have skipped along as we pleased. I felt resentful from the moment the gong rang for us to stah't. It had such a bossy, tyrannical sawt of sound."

"You'll not find it that way at Warwick Hall," was the emphatic answer. "There are bells for rising and chapel and meals, but the signal for exercise is a hunter's horn, blown on the upper terrace. There's something so breezy and out-of-doors in the sound that it is almost as irresistible a call as the Pied Piper of Hamelin's. You ought to see the doors fly open along the corridors, and the girls pour out when that horn blows. We can go in twos or threes or squads, any way we please, and in any direction, so long as we keep inside the grounds. There's an orchard to stroll through, and a wooded hillside, and a big meadow. On bad days there is over half a mile of gravel road that runs through the grounds to the trolley station, or we can take our exercise going round and round the garden walks. The garden is over there at the left of the Hall," she explained, waving her hand toward it. "Do you see that pergola stretching along the highest terrace? That is where the garden begins, and the ivy running over it was started from a slip that Madam Chartley brought from Sir Walter Scott's home at Abbotsford.

"It is the stateliest old garden you ever saw, and the pride of the school. There's a sun-dial in it, and hollyhocks from Ann Hathaway's cottage, and rhododendrons from Killarney. There's all the flowers mentioned in the old songs. Madam has brought slips and roots and seeds from all sorts of places, so that nearly every plant is connected with some noted place or person. I simply love it. In warm weather I get up early in the morning, and study my Latin out in the honeysuckle arbour. Latin is my hardest study, but it doesn't seem half so hard out there among the bees and hummingbirds, where it's all so sweet and still."

"Oh, will they let you do things like that?" came the same amazed question from all four at once.

"You wait and see," was the encouraging reply. "That isn't the beginning."

The four exchanged ecstatic glances.

"Oh, we haven't introduced ourselves," exclaimed Kitty, bethinking herself of formalities. "I am Katherine Walton, and this is my big sister, Allison. That is Lloyd Sherman and Elizabeth Lewis. They're almost as good as sisters, for they live together, and Lloyd's mother is Betty's godmother. And we're all from the same place, Lloydsboro Valley, Kentucky."

"And I am Juliet Lynn from Wisconsin. That is, I lived there till papa had to come to Washington. He's a Congressman now. I was sure that you were from Kentucky, and I've been hoping that you were new girls for the Hall ever since I heard you talking about some house-party where you all did such funny things."

"Oh, yes, that was one we had this summer at The Beeches," began Kitty, glibly, "when we all took turns—"

But, with a big-sister frown of warning, Allison said, in a low aside: "For pity's sake, don't stop to tell all that long rigmarole over *now*. We want to hear some more about the school."

"What is Madam Chartley herself like?" she asked, turning to Juliet. "She must be something of an old dragon if she can keep forty girls straight with so few rules. We've pictured her as a big British matron, dignified and imposing,—a sort of lioness rampant, you know, with a stern air, as if she was about to say in a deep voice, 'England—expects—every—man—to—do—his—duty,—sir!'"

"But she isn't that way at all!" cried Juliet, almost indignantly. "She's just as American as you are, for she was born and educated in this country. She has the gentlest voice and sweetest manner. Her hair is snow-white, and there's something awfully aristocratic about her, for she is—sort of—well, I hardly know how to express it, but just what you'd expect the 'daughter of a hundred earls' to be, you know. But you won't feel one bit in awe of her. The girls simply adore her."

"But isn't she something to be afraid of when you break the rules?" queried Kitty, anxiously. "When you have midnight feasts and pillow-case prowls and all that?"

Juliet shook her head. "We don't do those things. I tell you it isn't like any other boarding-school you ever heard of."

"Then I know I sha'n't like it," declared Kitty. "All my life I've looked forward to going off to school just for the jolly good times I'd have. You see we were only day-pupils at Lloydsboro Seminary, and there wasn't a chance for that kind of fun, except the one term when Lloyd and Betty boarded in the school while their family was away from home. We managed to stir up a little excitement then, and I'd hoped for all sorts of thrilling adventures here. I'm horribly disappointed that it's so tame and goody-goody."

Juliet's face coloured resentfully. "It isn't tame at all!" she declared. "It's only that we are always so busy doing pleasant things and going to interesting places that nobody cares for stolen spreads. Some girls don't like the place just at first, because it's so different from what they've been used to. But by the end of the term they're so in love with Warwick Hall and everything about it that nothing could induce them to change schools. There's only one girl I ever heard of who didn't like it."

"And why didn't she?" asked Lloyd and Allison, in the same breath.

"Well, she came from some ranch away out West, Wyoming or Nevada or some of those places, where she'd been as free and easy as a squaw, and she couldn't stand so much civilization. You see, from the minute you enter Warwick Hall you feel somehow that you're a guest of Madam Chartley's instead of a pupil. She uses the old family silver and the china has her great-grandfather's crest on it, and she brought over a London butler who grew up in the family service. She keeps him for the same reason that she keeps the peacocks, I suppose. They give such a grand air to the place.

"Lida Wilsy—that's the girl from the ranch—couldn't live up to so much stateliness, especially of the stony-eyed butler. Hawkins was too much for her. She told her roommate that she thought it was foolish to have so many forks and spoons at each place. One was enough for anybody to get through a dinner with. Life was too short for so much fuss and feathers. She never could learn which to use first, and she would get her silverware so hopelessly mixed up that by the time dessert was brought on maybe she would have nothing to eat it with but an oyster fork. I've seen her ready to go under the table from embarrassment. Not that she cared so much what the girls thought. She joked about it to them. Her father owned the biggest part of a silver mine, and they could have had Tiffany's whole stock of forks if they'd wanted them. It was Hawkins she was afraid of. Of course he was too well trained to show what he thought of her mistakes, but you couldn't help feeling his high and mighty inward scorn of such ignorance. It fairly oozed from his finger-tips."

Kitty's black eyes sparkled, anticipating times ahead when she would certainly make it lively for Hawkins.

"There's grandfathah!" cried Lloyd, catching sight of a white-haired old gentleman who had just come up on deck. "I want to tell him about the garden before we lose sight of it."

Juliet's glance followed her with interest as she darted away, for it was a distinguished-looking old gentleman who lifted his hat with elaborate courtesy at her approach. He was dressed in white duck, and the right coat-sleeve hung empty.

"It's Colonel Lloyd," explained Allison, noting Juliet's glance of curiosity. "He's bringing us all to school, for it wasn't convenient for mother or Mrs. Sherman to come."

"They don't look alike," remarked Juliet, surveying them with a puzzled expression. "But what is it about them—there is such a startling resemblance?"

"Everybody notices it," said Kitty. "When Lloyd was smaller, they used to call her the Little Colonel all the time, but especially when she was in a temper. They call her Princess now."

"Princess," echoed Juliet. "That name suits her exactly."

She cast another admiring glance at the slender, fair-haired girl, standing with her hand in her grandfather's arm, pointing out the beauties of the place they were slowly passing.

"And she will suit Warwick Hall," she added, with a sudden burst of schoolgirl enthusiasm, "just as the peacocks suit it, and the coat of arms, and Madam Chartley herself. She's got that same 'daughter-of-a-hundred-earls' air about her that Madam has."

"Oh, it all sounds so delightful and fascinating," sighed Betty, pushing back the brown hair that blew in little curls about her face, and smiling at the slowly disappearing Hall with a happy light in her brown eyes. "I can hardly wait for to-morrow."

The boat had glided on until only the high, square tower was left in view, with the red sunset glow upon it.

"'The splendour falls on castle walls
And snowy summits old in story'"—

Betty sang half under her breath, with a farewell flutter of her handkerchief, as the boat rounded a bend in the river which hid the tower from sight. Already she was in love with the place, and already, as Lloyd had predicted, she was fitting some line of Tennyson to it at every turn.

Acquaintance progressed rapidly in the next half-hour. Long before they reached Washington, Juliet knew, not only that she had guessed Allison's age correctly at seventeen, that Betty was sixteen, and Lloyd and Kitty a year younger, but that each girl in her own way would make a desirable friend. Incidentally she learned that Allison and Kitty had lived in the Philippines, and were daughters of the brave General Walton who had lost his life there in his country's service. When they parted at the boat-landing, it was with delightful anticipations of the next day, and with each one eager to renew an acquaintance so pleasantly begun.

If Warwick Hall suggested ancient stateliness on the outside, it was informal and frivolous enough within, when forty girls were taking possession of their rooms on the opening day of the school year. In and out like a flock of twittering sparrows, the old pupils darted from one room to another, exchanging calls and greetings, laughing over old jokes and reminiscences, and settling down into familiar corners with an ease that the new girls envied.

Juliet Lynn, quickly establishing herself in her last year's quarters, started down the corridor to announce at every door that she was the first one unpacked and settled. All the other rooms were in hopeless confusion, beds, chairs, and floors being piled with the contents of open trunks.

At the first door where she paused, a shower of shoes and slippers was the only answer to her triumphant announcement. At the next a laughing cry of "Help! help!" greeted her. At the third she was informed that there was standing-room only.

"Don't you believe it, Juliet!" called a gay voice from the chiffonier, where an earlier visitor was perched. "There's always room at the top. I've discovered where Min keeps her butter-scotch. Come in and have some."

"No, I'm going the rounds to see what everybody is about," she answered. "You're all in such a mess now, I'd rather look in later. I'm one of the early settlers, and have been in order for ages."

"What's the odds so long as you're happy?" called the girl on the chiffonier. "Besides, it's no better next door. They'll invite you to make yourself at home under the bed, as they did me. Come on back and tell us your summer's experiences. Min has had one dizzy whirl of adventures after another."

But Juliet kept on down the hall. She wanted to find what rooms had been assigned to the girls whom she had met the day before on the boat, and to hear their first impressions of Warwick Hall. Presently, through a half-open door, she caught sight of Betty, sitting at an open window overlooking the river. With chin in hand and elbows resting on the sill, she was gazing dreamily out at the willow-fringed banks, so absorbed in her thoughts that she did not hear Juliet's first knock. But at the second she started up and called cordially: "Oh, I'm so glad to see you! Come in!"

"Why, you're all unpacked and put away, too!" exclaimed Juliet, in surprise, looking around the orderly room. "I thought that I was the only one, but I see you've even hung your pictures."

"Yes, we don't know any of the other girls yet, so we didn't lose any time running back and forth to their rooms, as everybody else is doing. We've been through ever so long. Lloyd is out exploring the grounds with Allison, but I was too tired after all the sightseeing we have done. I'd be glad not to stir out of my room for a week."

She pushed a rocking-chair hospitably toward her guest, and leaned back in the opposite one.

"I don't want to sit down," said Juliet. "I'm just exploring. I think it's so much fun to poke around the first day and see how everybody is fixed. You don't mind, do you, if I walk around and look at your pictures?"

"No, indeed!" answered Betty, cordially. "Help yourself."

Catching a glimpse of herself in the mirror, she sat up straight in her chair, and adjusted the side-combs which were slipping out of her curly hair. It was a pleasing reflection that the mirror showed her, of a slim girl in a linen shirt-waist and a dark brown skirt just reaching to her ankles. But it held her gaze only long enough for her to see that her belt was properly pulled down and her stock all that could be desired. The friendly brown eyes and the trusting little mouth never needed readjustment. They always met the world with a smile, and thus far the world had always smiled back at them.

"Last year," said Juliet, as she wandered around, "the girl who had this room simply plastered the walls with posters. It was so sporty-looking. She had hunting scenes between these windows, and there was a frieze of hounds and a yard of puppies where you have that panel of photographs. Oh, what perfectly beautiful places!" she cried, moving nearer. "Do tell me about them. Is that where you live?"

"Yes, this is our Lloydsboro Valley corner—the Happy Valley we call it," answered Betty, crossing the room to point out the various places: "Locust," her home and Lloyd's, a stately white-pillared mansion at the end of a long locust avenue; "The Beeches," where the Waltons lived; the vine-covered stone church; the old mill; the post-office, and a row of snap shots showing Lloyd and her mounted on their ponies, Tarbaby and Lad.

"What good times you must have there!" sighed Juliet, presently.

Betty opened a drawer in the writing-desk and took out six little books, bound in white kid, her initials stamped in gold on each cover.

"Just see how many!" she exclaimed. "I started to keep a record of all my good times when I went to Lloyd's first house-party. When godmother gave me this volume, number one, I thought it would take a lifetime to fill it, but so many lovely things happened that summer that it was full in a little while. Then I went abroad in the fall, and that trip filled a volume. Now I am beginning the seventh."

Juliet stared at the pile of white books in amazement. "What a lot of work!" she cried. "Doesn't it take every bit of pleasure out of your good times, thinking that you'll have to write all about it afterward? I tried to keep a diary once, but it looked more like the report of a weather bureau than anything else, and my small brother got hold of it and mortified me nearly to death one night when we had company, by quoting something from it. It sounded dreadfully sentimental, although it hadn't seemed so when I wrote it. That's the trouble in keeping a journal, don't you think so? You'll often put down something that seems important at the time, but that sounds silly afterward."

"No," said Betty, hesitatingly. "I always enjoy going back to read the first volumes. It's interesting to see how one changes from year to year in opinions as well as handwriting. See how little and cramped the letters are in this first volume. It's good exercise, and, as I expect to write a book some day, every bit of practice helps."

Betty made the announcement as simply as if she had said she intended to darn a stocking some day, and Juliet looked at her in open-mouthed wonder. She had never encountered a girl of that species before, and more than ever she felt that her friendship would be worth cultivating. When she finally took her departure, there was no time for any further tour of inspection, but she ran into several rooms on the way back to her own to say, hastily: "Girls, do all you can to get that Kentucky quartette into our sorority! I'll tell you about them later. We must give them a grand rush to-morrow night at the old girls' welcome to the new. I hope I'll get to take Elizabeth Lewis. My *dears*, she's a perfect genius! She's written poems and plays that have been published, and she's at work on a *book!*"

As Juliet closed the door behind her, Betty took up the new volume in the series of little white records, and began turning the blank pages. Like the new school year, it lay spread out before her, white and fair, hers to write therein as she chose.

"And I'll try my hardest to make it the best and happiest record of them all," she said to herself. As she dipped her pen into the ink, there was a knock at the door, and a white-capped maid looked in.

"Madam Chartley would be pleased to see you at once in the pink room, miss," she announced, and Betty, much surprised, rose to answer the unexpected summons.

CHAPTER II.

"THE OLD GIRLS' WELCOME TO THE NEW"

As Betty opened the door, she ran into Kitty Walton, who at sight of her struck an attitude on the threshold, crossing her hands on her breast, and rolling her eyes upward until only the whites were visible.

"What new pose is this, you goose?" laughed Betty, shaking her gently by one shoulder.

"Don't laugh," was the solemn answer. "This is pious resignation to fate." Then her hands dropped and she turned to Betty tragically.

"I've just come from an interview with Madam Chartley," she explained. "And what do you think? That blessed old soul expects me to live up to the motto on her teacups! But how can I give Hawkins his just due *if* I do? I had the loveliest things planned for his tormenting, but I'd be ashamed to look her in the face if she ever found me out after this interview.

"Oh, Betty, I don't want to renounce the world and the flesh and all the other bad things this early in the term, but I'm afraid that I've already done it. She's laid a spell on all of us."

"Has she sent for Lloyd and Allison, too?"

"Yes, Allison was the first victim. She came back in a regular dare-to-be-a-Daniel mood, and announced that she intended to start in, heart and soul, for the studio honours this year. Then Lloyd had her turn, and she came back looking like Joan of Arc when she'd been listening to the voices. I vowed she shouldn't have that effect on me, but here I am, perfectly docile as you see, fangs drawn and claws cut. I tremble for the effect on you, sweet innocent. Your wings will sprout before you get back."

Betty laughed and hurried past her down the stairs. Evidently it was Madam's custom to make the acquaintance of her new girls in this way, one at a time. Only fifteen freshmen were admitted each year, so it was possible for her to take a personal interest in every pupil.

Betty's heart fluttered expectantly as she paused an instant in the door of the pink room. Madam Chartley had looked very imposing and dignified as she presided at the lunch-table that noon, with the stately Hawkins behind her chair and the stately portraits looking down from the walls.

She looked now as if she might be the original of one of these old portraits herself, as she sat there in the high-backed chair, with the griffins carved on its teakwood frame. Her gray gown trailed around her in graceful folds. There was a soft fall of lace at wrists and throat, and her white hair had a sheen like silver against the pink brocade with which the chair was upholstered.

With a smile which seemed to take Betty straight into her confidence, she held out her hand and drew her to a seat beside her. An old-fashioned silver tea-service stood on a table at her elbow, and when the maid had brought hot water, she busied herself in filling a cup for Betty.

"There!" she said, as she passed it to her. "There's nothing like a cozy chat over a cup of tea for warming acquaintances into friends."

Betty wondered, as she took a proffered slice of lemon, if Madam began all her interviews in this way, and if she was to hear the same little sermon about the crest on the ancestral teacups that Kitty had heard. It certainly was an interesting crest. She lifted the fragile bit of china for a closer survey. A mailed arm, rising out of a heart, clasped a spear in its hand, and under it ran the motto, "I keep tryst."

"MADAM'S CONVERSATION LED FAR AWAY FROM THE CREST AND ITS LESSON"

But Madam's conversation led far away from the crest and its lesson. At first it was about a quaint old English inn, where is served delicious toasted scones with five o'clock tea. When she mentioned that, it was as if they had discovered a mutual friend, for Betty cried out joyfully that she had been there, and had spent a long rainy afternoon in one of its rooms, where Scott had written many chapters of "Kenilworth." Betty remembered afterward that not a word was said about school and its obligations. It was of the Old Curiosity Shop they spoke, and the House of Seven Gables. Madam promised to show her the autographs of Dickens and Hawthorne, which she had in her collection, and a pen which had once belonged to George Eliot.

Then Betty found that Madam had known Miss Alcott, and, before she realized what she was doing, she had thrown herself down impulsively on the stool at her feet, and, with both hands clasping the griffin's head on the arm of the high-backed chair, was asking a dozen eager questions about "Little Women" and the author who had been her first inspiration to write.

Nearly an hour later, when she went back to her room, it was with something singing in her heart that made her very solemn and very happy. It was the immortal music of the Choir Invisible. She had been in the unseen company of earth's best and noblest, and felt in her soul that some day she, too, would have a right to be counted in that chorus, having done something really great and worth while.

That evening after dinner Kitty bounced into the room where Allison sat talking with Lloyd and Betty during recreation hour.

"To-morrow night there's to be the Old Girls' Welcome to the New!" she cried. "Come on in, Juliet, and tell them about it."

Juliet thrust her head through the half-open door.

"Haven't time to stop," she answered, "but I'll tell this much. It's the first of the great social functions. Everybody wears her party clothes and a sweet smile. It's the first lesson of the year in How to attain Ease under New and Exacting Conditions. No matter how the seniors snub you later on, in order to teach you your proper place, you'll all be birds of a feather that one time, and flock together as peaceably as pet hens.

"Each new girl has an escort appointed by the entertaining committee, who sends her flowers and calls for her and sees that her programme is filled. So there are never any wallflowers the first night. No, Allison, it isn't a dance. The programmes are for progressive conversation. Somewhere in the background there's a piano playing waltzes and two-steps, and so forth, but you talk out the numbers instead of dancing them. Changing partners so often keeps you from getting bored, and strangers can tell who is talking to them, for there are the names on their programmes. You can refer to that when anybody comes up to claim you. I'm to take Lloyd, and Sybil Green is to take Kitty. I haven't found out the other assignments yet. I'll let you know as soon as I do. Continued in our next."

With an airy wave of the hand she withdrew, leaving them to an animated discussion of what to wear.

"You must remember that this isn't the only time you're to appear in public, Katherine Walton," said Allison, severely, when Kitty proposed her best array. "There's to be a reception at the White House next week, and Friday night we're to go in to Washington to see Jefferson in 'Rip Van Winkle,' and there's to be a studio tea soon, and a recital, and all sorts of things. I saw the bulletin of the term's entertainments in the hall this evening."

"*We*'ll never be seen at those things," insisted Kitty.

"We'll scarcely be a drop in the bucket. But to-morrow night, isn't the whole affair for us? We'll be the whole show. We'll be *it*, Allison, and 'it's my night to howl.' I intend to wear my rose-pink mull and a rosebud in my raving tresses, and carry the gorgeous spangled fan that the dear old admiral gave me in Manila. So there!"

"Then don't come near me," said Allison, with a warning shake of her head, "for I am going to wear my cerise crêpe de chine. It's lovely by itself, but by the side of anything the shade of your pink mull it's the most hideous, sickly colour you ever saw. I *wish* you'd wear that pale green dress, Kitty. You look sweet in that, and it goes so well with mine."

"But, my dear sister," laughed Kitty, "I don't expect to spend any time getting acquainted with *you*. I'll probably not be near you the whole evening. It's not expected that, just because we are from Kentucky, we have to pose as those two devoted creatures on the State seal,—stand around with our hands clasped, exclaiming 'United we stand, divided we fall!' to every one that comes up."

"Nevah mind, Allison," said Lloyd, laughing at Kitty's dramatic gestures and her sister's worried expression. "I'll play 'State seal' with you. I have a pale green almost the shade of Kitty's, and I'll wear the coral clasps and chains that were Papa Jack's mothah's. He gave them to me just before I left home. I'll show them to you."

She began to rummage through her trunk. Betty sat looking at the ceiling, trying to decide the momentous question of dress for herself. Finally she announced: "I'll just wear white, then I'll harmonize with everybody, and can run up to the first one of you I happen to see when I need a spark of courage. I know I'll be terribly embarrassed. It makes me cold right now to think of meeting so many strangers."

But Betty's courage needed no reinforcing next evening, when Maria Overlin, one of the seniors, took her in charge. The reception took place in what had been the ballroom, in the days when Warwick Hall was noted for its brilliant entertainments. Even its first hostess could not have received her distinguished guests with courtlier grace than Madam Chartley received her pupils, when, to the music of a stately minuet, they filed past her down the long line of teachers.

For once, each of the new girls, no matter how timid or inexperienced in social ways, tasted the sweets of popularity, and the four whom Juliet Lynn had dubbed the Kentucky quartette were overwhelmed with attentions.

Juliet, who had hoped to escort Betty, was glad that Lloyd had fallen to her lot when she saw what an admiring little court flocked around her wherever she turned. In the pale green dress, with its clasps of pink coral carved in the shape of tiny butterflies, she looked more princess-like than ever. She wore a bracelet of the coral butterflies also, and a slender circlet of them about her throat. They gave a soft pink flush to her cheeks.

No sooner had she passed the receiving line than she was surrounded by a group of white-gowned girls clamouring for an introduction and a place on her programme.

"Whose initials are these?" she whispered to Juliet presently when the card was all filled and there were still several girls asking to be allowed to write their names on it.

"Couldn't I give Miss Bartlett this line where there's nothing but G. M. scrawled on it?"

"Mercy, no!" exclaimed Juliet. "That's for Gabrielle Melville. It would never do for you two to miss each other to-night. I put them down for her, as she's to play later in the evening on the violin, you know, and I knew she'd never get here in time to do it herself. She always has such frantic times dressing. Just struggles into her things, never can find half her clothes, and what she does manage to fall into catches and rips in the struggle. Her hat is always over one ear, and her belts never make connection in the back, but she's so adorable that nobody minds her wild toilets. They laugh and say, 'Oh, it's just Gay.' That's her nickname, you know. Here's Emily Chapman coming to claim you. Emily, you can tell Lloyd some things about Gay, can't you?"

"I rather think so," laughed Emily. "We roomed together last year, and I got her again this term. It took a fight, though, for she's the most popular girl in school."

"Is she pretty?" asked Lloyd.

"We think so, don't we, Juliet? If she had any enemies, they might say that she has red hair and a pug nose. But that would be exaggerating. Her hair is that beautiful bronzy auburn that crinkles around her face and blows in her eyes till she always seems to be bringing a breeze with her."

"And her nose isn't pug exactly," chimed in Juliet. "There's just a darling, saucy little tip to it, that seems to suit her. She wouldn't be half as pretty with the approved Gibson girl kind, no matter how perfect it was."

"And her complexion is so lovely," Emily resumed, enthusiastically. "And her eyes are a jolly, laughing kind of brown, with an amber sparkle in them, except when she gets into one of her intense, serious moods. Then they are almost black, they're so deep and velvety. She's never twice in the same mood. Oh! There she comes now."

A side door opened, and a slim little thing all in white, with a violin under her arm and a distracted pucker on her face, hurried up to the piano. Nervously feeling her belt to make sure that she was presentable before turning her back on the audience, she whispered to the girl who was to play her accompaniments, and began tuning the violin. Then, tucking it under her chin as if she loved it, she listened an instant to the piano prelude, and drew her bow softly across the strings.

"Good!" whispered Emily. "It's that Mexican swallow song. She always has such a rapt expression on her face when she plays that. She makes me think of St. Cecilia. She's so earnest in all she does. If it's no more than making fudge, she throws her whole soul into it, just that way. She's as intense as if the fate of a nation depended on whatever she happens to be doing."

As Lloyd joined loudly in the applause which followed the performance, another girl came up to claim her attention. It was Myra Carr, the senior who had taken Allison under her wing.

"Doesn't Gay play splendidly?" she exclaimed, not knowing that she had been the previous topic of conversation. "We think she's a genius. She improvises little things sometimes in the twilight that are so sweet and sad they make you cry. Then she's unconventional enough to be a genius. She's always shocking people without meaning to, and so careless, she'd lose her head if nature hadn't attended to the fastenings.

"We all love her dearly, but we vowed the last time we went sightseeing that she should never go with us again unless she let us tie her up in a bag, so that nothing could drop out by the way. First she lost her hat. It blew off the trolley-car, one of those 'seeing Washington' affairs, you know. She had to go bareheaded all the rest of the way. Then she lost her pocketbook, and such a time as we had hunting that. The time before, she lost a locket that had been a family heirloom, and we missed our train and got caught in a shower looking for it."

"Where does she live?" asked Lloyd, watching the bright face that was making its way toward them across the crowded room.

"At Fort Sam Houston, down in San Antonio. Her father is an army officer at that post."

There was no time for further discussion, for Gabrielle was coming toward her with outstretched hand.

"This is Juliet's Princess, isn't it?" she asked, with a smile that captivated Lloyd at once, flashing over the whitest of little teeth. "You're getting all sorts of titles to-night. I heard a girl speak of you as a mermaid in that pale sea-green gown and corals, but I've come over here on purpose to call you the 'Little Colonel.' You don't know how much good it does me to hear a military title once more. Out at the fort it's all majors and captains and such things."

Then, dropping her grown-up society manner, she suddenly giggled, turning to include Emily in the conversation.

"Oh, girls, I had the worst time getting dressed this evening that I ever had in my life. When I unpacked my trunk yesterday, everything was so wrinkled that there was only one dress I could wear without having it pressed; this white one. So I laid it out, but, when I went to put it on to-night, I found that mamma had made a mistake in packing, and put in Lucy's skirt instead. Lucy is my older sister," she explained to Lloyd. "We each had a dotted Swiss this summer, made exactly alike, but Lucy is so much taller than I that her skirts trail on me. Just look how imposing!"

She swept across the floor and back to show the effect of her trail.

"Of course there was nothing to do at that late hour but pin it up in front and go ahead. I'm afraid every minute that I'll trip and fall all over myself, but I do feel so dignified when I feel my train sweeping along behind me. The pins keep falling out all around the belt, and I can't help stepping on the hem in front. I love trains," she added, switching hers forward with a grand air that was so childlike in its enjoyment that Lloyd felt impelled to hug her. "It gives you such a dressed-up, peacocky feeling."

Then she looked up in her most soulful, intense way, as if she were asking for important information. "Do you know whether it's true or not? *Does* a peacock stop strutting if it happens to see its feet? My old nurse told me that, and said that it shows that pride always goes before a fall. I never was where they kept peacocks before I came to Warwick Hall, and I've spent hours watching

Madam's to see if it is true. But they are always so busy strutting, I've never been able to catch them looking at their feet."

She glanced at her own feet as she spoke, then gasped and, covering her face with her hands, sank limply into a chair in the corner behind her.

"What's the matter?" cried Juliet, alarmed by the sudden change.

"Look! Oh, just *look!*" was the hysterical answer, as she thrust out both feet, and sat pointing at them tragically, with fingers and thumbs of both hands outspread.

"No wonder they felt queer. I was so intent on getting my dress pinned up, and in rushing out in time to play, that I couldn't take time to analyze my feelings and discover the cause of the queerness. Madeline blew in at a critical point to borrow a pin, and that threw me off, I suppose."

From under the white skirt protruded two feet as unlike as could well be imagined. One was cased in dainty white kid, the other in an old red felt bedroom slipper, edged with black fur.

"And it would have been all the same," sighed Gay, "if I had been going to an inaugural ball to hobnob with crowned heads. And I had hoped to make *such* a fine impression on the Little Colonel," she added, in a plaintive tone, with a childlike lifting of the face that Lloyd thought most charming.

If the mistake had been made by any other girl in the school, it would not have seemed half so ridiculous, but whatever Gay did was irresistibly funny. A laughing crowd gathered around her, as she sat with the red slipper and the white one stretched stiffly out in front of her, bewailing her fate.

"Anyhow," she remarked, "I'll always have the satisfaction of knowing that I put my best foot foremost, and if they had been alike I couldn't have done that. Now could I?" And the girls laughed again, because it was Gay who said it in her own inimitable way, and because the old felt slipper looked so ridiculous thrust out from under the dainty white gown. As others came crowding up to see what was causing so much merriment in that particular corner, Gay attempted to slip out and go to her room to correct her mistake. But Sybil Green, pushing through the outer ring, came up with Allison and Kitty.

"Gay," she began, "here are the girls that you especially wanted to meet: General Walton's daughters."

Gay's face flushed with pleasure, and, forgetting her errand, she impulsively stretched out a hand to each, and held them while she talked.

"Oh, I'm so glad to meet you!" she cried. "I wish that I had known that you girls were here yesterday before papa left. He is Major Melville, and he was such a friend of your father's. He was on that long Indian campaign with him in Arizona, and I've heard him talk of him by the hour. And last week"—here she lowered her voice so that only Allison and Kitty heard, and were thrilled by the sweet seriousness of it. "Last week he took me out to Arlington to carry a great wreath of laurel. When he'd laid it on the grave, he stood there with bared head, looking all around, and I heard him say, in a whisper, 'No one in all Arlington has won his laurels more bravely than you, my captain.' You see it was as a captain that papa knew him best. He would have been so pleased to have seen you girls."

Kitty squeezed the hand that still held hers and answered, warmly: "Oh, you dear, I hope we'll be as good friends as our fathers were!" And Allison answered, winking back the tears that had sprung to her eyes: "Thank you for telling us about the laurel. Mother will appreciate it so much."

While this conversation was going on at Lloyd's elbow, Betty came up to her on the other side. "Please see if my dress is all right in the back," she whispered. "It feels as if it were unfastened." Then, as Lloyd assured her it was properly buttoned, she added, in an undertone: "Have you met Maud Minor? She's one of the new girls."

Lloyd shook her head.

"Then I'm going to introduce you as soon as I can. She knows Malcolm MacIntyre."

"Knows Malcolm!" exclaimed Lloyd, in amazement. "Where on earth did she ever meet him?"

"At the seashore last summer. She can't talk about anything else. She thinks he is so handsome and has such beautiful manners and is so adorably romantic. Those are her very words. She has his picture. Evidently he has talked to her about you, for she's so curious to know you. She asked a string of questions that I thought were almost impertinent."

"Where is she?" asked Lloyd.

"There, that girl in white crossing the room with the fat one in lavender."

Lloyd gave a long, critical look, and then said, slowly: "She's the prettiest girl in the room, and she makes me think of something I've read, but I can't recall it."

"I know," said Betty, "but you'll laugh at me if I say Tennyson again. It's from 'Maud'—

"'I kissed her slender hand.
She took the kiss sedately.
Maud is not seventeen,
But she is tall and stately.'

"But she is not as sedate as she looks," added Betty, truthfully. "I'd like her better if she didn't gush. That's the only word that will express it. And it seemed queer for her to take me into her confidence the minute she was introduced. Right away she gave me to understand that she'd had a sort of an affair with Malcolm. She didn't say so in so many words, but she gave me the impression that he had been deeply interested in her, in a romantic way, you know."

Lloyd looked at Maud again, more critically this time, and with keener interest. Then her thoughts flew back to the churchyard stile where they had paused in their gathering of Christmas greens one winter day. For an instant she seemed to see the handsome boy looking down at her, begging a token of the Princess Winsome, and saying, in a low tone, "I'll be whatever you want me to be, Lloyd."

Juliet's voice broke in on her reverie. "Miss Sherman, allow me to present Miss Minor."

Maud was slightly taller than Lloyd, but it was not her extra inches alone which seemed to give her the air of looking down on every one. It was her patronizing manner. Lloyd resented it. Instinctively she drew herself up and responded somewhat haughtily.

"My dear, I've been simply *dying* to meet you," began Maud, effusively. "Ever since I found out that you were the girl Malcolm MacIntyre used to be so fond of."

Lloyd responded coldly, certain that Malcolm had not discussed their friendship in a way to warrant this outburst from a stranger.

"Do you know his brothah Keith, too?" she asked. "We're devoted to both the boys. You might say we grew up togethah, for they visited in the Valley so much. We've been playmates since we were babies. You must meet the Walton girls. They are Malcolm's cousins, you know."

Before Maud realized how it came about, Lloyd had graciously turned her over to Allison and Kitty, and made her escape with burning cheeks and a resentful feeling. Maud's words kept repeating themselves: "So adorably romantic. The girl Malcolm *used to be* so fond of!" They made her vaguely uncomfortable. She wondered why.

For another hour she went on making acquaintances and adding to her store of information about Warwick Hall. They couldn't have chafing-dishes in their rooms, one frivolous sophomore told her. The insurance companies objected after one girl spilled a bottle of alcohol and set fire to the curtains. But once a week those who pined for candy could make it over the gas-stove in the Domestic Science kitchen. Those who were too lazy to make it could buy it Monday afternoons from Mammy Easter, an old coloured woman who lived in a cabin on the place. She was famous for her pralines, the sophomore declared. "We have jolly charades and impromptu tableaux up in the gymnasium sometimes. Oh, school at the Hall is one grand lark!"

"Don't you believe it," said the spectacled junior who monopolized Lloyd next. "It's a hard dig to keep up to the mark they set here. But I must say it is an agreeable kind of a dig," she added.

"It's good just to wake up in the morning and know there's going to be another whole day of it. The classes are so interesting, and the teachers so interested in us, that they bring out the very best in everybody. Even a grasshopper would have its ambition aroused if it stayed in this atmosphere long."

She peered at Lloyd through her glasses as if to satisfy herself that she would be understood, and then added, confidentially: "I can fairly feel myself grow here. I feel the way I imagine the morning-glories do when they find themselves climbing up the trellis. They just stretch out their hands and everything helps them up,—the sun and the soil, the wind and the dew. And here at Warwick Hall there's so much to help. Even the little glimpses we get over the garden wall into the outside world of Washington, with its politics and great men. But those two people over there help me most of all." She nodded toward Madam Chartley and

Miss Chilton, the teacher of English, who were now seated together on a sofa near the door.

"When I look at them I feel that the morning-glory vine must climb just as high as it possibly can, and shake out a wealth of bells in return for all that has been given toward its growth. Don't you?"

"Yes," answered Lloyd, slightly embarrassed by the soulful gaze turned on her through the spectacles. "Betty would enjoy knowing you," she exclaimed. "She is always saying and writing such things."

"Oh, I thought that you were the one that writes," answered the junior. "Aren't you the one the freshmen are going to elect class editor for their page of the college paper?"

"No, indeed!" protested Lloyd, laughing at the idea. "Come across the room with me and I'll find Betty for you."

"There won't be time to-night," responded the junior, "for there goes the music that means good night. They always play 'America' as a signal that it's time to go."

"What makes you so quiet?" asked Betty, a little later, as they slowly undressed. She had chattered along, commenting on the events of the evening, ever since they came to their room, but Lloyd had seemed remarkably unresponsive.

"Oh, nothing," yawned Lloyd. "I was just thinking of that fairy-tale of the three weavers. I'll turn out the light."

As she reached up to press the electric button, she thought again, for the twentieth time, "I wonder what it was that Malcolm told Maud Minor." Then she nestled down among the pillows, saying, sleepily, to herself: "Anyway, I'm mighty glad that I nevah gave him that curl he begged for."

CHAPTER III.

AN EXCURSION

It was a Sabbath afternoon in October, sunny and still, with a purple haze resting on the distant woodlands across the river. A warm odour of ripe apples floated across the old peach orchard, for a few rare pippin-trees stood in its midst, flaunting the last of their fruitage from gnarled limbs, or hiding it in the sear grass underneath.

Here and there groups of bareheaded girls wandered in the sun-flecked shade, exchanging confidences and stooping now and then to pounce joyfully upon some apple that had hitherto evaded discovery. Betty, who had been reading aloud for nearly an hour to a little group under one of the largest trees, closed her book with a yawn. Lloyd and Kitty leaned lazily back against the mossy trunk, and Allison, with her arms around her knees, gazed dreamily across the river. The only one who did not seem to have fallen under the drowsy spell of the Indian summer afternoon was Gay. Up in the tree above them, she lay stretched out along a limb, peering down through the leaves like a saucy squirrel.

"What a Sleepy Hollow tale that was!" she exclaimed. "It just suits the day, but it has hypnotized all of you. Do wake up and be sociable."

She began breaking off bits of twigs and dropping them down on the heads below. One struck Lloyd's ear, and she brushed it off impatiently, thinking it was a bug. Gay laughed and began teasingly:

"There was a young maiden named Lloyd,
Whom reptiles always annoyed.
An innocent worm would cause her to squirm,
And cloyed—toyed—employed—

I'm stuck, Betty. Come to the rescue with a rhyme."

"So with germicide she's overjoyed," supplied Betty, promptly.

"That's all right," said Kitty, waking up. "Let's each make a Limerick. Five minutes is the limit, and the one that hasn't his little verse ready when the time is up will have to answer truthfully any question the others agree to ask."

"No," objected Lloyd. "I'd be suah to be it. I can make the rhymes, but the lines limp too dreadfully for any use."

"We won't count that," promised Kitty, looking at her chatelaine watch. "Now, one, two, three! Fire away!"

There was silence for a little space, broken only by the soft cooing of a far-away dove. Then Betty looked up with a satisfied smile. The anxious pucker smoothed out of Lloyd's forehead, and Allison nodded her readiness.

"Lloyd first," called Kitty, looking at her watch again.

A mischievous smile brought the dimples to the Little Colonel's face as she began:

"There's a girl in our school called Kitty,
Evidently not from the city.
With screeches and squawkin's
She upset the nerves of poah old Hawkins.
Oh, her behaviour was not at all pretty."

A burst of laughter greeted Lloyd's attempt at verse-making, for the subject which she had chosen recalled one of Kitty's outbreaks the first week of school, when the temptation to upset Hawkins's dignity was more than she could resist. No one of them who had seen Hawkins's wild exit from the linen closet the night she hid on the top shelf, and raised his hair with her blood-curdling moans and spectral warnings (having blown out his candle from above), could think of the occurrence without laughing till the tears came to their eyes.

"Now, Allison," said Kitty, when the final giggle had died away. "It's your turn." Allison referred to the lines she had scribbled on the back of a magazine:

"There is a young maiden, they say,
Who grows more beloved every day.
When we talk or we ramble, there's always a scramble
To be next to the maid who is *Gay*."

"Whew! Thanks awfully!" came the embarrassed exclamation from the boughs above, and Betty cried, in surprise: "Why, I wrote about her, too. I said:

"Like the bow on the strings when she plays,
So she crosses with music our days.
Our hearts doth she tune to the gladness of June,
And the smile that brings sunshine is Gay's."

"My dear, that's no Limerick, that's poetry!" exclaimed Kitty, and Gay called down: "It's awfully nice of you, girls, but please change the subject. I'm so covered with confusion that I'm about to fall off this limb."

"Well, here's something mean enough to brace you up," answered Kitty. "It's about Maud Minor. It's hateful of me to write it, but I happened to see her going down the terrace steps and it just popped into my head:

"There is a young lady named Maud,
Whose manners are overmuch thawed.
She'll beat an oil-well. When they'd gushed for a spell
It would take a back seat and applaud."

"What's the matter, Kitty?" asked Betty, "I thought you admired her immensely."

"I did that first week, but it's just as I say. She gushes over me so, simply because I am Malcolm's cousin. I know very well that I am not the dearest, cutest, brightest, most beautiful and angelic being in the universe, and she isn't sincere when she insists that I am. She overdoes it, and is so dreadfully effusive that I want to run whenever she comes near me. I wish she wasn't going on the excursion to-morrow."

"She doesn't worry me," said Gay. "I meet her on her own ground and fire back her own adjectives at her, doubled and twisted. She has let me alone for some time."

The discussion of Maud led their thoughts away from Gay's Limerick, and Kitty forgot to ask for it. They sat in silence again, and the plaintive calling of the dove sounded several times before any one spoke.

"It's so sweet and peaceful here," said Betty, softly. "It makes me think of Lloydsboro Valley. I could shut my eyes and almost believe I was back in the old Seminary orchard."

"I'm glad we're not," said Allison. "For then we'd miss to-morrow's excursion. And I like having our holiday on Monday instead of Saturday, as we did there."

"What excursion are you talking about?" asked Gay, lazily swinging her foot over the limb.

Betty explained. "We're going to see some rare old books and illuminated manuscripts. Miss Chilton has a friend in Washington who has one of the finest private collections in the country, and she offered to take any of the freshman class who cared to go. Ten of us have accepted the invitation. We're going to the Congressional Library in the morning, take lunch at some restaurant, and then call on this lady early in the afternoon. It will be the only chance to see them, as she is going abroad very soon, and the house will be closed for the winter."

"There are other things in the collection besides books," said Allison "Some queer old musical instruments,—a harpsichord and a lute, and an old violin worth its weight in gold. Some of the most noted violinists in the world have played on it."

"Oh, I know!" cried Gay, raising herself to a sitting position and throwing away the core of the apple she had been eating. "That's the excursion I missed last year when I sprained my ankle. I never was so disappointed in my life. I'm going right now to ask Miss Chilton to take me, too. I'm wild to get my fingers on that violin."

Swinging lightly down from the limb to the ground, she twisted around like a contortionist in a vain attempt to see her back.

"There!" she exclaimed, feeling her belt with a sigh of relief. "For a wonder there's nothing torn or busted this trip. I must be reforming Girls, what do you think! I haven't lost a single thing for a whole week."

"Don't brag," warned Lloyd. "Mom Beck would say you'd bettah scratch on wood if you don't want yoah luck to change."

Gay shrugged her shoulders at the superstition, but she reached over and lightly scratched the pencil thrust through Betty's curly hair.

"There goes the first bell for vespers," said Kitty, as they strolled slowly back toward the Hall, five abreast and arm in arm. With one accord they began to hum the hymn with which the service always opened,—"Day is dying in the west."

"It's going to be a fair day to-morrow," prophesied Gay, pausing an instant on the chapel steps. "There's Miss Chilton. I'll run over and ask her now."

"It's all right," she whispered several minutes later, when she slipped into the seat next Lloyd. "I can go. It'll be the greatest kind of a lark."

As Sybil Green passed through the hall next morning, where the excursionists were assembling, Gay stopped her and began slowly revolving on her heels. "Now view me with a critic's eye," she commanded. "Gaze on me from chapeau to shoe sole, and bear witness that I am properly girded up for the occasion. See how severely neat and plain I am. See how beautifully my belts make connection in the back. Three big, stout safety-pins will surely keep my skirt and shirt-waist together till nightfall, and there's not a thing about me that I can possibly lose."

She was still turning around and around. "Not a watch, ring, pin, or bangle! Not even a pocketbook. Miss Chilton is carrying my car-fare, and my handkerchief is up my sleeve."

"You might lose your balance or your presence of mind," laughed Sybil. "You'll have to watch her, girls. How spick and span you all look," she added, as they trooped past, behind Miss Chilton, most of them in freshly laundered shirt-waist suits, for the Indian summer day was as warm and sunny as June.

"It would be just about Gay's luck to run into a watering-cart or lean up against a freshly painted door, in that pretty pongee suit," she thought, watching them out of sight.

But for once Gay's lucky star was in the ascendant. The trip to the library left her without spot or wrinkle, and as she followed Miss Chilton into the restaurant she could not help smiling at her reflection in the mirror. It looked so trim and neat.

The restaurant was crowded. The waiters rushed back and forth, balancing their great trays on their finger-tips in a reckless way that made Gay dodge every time they passed.

"Oh, you needn't laugh," she exclaimed, when some one jokingly called attention to her. "I'm born to trouble; and I have a feeling that something is going to happen before the day is over."

Something did happen almost immediately, but not to Gay. Two of the pompous coloured men collided just as they were passing Miss Chilton's table. One tray dropped to the floor with a tremendous crash of breaking dishes. The other was caught dexterously in mid-air, but not before its contents had turned a somersault and wrought ruin all around it. A bowl of tomato soup splashed over Lloyd's immaculate shirt-waist and ran in two long red streaks across the shoulders of her duck jacket, which she had hung on her chair-post. Her little gasp of dismay was followed by one from Maud Minor, whose dainty gray silk waist was spattered plentifully with coffee.

There was a profusion of apologies from the waiters and a momentary confusion as the wreck was cleared away. In the midst of it, Miss Chilton was pleased and gratified to hear a low-pitched voice at the table behind her say: "Those are Warwick Hall girls. I recognize their chaperon, but I would have known them anywhere from the ladylike way they treated the affair. So quiet and self-controlled, not a bit of fuss or excitement, and it probably means that the day's outing will be spoiled for two of them."

The girls proceeded with their dessert, but Miss Chilton sat considering.

"If you girls were only familiar with the city," she said at last, looking at her watch, "I could let you go to some shop and get new shirt-waists, and you could meet me at my friend's afterward. But even if you could find your way to the shop, I would be afraid to risk your finding her house. You would have to change cars and walk a block after leaving the last one. I must keep my engagement with her promptly, for she is an extremely busy woman, and has granted this view of her library as a personal favour to me."

"Do let me take them, Miss Chilton," urged Gay, eagerly. "I'm the only old girl in the crowd. I learned my way all about town during last Christmas vacation. We could meet you in time to see part of the things. All I care for is that violin. *Please* say yes. I'll be the strictest, most dignified chaperon you ever heard of."

Miss Chilton laughed at the expression of ferocity which Gay's face suddenly assumed to convince her that she could play the part she begged for.

"Really that seems to be the only way out of the difficulty," she answered. "I'll give you a note to the department store which Madam Chartley always patronizes, so that you can have your purchases charged."

"What if we can't find anything to fit," suggested Maud, "and it should take such a long time to alter them that we'd be too late to meet you?"

Miss Chilton considered again. "It's almost preposterous to imagine that, but it is always well to provide for every emergency. If anything unforeseen should happen to delay you, or you can't find the proper things to make yourselves presentable, just go to the station and take the first car back to the school. I'll inquire of the ticket agent, and if you've left a card saying 'gone on,' I'll know that you are safe. If you've left no word, I'll put these girls on the car for home, and come back and institute a search for you."

While the others busied themselves with finger-bowls, she wrote a hasty note on a leaf torn from her memorandum book, which she gave to Maud. Then she handed a card to Gay.

"You are the pilot, so here is my friend's address on this card. I've marked the line of cars you're to take, and the avenue where you change."

"Better let Lloyd take it," suggested Kitty. But, with a saucy grimace, Gay folded it and slipped it under her belt.

"There!" she said, fastening it with a big black pin she borrowed from Allison. "I've woven that pin in and out, first in the ribbon and then through the card, till it's as tight as if it had grown there."

"Can't you take us down an alley?" asked Lloyd. "It mawtifies me dreadfully to have to go down the street looking like this."

"The car-line that passes this door goes directly to the department store," answered Gay. "It's only a few blocks away, but we'll take it. That tomato soup on you certainly does look gory."

Maud had taken the veil from her hat and thrown it over her shoulders in a way to hide the coffee stains. "Never mind," she said, carelessly, as they left the restaurant. "Just hold your head up and sail along with your most princess-like air, and people will be so busy admiring you that they won't have time to look at your soupy waist."

"Ugh! It smells so greasy and horrid," sniffed the Little Colonel, ignoring Maud's remark. "It's just like dishwatah and bacon rinds. I want to get away from it as soon as possible."

"Misses' white shirt-waists?" repeated the saleswoman in the big department store, when they reached it a few minutes later. "Certainly. Here is something pretty. The newest fall goods."

She led them to a counter piled high with boxes, and they made a hasty selection. Some alteration was needed in the collar of the one Lloyd chose, and in the sleeves of Maud's. While they waited in the fitting-room, turning over some back numbers of fashion-plates and magazines, Gay amused herself by wandering around the millinery department, trying on hats. Presently she found one so becoming that she ran back to them, delighted.

"It isn't once in a thousand years that I find a picture hat that looks well with my pug nose!" she cried. "But gaze on this!"

She revolved slowly before them, so radiantly pleased over her discovery that she looked unusually pretty. Both girls exclaimed over its becomingness. Then Lloyd's gaze wandered from the airy structure of chiffon and flowers down Gay's back to her waist-line.

"Mercy, child!" she exclaimed. "You've lost your belt. Every one of those three safety-pins is showing, and they each look a foot long!"

Gay's hand flew wildly to the back of her dress, but she felt in vain for a belt under which to hide the pins. She turned toward them with a hopeless drooping of the shoulders.

"*How* did I lose it?" she demanded, helplessly. "It had the safest, strongest kind of a clasp. When do you suppose I did it, and where? I must have been a sight parading the street this way like an animated pincushion."

She passed her hand over the obtrusive pins again. "I certainly had it on when we left the restaurant. Yes, and after we got on the car to come here, for I remember just after you paid the fare I ran my fingers down inside of it to make sure that Miss Chilton's card was still safely pinned to it."

Then she rolled up her eyes and fell limply back against the wall.

"Girls!" she exclaimed, in a despairing voice, "the card is lost with it, too. I've no more idea than the man in the moon where Miss Chilton's friend lives, or what her name is, or what car-line to take to get there. Do either of you remember hearing her say anything that would throw any light on the subject?"

Neither Lloyd nor Maud could remember, and the three stood staring at each other with startled faces.

"Maybe you dropped your belt coming up in the elevator," suggested Maud. "You might inquire. As soon as we get our clothes on, we'll help you hunt."

Gay flew to lay aside the picture hat for her own, and, with her hands clutching her dress to hide the unsightly safety-pins, started on her search through the store.

"We came straight past the ribbon counter and the embroideries to the silks, and then we turned here and took the elevator," she said to herself, retracing her steps. But inquiries of the elevator boy and every clerk along the line failed to elicit any information about the lost belt.

"No, it was only an ordinary belt that no one would look at the second time," she explained to those who asked for a description. "Just dark blue ribbon with a plain oxidized silver clasp. But there was an address pinned to it that is very important for me to find."

The floor-walker obligingly joined in the search, going to the door and scanning the pavement and the street-crossing at which they had left the car, but to no purpose.

"I can buy a new belt and have it charged," she said to Lloyd, when she came back to report, "but there is no way to get the lost address. If I could only remember the name, I could look for it in the directory, but I never heard it. Miss Chilton always spoke of the lady as 'my friend.'"

"I heard her speak it once," said Lloyd, "but I can't remembah it now."

"Go over the alphabet," suggested Maud. "Say all the names you can think of beginning with A and then B, and so on. Maybe you will stumble across one that you recognize as the right one."

Lloyd shook her head. "No, it was an unusual name, a long foreign-sounding one. I wondahed at the time how she could trip it off her tongue so easily."

"Then we're lost! Hopelessly, helplessly undone!" moaned Gay. "All our lovely outing spoiled! You won't get to see the books, nor I the violin. I know you are hating me horribly. There's nothing to do but go back to Warwick Hall, and leave a note with the ticket agent for Miss Chilton."

The tears stood in her eyes, and she looked so broken-hearted that Lloyd put her arms around her, insisting that it didn't make a mite of difference to her. That she didn't care much for the old books, anyhow, and for her not to grieve about it another minute.

Maud's face darkened as she listened. Presently she said: "I don't care particularly about the books, either, but I don't see any use of our losing the entire holiday. You know your way about the city, Gay; I have some car-fare in my purse, and so has Lloyd. We can go larking by ourselves."

The dressmaker came back with Maud's waist. She put it on, and Gay went for her belt. While Lloyd was still waiting for her waist, Maud sauntered out of the fitting-room, and asked permission to use the telephone. She was still using it when Gay joined them.

"Wait a minute," Maud called to her invisible auditor, and, still holding the receiver, turned toward the girls.

"Such grand luck!" she exclaimed, in a low tone. "I just happened to think of a young fellow I know here in town—Charlie Downs. He is always ready for anything going, and, when I telephoned him the predicament we are in, he said right away he would meet us down here and take us all to the matinée."

"Charlie Downs," echoed Gay. "I never heard of him."

"That doesn't make any difference," Maud answered, hurriedly. Then, in a still lower tone, with her back to the telephone: "He's all right. He's a sort of a distant relative of mine,—that is, his cousin married into our family. I can vouch for Charlie. He's a young medical student, and he's in old Doctor Spencer's office. Everybody knows Doctor Spencer, one of the finest specialists in the country."

She turned toward the telephone again, but Gay stopped her. "It's out of the question, Maud, for us to accept such an invitation. It's kind of him to ask us, but you're in my charge, and I'll have to take the responsibility of refusing."

"Well, I never heard the like of that!" said Maud, angrily, looking down on Gay in such a scornful, disgusted way that Lloyd would have laughed had the situation not been so tragic. Gay, trying to be commanding, reminded her of an anxious little hen, ruffling its feathers because the obstinate duckling in its brood refused to come out of the water.

"Madam Chartley wouldn't like it," urged Gay.

"Then she should have made rules to that effect. You know there's not a single one that would stand in the way of our doing this."

"Yes, there is. It's an unwritten one, but it's the one law of the Hall that Madam expects every one to live up to."

"May I ask what?" Maud's tone was freezingly polite.

"The motto under the crest. It's on everything you know, the old earl's teacups, the stationery, and everything—'Keep tryst.'"

"Fiddlesticks for the old earl's teacups!" said Maud, shrugging her shoulders. "It's unreasonable to expect us to keep tryst with Miss Chilton now."

"Not that," said Gay, ready to cry. "We're to keep tryst with what she expects of us. She expects us to do the right thing under all circumstances, and you know the right thing now is to go home. We were recognized at the restaurant as Warwick Hall girls, and we might be again at the matinée. What would people think of the school if they saw three of the girls there with a strange young man without a chaperon?"

"You're the chaperon. If you'd do to take us shopping, you'd do for that."

"Oh, Maud, don't be unreasonable," urged Gay. "It's entirely different. Don't be offended, please, but we can't go. It's simply out of the question."

"Indeed it isn't," answered Maud, turning again to the telephone. "Go home if you want to, but Lloyd and I will do as we please. I'll accept for us."

This time Lloyd stopped her. "Wait! Let's telephone out to the Hall and ask Madam."

Maud shrugged her shoulders. "You know very well she'd say no if you asked her beforehand." Then the two heard one side of her conversation over the telephone.

"Hello, Charlie! Sorry to keep you waiting so long."

"The girls are afraid to go."

"What's that?"

"I don't suppose so."

"I'm perfectly willing. I'll ask them."

Then turning again, with the receiver in her hand: "He says that the matinée will probably be over before the second train out to the Hall, and, if it isn't, we can leave a little earlier and be at the station before Miss Chilton gets there, and she need never know but what we've just been streetcar riding, as we first planned."

"Then that settles it!" exclaimed Lloyd. "If he said that, I wouldn't go with him for anything in the world."

"Why?" demanded Maud. Her eyes flashed angrily.

"Because—because," stammered Lloyd. "Well, it'll make you mad, but I can't help it. Papa Jack said one time that an honourable man would never ask me to do anything clandestine. And it would be sneaking to do as he proposes."

Maud was white with rage, and the hand that held the receiver trembled. "Have the goodness to keep your insulting remarks to yourself in the future, Miss Sherman."

"Please don't go," begged Gay. "I feel so responsible for getting you home safely, and it *would* be sneaking, you know, to pretend we'd been simply trolley-riding when we'd been off with him."

"You're nasty little cats to say such things!" stormed Maud. "I don't want to have anything more to do with either of you. Go on home and leave me alone. Hello! Hello, Charlie!"

They heard her make an engagement to meet him at the drug-store on the next corner. Then she sailed out of the store past them, without a glance in their direction. Gay began fumbling up her sleeve for her handkerchief. The tears were gathering too fast to be winked back.

"It's all my fault," she sobbed. "Oh, if I hadn't lost that unlucky belt. To think that I begged to be a chaperon, and then wasn't fit to be trusted."

Lloyd tried vainly to comfort her. A little later two disconsolate-looking girls took the first afternoon train out to Warwick Hall, and stole up to Lloyd's room. As Betty was with Miss Chilton, no one knew of their arrival, and they spent several uncomfortable hours agonizing over the question of what they should say when they were called to account. They decided at last that they would give no more information about Maud than that a distant relative had called for her.

At five o'clock, Miss Chilton reached the ticket-office with her little brood, and found Lloyd's card with the words "gone on" scribbled in one corner. Lloyd and Gay, watching at the window for their arrival, saw with sinking hearts that Maud was not with them. They hoped that she would come on the same train, and would be forced to make her own explanations. But they were not called upon to explain her disappearance. Miss Chilton, almost distracted with an attack of neuralgic headache, went to her room immediately, and sent down word that she would not appear at dinner.

"She'll surely come on the next train," Gay whispered to Lloyd, but the whistle sounded at the station, and they watched the clock in vain. Ample time passed for one to have walked the distance twice from the station to the Hall, but no one came.

It was half-past six when they filed down to dinner. The halls were lighted, and all the chandeliers in the great dining-room glowed.

As they passed the window on the stair-landing, Lloyd pressed her face against the pane and peered out into the darkness. Gay, just behind her, paused and peered also.

"What do you suppose has happened?" she whispered. "It's as dark as a pocket, and Maud hasn't come yet."

CHAPTER IV.

"KEEP TRYST"

Lloyd and Betty were starting to undress when there was a light tap at the door, and Gay's head appeared. In response to their eager call, she came in, and, shutting the door behind her, stood with her back against it.

"No, I can't sit down," she answered. "It's too late to stop. I only ran in to tell you that Maud got home about five minutes ago. 'Charlie' came with her as far as the door and Madam has just sent for her to demand an explanation. She told her roommate that she knew she was in for a scolding, and that, as one might as well be killed for a sheep as a lamb, she made her good time last as long as she could. After the matinée they had a little supper at some roof-garden or café or something of the kind, where there was a band concert. Then he brought her out on the car, and they strolled along the river road home. The moon was just beginning to come up. She's had a beautiful time, and thinks she has done something awfully cute, but she'll think differently by the time Madam is through with her."

"Will she be very terrible?" asked Lloyd, pausing with brush in hand.

"I don't know," answered Gay. "Nothing like this has happened since I have been at the Hall, but I've heard her say that this is not a reform school, and girls who have to be punished and scolded are not wanted here. If they can't measure up to the standard of good behaviour, they can't stay. As long as this is the first offence, she'll probably be given another trial, but I'd not care to be in her shoes when Madam calls her to judgment."

No one ever knew what passed between the two in the up-stairs office, but Maud sailed down to breakfast next morning as if nothing had happened. The only difference in her manner was when Lloyd and Gay took their places opposite her at the table. They glanced across with the usual good morning, but she looked past them as if she neither saw nor heard.

"Cut dead!" whispered Lloyd. Gay giggled, as she unfolded her napkin. "I'm very sure she has no cause to be angry with us. We are the ones who ought to act offended."

Soon after breakfast they were called into Miss Chilton's room, but to their great relief found that she already knew what had happened, and that they were to be questioned only about their own part in the affair. So presently Gay passed out to her Latin recitation, and Lloyd wandered around the room, waiting for the literature class to assemble.

Miss Chilton's room was the most attractive one in the Hall. It looked more like a cheerful library than a schoolroom. Low book-shelves lined the walls, with here and there a fine bust in bronze or Carrara marble. Pictures from many lands added interest, and the wicker chairs, instead of being arranged in stiff rows, stood invitingly about, as if in a private parlour. There were always violets on Miss Chilton's desk, and ferns and palms in the sunny south windows. The recitations were carried on in such a delightfully informal way that the girls looked forward to this hour as one of the pleasantest of the day.

This morning, to their surprise, instead of questioning them about the topic they had studied, Romance of the Middle Ages, she announced that she had a story which Madam Chartley had requested her to read to them, and she wished such close attention paid to it that afterward each one could write it from memory for the next day's lesson.

"I have a reason for wishing to impress this little tale indelibly on your minds," she said, "so I shall offer this inducement for concentrating your attention upon it: five credits to each one who can hand in a full synopsis of the story, and ten to the one who can reproduce it most literally and fully."

There was a slight flutter of expectancy as the class settled itself to listen, and, opening the little green and gold volume where a white ribbon kept the place, she began to read:

"Now there was a troubadour in the kingdom of Arthur, who, strolling through the land with only his minstrelsy to win him a way, found in every baron's hall and cotter's hut a ready welcome. And while the boar's head sputtered on the spit, or the ale sparkled in the shining tankards, he told such tales of joust and journey, and feats of brave knight errantry, that even the scullions left their kitchen tasks, and, creeping near, stood round the door with mouths agape to listen.

"Then with his harp-strings tuned to echoes of the wind on winter moors, he sang of death and valour on the field, of love and fealty in the hall, till those who listened forgot all save his singing and the noble knights whereof he sang.

"One winter night, as thus he carolled in a great earl's hall, a little page crept nearer to his bench beside the fire, and, with his blue eyes fixed in wonderment upon the graybeard's face, stood spellbound. Now Ederyn was the page's name, an orphan lad whose lineage no man knew, but that he came of gentle blood all eyes could see, although as vassal 'twas his lot to wait upon the great earl's squire.

"It was the Yule-tide, and the wassail-bowl passed round till boisterous mirth drowned oftentimes the minstrel's song, but Ederyn missed no word. Scarce knowing what he did, he crept so close he found himself with upturned face against the old man's knee.

"'How now, thou flaxen-haired,' the minstrel said, with kindly smile. 'Dost like my song?'

"'Oh, sire,' the youth made answer, 'methinks on such a wing the soul could well take flight to Paradise. But tell me, prithee, is it possible for such as *I* to gain the title of a knight? How doth one win such honours and acclaim and reach the high estate that thou dost laud?'

"The minstrel gazed a little space into the Yule log's flame, and stroked his long hoar beard. Then made he answer:

"'Some win their spurs and earn the royal accolade because the blood of dragons stains their hands. From mighty combat with these terrors they come victorious to their king's reward. And some there be sore scarred with conquest of the giants that ever prey upon the borders of our fair domain. Some, who have gone on far crusades to alien lands, and there with heart of gold and iron hand have proved their fealty to the Crown.'

"Then Ederyn sighed, for well he knew his stripling form could never wage fierce combat with a dragon. His hands could never meet the brawny grip of giants. 'Is there no other way?' he faltered.

'I wot not,' was the answer. 'But take an old man's counsel. Forget thy dreams of glory, and be content to serve thy squire. For what hast such as thou to do with great ambitions? They'd prove but flames to burn away thy daily peace.'

"With that he turned to quaff the proffered bowl and add his voice to those whose mirth already shook the rafters. Nor had he any further speech with Ederyn. But afterward the pretty lad was often in his thoughts, and in his wanderings about the land he mused upon the question he had asked.

"Another twelvemonth sped its way, and once again the Yule log burned within the hall, and once again the troubadour knocked at the gate, all in the night and falling snow. And as before, with merry jests they led him in and made him welcome. And as before, was every mouth agape from squire's to scullion's, as he sang.

"Once more he sang of knights and ladyes fair, of love and death and valour; and Ederyn, the page, crept nearer to him till the harp-strings ceased to thrill. With head upon his hands, he sat and sighed. Not even when the wassail-bowl was passed with mirth and laughter did he look up. And when the graybeard minstrel saw his grief, he thought upon his question of the Yule-tide gone.

"'Ah, now, thou flaxen-haired,' he whispered in his ear. 'I bear thee tidings which should make thee sing for joy. There is a way for even such as thou to win the honours thou dost covet. I heard it in the royal court when last I sang there at the king's behest.'

"Then all aquiver with his eagerness did Ederyn kneel, with face alight, beside the minstrel's knee to hear.

"'Know this,' began the graybeard. ''Tis the king's desire to 'stablish round him at his court a chosen circle whose fidelity hath stood the utmost test. Not deeds of prowess are required of these true followers, with no great conquests doth he tax them, but they must prove themselves trustworthy, until on hand and heart it may be graven large, "*In all things faithful.*"

"'To Merlin, the enchanter, he hath left the choice, who by some strange spell I wot not of will send an eerie call through all the kingdom. And only those will hear who wake at dawn to listen in high places. And only those will heed who keep the compass needles of their souls true to the north star of a great ambition. The time of testing will be long, the summons many. To duty and to sorrow, to disappointment and defeat, thou may'st be called. No matter what the tryst, there is but one reply if thou wouldst win thy knighthood. Give heed and I will teach thee now that answer.'

"Then smiting on his harp, the minstrel sang, so softly under cover of the noise, that only Ederyn heard. Through all the song ran ever this refrain. It seemed a brooklet winding in and out through some fair meadow:

""'Tis the king's call. O list!
Thou heart and hand of mine, keep tryst—
Keep tryst or die!'

"Then Ederyn, with his hand upon his heart, made solemn oath. 'Awake at dawn and listening in high places will I await that call. With the compass needle of my soul true to the north star of a great ambition will I follow where it leads, and though through fire and flood it take me, I'll make but this reply:

""'Tis the king's call. O list!
Thou heart and hand of mine, keep tryst—
Keep tryst or die!'

"Pressing the old man's hand in gratitude (he could say no word for the strange fulness in his throat that well-nigh choked him), he rose from his knees and left the hall to muse on what had passed.

"That night he climbed into the tower, and, with his face turned to the east, kept vigil all alone. Below, the rioters waxed louder in their mirth. The knife was in the meat, the drink was in the horn. But he would not join their revels, lest morning find him sunk in sodden sleep, heavy with feasting and witless from wine.

"As gray dawn trailed across the hills, he started to his feet, for far away sounded the call for which he had been waiting. It was like the faint blowing of an elfin horn, but the words came clearly.

"'Ederyn! Ederyn! One awaits thee at nightfall in the shade of the yew-tree by the abbey tower! Keep tryst!'

"Now the abbey tower was the space of forty furlongs from the domain of the earl, and full well Ederyn knew that only by especial favour of his squire could he gain leave of absence for this jaunt. So, from sunrise until dusk, he worked with will, to gain the wished-for leave. Never before did buckles shine as did the buckles of the squire entrusted to his polishing. Never did menial tasks cease sooner to be drudgery, because of the good-will with which he worked. And when the day was done, so well had every duty been performed, right willingly the squire did grant him grace, and forthwith Ederyn sped upon his mission.

"The way was long, and, when he reached the abbey tree, he fell a-trembling, for there a tall wraith stood within the shadows of the yew. No face had it that he could see, its hands no substance, but he met it bravely, saying: 'I am Ederyn, come to keep the king's tryst.'

"And then the spectre's voice replied: 'Well hast thou kept it, for 'tis known to me the many menial tasks thou didst perform ere thou couldst come upon thy quest. In token that we two have met, here is my pledge that thou may'st keep to show the king.'

"He felt a light touch on the bosom of his inner vestment, and suddenly he stood alone beside the gruesome abbey. Clammy with fear, he knew not why, he drew his mantle round him and sped home as one speeds in a fearsome dream. And that it was a dream he half-believed, when later, in the hall, he served at meat those gathered round the old earl's board. But when he sought his bed, and threw aside his outer garment, there on his coarse, rough shirt of hodden gray a pearl gleamed white above his heart, where the wraith's cold hand had touched him. It was the token to the king that he had answered faithfully his call.

"Again before the dawn he climbed into the tower, and, listening when the voices of the world were still, heard clear and sweet, like far-blown elfin horn, another summons.

"'Ederyn! Ederyn! One awaits thee at the midnight hour beside black Kilgore's water. Keep tryst!'

"Again to gain his squire's permission he toiled with double care. This time his task was counting all the spears and halberds, the battle-axes and the coats of mail that filled the earl's great armament. And o'er and o'er he counted, keeping careful tally with a bit of keel upon the iron-banded door, till the red lines that he marked there made his eyes ache and his head swim. At last the task was finished, and so well the squire praised him, and for his faithfulness again was fain to speed him on his way.

"It was a woful journey to the waters of Kilgore. Sleep weighed on Ederyn's eyelids, and haltingly he went the weary miles, footsore and worn. But midnight found him on the spot where one awaited him, another wraith-like envoy of the king, and it, too, left a touch upon his heart in token he had kept the tryst. And when he looked, another pearl gleamed there beside the first.

"So many a day went by, and Ederyn failed not in his homely tasks, but carried to his common round of duties all his might, as if they were great feats of prowess. Thus gained he liberty to keep the tryst with every messenger the king did send.

"Once he fared forth along a dangerous road that led he knew not where, and, when he found it crossed a loathly swamp all filled with slime and creeping things, fain would he have fled. But, pushing on for sake of his brave oath, although with fainting heart, he reached the goal at last. This time his token made him wonder much. For when he wakened from his swoon, a shining star lay on his heart above the pearls.

"Now it fell out the squire to whom this Ederyn was page was killed in conflict with a robber band, and Ederyn, for his faithfulness, was taken by the earl to fill that squire's place. Soon after that, they left the hall, and journeyed on a visit to a distant lord. 'Twas to the Castle of Content they came, where was a joyous garden. And now no menial tasks employed the new squire's time. Here was he free to wander all the day through vistas of the joyous garden, or loiter by the fountain in the courtyard and watch the maidens at their tasks, having fair speech with them among the flowers. And one there was among them, so lily-like in face, so gentle-voiced and fair, that Ederyn well-nigh forgot his oath, and felt full glad when for a space the king's call ceased to sound. And gladder was he still, when, later on, the earl's long visit done, he left young Ederyn behind to serve the great lord of the castle, for so the two friends had agreed, since Ederyn had pleased the old lord's fancy.

"Yet was he faithful to his vow, and failed not every dawn to mount to some high place, when all the voices of the world were still, and listen for the sound of Merlin's horn. One morn it came:

"'Ederyn! Ederyn! One waits thee far away. By the black cave of Atropos, when the moon fulls, keep thy tryst!'

"Now 'twas a seven days' journey to that cave, and Ederyn, thinking of the lily maid, was loath to leave the garden. He lingered by the fountain until nightfall, saying to himself: 'Why should I go on longer in these foolish quests, keeping tryst with shadows that vanish at the touch? No nearer am I to a knight's estate than, when a stripling page, I listened to the minstrel's tales.'

"The fountain softly splashed within the garden. From out the banquet-hall there stole the sound of tinkling lutes, and then the lily maiden sang. Her siren voice filled all his heart, and he forgot his oath to duty. But presently a star reflected in the fountain made him look up into the jewelled sky, where shone the polar constellation. And there he read the oath he had forgotten: 'With the compass needle of my soul true to the north star of my great ambition, I will follow where it leads.'

"Thrusting his fingers in his ears to silence the beloved voice of her who sang, he madly rushed from out the garden into the blackness of the night. The Castle of Content clanged its great gate behind him. He shivered as he felt the jar through all his frame, but, never taking out his fingers, on he ran, till scores of furlongs lay between him and the tempting of that siren voice.

"It was a strange and fearsome wood that lay between him and the cave. All things seemed moaning and afraid. He saw no forms, but everywhere the shadows shuddered, and moans and groans pursued him till nameless fears clutched at his heart with icy chill. Then suddenly the earth slipped way beneath his feet, and cold waves closed above his head. He knew now he had fallen in the pool that lies upon the far edge of the fearsome wood,—a pool so deep and of such whirling motion that only by the fiercest struggle may one escape. Gladly he would have allowed the waters to close over him, such cold pains smote his heart, had he not seemed to hear the old minstrel's song. It aroused him to a final effort, and he gasped between his teeth:

"'Tis the king's call! O list!
Thou heart and hand of mine, keep tryst—
Keep tryst or die!'

"With that, in one mighty struggle he dragged himself to land. A bow-shot farther on he saw the cave, and by sheer force of will crept toward it. What happened then he knew not till the moon rose full and high above him. A form swathed all in black bowed over him.

"'Ederyn,' she sighed. 'Here is thy token that the king may know that thou hast met me face to face.'

"He thought it was a diamond at first, that sparkled there beside the star, but when he looked again, lo, nothing but a tear.

"Then went he back unto the joyous garden by slow degrees, for he was now sore spent. And after that the summons came full often. Whenever all the world seemed loveliest and life most sweet, then was the call most sure to come. But never once he faltered. Never was he faithless to the king's behest. Up weary mountain steps he toiled to find the sombre face of Disappointment there in waiting, and Suffering and Pain were often at his journey's end, and once a sore Defeat. But bravely as the months went by he learned to smile into their eyes, no matter which one handed out to him the pledge of Duty well performed.

"One day, when he no longer was a beardless youth, but grown to pleasing stature and of great brawn, he heard the hoped-for call of which he long had dreamed: 'Ederyn! Ederyn! The king himself awaits thee. Midsummer morn at lark-song, keep tryst beside the palace gate.'

"As travellers on the desert, spent and worn, see far across the sand the palm-tree's green that marks life-giving wells, so Ederyn hailed this summons to the king. The soul-consuming thirst that long had urged him on grew fiercer as the well of consummation came in sight. Hope shod his feet with wings, as thus with every nerve a-strain he pushed toward the final tryst. So fearful was he some mishap might snatch the cup away ere it had touched his thirsty lips, that three full days before the time he reached the Vale of Avalon, and sat him down outside the entrance to the palace.

"Now there came prowling through the wood that edged the fair domain the gnarled dwarfs that do the will of Shudderwain. And Shudderwain, of all the giants thereabouts, most cruel was and to be feared. Knowing full well what pleasure it would give the bloody monster, these dwarfs laid evil hands on Ederyn. Sleeping they found him, and bound him with hard leathern thongs, and then with gibes and impish laughter dragged him into a dungeon past the help of man.

"Two days and nights he lay there, raging at fate and at his helplessness, till he was well-nigh mad, bethinking him of all his baffled hopes. And like a madman gnawed he on the leathern thongs till he was free, and beat his hands against the stubborn rock that would not yield, and threw himself against the walls that held him in.

"The dwarfs from time to time peered through the slatted window overhead and mocked him, pointing with their crooked thumbs.

"'Ha! ha! Thou'lt keep no tryst,' they chattered. 'But if thou'lt swear upon thy oath to go back to the joyous garden, and hark no more for Merlin's call, we'll let thee loose from out this Dungeon of thy Disappointment.'

"Then was Ederyn tempted, for the dungeon was foul indeed, and his heart cried out to go back to the lily maiden. But once more in his ears he thrust his fingers and cried:

"'To the king's call alone I'll list!
Oh, heart and hand of mine, keep tryst—
Keep tryst or die!'

"On the third night, with the quiet of despair he threw him prone upon the dungeon floor and held his peace, no longer gnawing on his thongs or beating on the rock. A single moonbeam straggled through the slatted window, and by its light he saw a spider spinning out a web. Then, looking dully around, he saw the dungeon was hung thick with other webs, foul with the dust of years. Great festoons of the cobweb film shrouded his prison walls. As up and down the hairy creature swung itself upon its thread, the hopeless eyes of Ederyn followed it.

"All in a twinkling he saw how he might profit by the spider's teaching, and clapped his hand across his mouth to keep from shouting out his joy, so that the dwarfs could hear. Now once more like a madman rushing at the walls, he tore down all the dusty webs, and twisted them together in long strands. These strands he braided in thick ropes and tied them, knotting them and twisting and doubling once again. All the while he kept bewailing the stupid way in which he wasted time. 'Three days ago I might have quit this den,' he sighed, 'had I but used the means that lay at hand. Full well I knew that heaven always finds a way to help the man who helps himself. No creature lives too mean to be of service, and even dungeon walls must harbour help for him who boldly grasps the first thing that he sees and makes it serve him.'

"So fast and furiously he worked that, long before the moonbeam faded, his cobweb rope was strong enough to bear his weight, and long enough to reach twice over to the slatted window overhead. By many trials he at last succeeded in throwing it around a spike that barred the window, and, climbing up, he forced the slats apart and clambered through. Then tying the rope's end to the window, he slid down all the dizzy cliffside in which the dwarfs had dug the dungeon, and dropped into the stream that ran below.

"Lo, when he looked around him it was dawn. Midsummer morn it was, and, plunging through the wood, he heard the lark's song rise, and reached the palace gate just as it opened to the blare of trumpets for the king's train to ride forth. When Ederyn saw the royal cavalcade, he shrunk back into the wayside bushes, so ill-befitting did it seem that he should come before the king in tattered garments, with blood upon his hands where the sharp rocks had cut, and with foul dungeon stains.

"But that the king might know he'd ever proven faithful, he sank upon his knees and bared his breast at his approach. There all the pledges glistened in the sunlight, in rainbow hues. There Pain had dropped her heart's blood in a glittering ruby, and Honour set her seal upon him in a golden star. A diamond gleamed where Sorrow's tear had fallen, and amethysts glowed now with purple splendour to mark his patient meeting with Defeat. But mostly were the pledges little pearls for little duties faithfully performed; and there they shone, and, as the people gazed, they saw the jewels take the shape of letters, so that the king read out before them all, '*Semper fidelis*.'

"Then drew the king his royal sword and lightly smote on Ederyn's shoulder, and cried: 'Arise, Sir Knight, Sir Ederyn the Trusty. Since I may trust thee to the utmost in little things as well as great, since thou of all men art most worthy, henceforth by thy king's heart thou shalt ride, ever to be his faithful guard and comrade.'

"So there before them all he did him honour, and ordered that a prancing steed be brought and a good sword buckled on his side.

"Thus Ederyn won his sovereign's favour. Soon, by his sovereign's grace permitted, he went back to the joyous garden to woo the lily maiden. When he had won his bride and borne her to the palace, then was his great reward complete for all his years of fealty to his vow. Then out into the world he went to guard his king. Henceforth blazoned on his shield and helmet he bore the crest—a heart with hand that grasped a spear, and, underneath these words:

"*I keep the tryst!*"

Slipping the white ribbon back between the pages to mark the place, Miss Chilton laid the little green and gold volume on the table, and smiled at the circle of attentive faces.

"I am sure you understand why I have read this story," she said. "It is the motto of the school. Tradition has it that Sir Ederyn was an ancient member of Madam Chartley's family. At any rate, it has borne his crest for many, many generations, and there could be no better motto for a school. The world expects us to do certain things. We must keep tryst with these expectations. You all know what happened yesterday. Madam looks for a certain course of conduct from her girls. She does not make rules. She only expects what the inborn instinct of a true lady would prompt you to do or to be. I am sure that after this explanation none of you will fail to keep tryst with her expectations."

That was the only public reference to Maud's escapade. She left the room with a very red face when the class was dismissed. The little story put her so plainly in the wrong before the other girls that it made her cross and uncomfortable.

Every member of the class had five marks to her credit, and Betty was the lucky one whose almost literal reproduction of the story gave her ten. She copied it all down in her white record afterward, adding a verse that she had once seen in an autograph album:

"Life is a rosary
Strung with the beads of little deeds,
Done humbly, Lord, as unto thee."

She repeated the verse aloud to Lloyd. "I'd like to make that kind of a rosary. I'd like to act out that story. It just strikes my fancy. It would be such a satisfaction to lay aside a token each night, as Ederyn did, that I had kept tryst with duty,—had perfect lessons, or lived through a day just as nearly right as I possibly could."

She went on writing after she had made the remark, but Lloyd, pleased by the thought, sat staring at the lamp. It was nearly bedtime, and presently, putting aside her book, she rose and crossed over to the bureau. In a sandalwood box in the top drawer was a broken fan-chain of white beads—tiny Roman pearls that she had bought in a shop in the Via Crucia. She had intended to string them sometime, mixing with them here and there some curious blue beads she had seen made at a glass-blower's in Venice—large blue ones with tiny roses on the sides.

Betty, busy with her diary, did not notice how long Lloyd stood with her back toward her, pouring the little Roman pearls from one hand to the other.

"It seems almost babyish," Lloyd was saying to herself. "But othah girls keep memory-books and such things, and this is such a pretty idea. No one need know. Yes, I'll begin the rosary this very night, for every lesson was perfect to-day, and I truly tried my best in everything."

Hesitating an instant longer, she rummaged through the drawer for a piece of fine white silk cord which she remembered having placed there. When she found it, she knotted one end securely, and then slowly slipped one little pearl bead down against the knot.

"There!" she thought, with a hasty glance over her shoulder at Betty, as she dropped the string back into its box. "There's one token that I've kept tryst, even if I nevah earn any moah. I'm going to have that string half-full by vacation."

CHAPTER V.

A MEMORY-BOOK AND A SOUVENIR SPOON

The string of white beads grew steadily, but work went hand in hand with play at Warwick Hall, as Kitty's memory-book testified. She brought it out to liven the recreation hour one rainy afternoon, late in the term, when they were house-bound by the weather. Its covers, labelled "Gala Days and Bonfire Nights," were bulging with souvenirs of many memorable occasions. She sat on the floor with it spread open on her lap. Betty was on one side and Lloyd on the other, while Gay leaned against her back and looked over her shoulder.

Kitty opened her treasure-house of mementos with a giggle, for on the first page was a water-colour sketch of Gay as she had appeared on the welcoming night. She had painted her with two enormous feet protruding from her flowing skirts, one cased in a party slipper with an exaggerated French heel, the other in a down-trodden bedroom slipper painted a brilliant crimson.

"You mean thing!" cried Gay, laughing over the ridiculous caricature of herself.

"That isn't a circumstance to some of them," remarked Allison, who was virtuously spending her recreation hour in sewing buttons on her gloves and mending a rip in the lining of her coat-sleeve. "Wait till you come to the programme of the recital given by the students of voice, violin, and piano. The pictures she made all around the margin of it are some of the best she has done. The sketch of Susie Tyndall, tearing her hair and shrieking out the 'Polish Boy,' is simply killing."

"Kitty Walton," exclaimed Gay, as she bent over the grotesquely decorated programme, "where do you keep this book o' nights? I'll surely have to steal it. Think what it will be worth to us when we are old ladies. There's one thing certain, you could never pose as a saintly old grandmother with such a record for mischief as this to bear witness against you."

Kitty looked up with a startled expression. "You know, it never occurred to me before that I'd ever look at this book through spectacles. I wonder if I'll find it as amusing then, when I'm dignified and rheumatic, as I do now."

"I'm sure *that* will be pleasant to recall," said Betty, pointing to a withered rose pinned to the next page. "That will properly impress your grandchildren."

Underneath the rose was written the date of a private reception granted the Warwick Hall girls at the White House.

"I had such a lovely time that afternoon," sighed Betty. "It was so much nicer to go as we did, for a friendly little visit under Madam's wing, than to have pushed by in a big public mob. Wasn't Cora Basket funny? She was so overawed by the honour that she fairly turned purple. Her roommate vows that, when she wrote home, she began, 'Preserve this letter! The hand that is now writing it has been shaken by the President of the United States of America!'"

"Cordie Brown was funnier than Cora," said Allison. "She wanted to impress people with the idea that the affair was nothing to her. That it rather bored her, in fact. She went around with her nose in the air, trying to appear so superior and indifferent, as if crowned heads and their ilk made her tired."

"What's this?" demanded Lloyd, as they turned the next leaf, through which a single long black hair had been drawn. Underneath was the gruesome legend, "Dead men tell no tales."

"Oh, that's only a 'hair from the tail of the dog of the child of the wife of the wild man of Borneo,'" laughed Kitty, attempting to turn the page; but Lloyd, laying both palms across it, held it fast.

"You know it's not, you naughty thing. You've been up to some prank."

"It a p. j. A private joke," explained Kitty, bending over the book and laughing till her forehead touched her knees. "I'm dying to tell you, for it's the funniest thing in the collection. It happened at the Hallowe'en party, and I promised not to tell."

"Promised whom?" demanded Betty.

"Can't tell that, either," was all that Kitty would say. She flipped over the next leaf. A gilded wishbone was fastened to the page by the bit of red ribbon run through it.

"That's 'In Memoriam' of the grand spread at the Thanksgiving Day feast. And this button pasted on just below it, popped off the glove of Mademoiselle La Tosto the afternoon she came to the Studio Tea and Art reception. You know how the girls buzzed around her like a swarm of bees, begging for her autograph. I'd rather have this button than a dozen autographs, for it dropped off her glove as she clapped her hands in that vivacious Frenchy way of hers, when she saw my caricature of Paderewski that the girls stuck up on the wall. Understand, young ladies, she was *applauding* it. I walked on air all afternoon."

"Why undah the sun have you saved this tea leaf?" asked Lloyd, pointing to one pasted carefully in the corner of the next page.

"Don't you remember the day that we went down to Mammy Easter's cabin, and her old black grandmother was there, and told our fortunes? She was a regular old hag, Gay. I wish you could have seen her,—teeth all gone; skin puckered as a dried apple; she looked more monkey than human. But she's a fine fortune-teller. I made a few hieroglyphics to recall what she said. This mark is supposed to be a coach and four. She said that Allison was to wed wid de quality and ride in a car'age, but sorrow would be her po'shun if she walked proud. She said that I'm bawn to trouble as de spah'ks fly upwa'd, case I won't hah'k to counsel, and that I mustn't marry the first man that axes me, and I mustn't marry the second man that axes me, but the third man that axes me, him I can safely marry. This tea leaf stands for the third man. I'm to have three sons and one daughter, and my luck will come to me through running water when the weather-vane points west."

Kitty pointed to several pencil scratches beside the tea leaf, intended to signify a brook and a weather-vane on a steeple.

"What did she say about Betty?" asked Gay.

Kitty studied the next line of hieroglyphics a moment. "Oh, I see now. I intended this for a ship. She said there was a veil done hanging ovah her future, so she couldn't rightly tell, but she could see ships coming and going and crowds of people, and she could see that her fortune was mixed up with a great many other persons. She said that the teacup held gold for her, and the signs all 'pinted friendly.'"

"And Lloyd?" queried Gay, trying to decipher the next line of pencil marks. "Surely that's not a cat I see."

"A cat, a teapot, and a ball of knitting," laughed Kitty. "I supposed that Lloyd's fortune would be something thrilling, but according to the old darky, it's to be the tamest of all. She said, 'I see a rising sun, and a row of lovahs, but I don't see you a-taking any of 'em, honey. Yo' ways am ways of pleasantness and all yo' paths am peace, but I'se powahful skeered dat you'se gwine to be an ole maid. I sholy is.'"

"Is that so, Lloyd?" asked Gay, leaning over Kitty's shoulder to laugh at the Little Colonel's teased expression. Kitty answered for her.

"Not if we can help it. We want her for a cousin, and we think that she ought to marry Malcolm just for the sake of being able to claim us as her dear relations. Look how she's blushing, girls."

"I'm not!" was the indignant answer. "You're just trying to make me get red, because you know I do it so easily."

She turned the page hastily and began to talk about its contents to change the subject. There were scraps of ribbon, as they went farther on, a burnt match, a peacock feather, a tiny block of wood with a hole shot through it, a strand of embroidery silk, a faded pansy,—a hundred bits of worthless rubbish which an unknowing hand would have swept into the waste-basket; but to Kitty each one was a key to unlock some happy memory of her swiftly passing school-days. As the four heads, brown and golden, black and auburn, bent over the book, the rain beat against the windows in torrents.

With needle in air, Allison sat a moment watching the water stream down the pane. "This makes me think of that afternoon in old Lloydsboro Seminary," she said, musingly, "when Ida Shane read the 'Fortunes of Daisy Dale' aloud to us. I wonder what has become of Ida. She was living in a little country town up in the mountains the last time I heard of her, taking in sewing and doing her own work."

"She's the girl who caused so much excitement at the Seminary," Betty explained to Gay. "The one who got our Shadow Club into disgrace. She tried to elope one night, but the teachers found it out and sent her home. It didn't do any good, for she ran away with Ned Bannon the next summer, and they were married by a justice of the peace. I don't see how Ida could do it when she'd always been so romantic, and planned to have her wedding just like Daisy Dale's, in cherry blossom time, and in the little stone church at Lloydsboro, with the vines over the belfry. It's so quaint and English looking, just like the one that Daisy was married in. Instead of being all in white, she was married in the dress she happened to have on when she ran away,—just an old black walking skirt and plaid shirt-waist. No veil, no trail, and no orange-blossoms, and she had counted on having all three. It was so prosy and commonplace after the grand things she had planned."

"She's had it prosy enough ever since, too," remarked Allison. "Ned drinks so hard that he can't keep a position. She didn't reform him one single bit, and I reckon she understands now why her aunt objected so strongly to her marrying him. Poor Ida, to think of her having to take in sewing to keep her from actual starvation! It's awful!"

"Poah Ida!" echoed Lloyd. "I don't see how she does it. When she was in the Seminary, she couldn't do anything with her needle but embroidah. I used to have Mom Beck do her mending and darning when she did mine."

"Thank fortune *my* mending is done!" exclaimed Allison, dropping her thimble into her work-bag, and throwing her coat across a chair. "It's almost time for the bell. I must take Juliet Lynn the papers I promised her."

Lloyd and Betty, looking at the clock, scrambled to their feet, and a moment after only Gay and Kitty were left on the rug with the memory-book open between them.

"Do you think that Lloyd really cares for your cousin?" asked Gay.

"No," was the emphatic answer. "You can make her blush that way about anybody, and I love to tease her. When she first came back from Arizona, I used to think she liked Phil Tremont, a boy she met out there, and then I thought maybe it was Joyce's brother Jack. She talked so much about the duck hunts they had together, and what a splendid fellow he was, and how much her father admired him. But the Princess is so particular that I believe the old darky told her fortune truly. If she's so particular at fifteen, 'I'se powahful skeered she's gwine to be an old maid. I sholy is.' For what will she be at twice fifteen?"

Gay laughed at the imitation of the old coloured woman, then asked: "But doesn't your cousin come up to her standard? According to Maud Minor he is as handsome as a Greek god, as accomplished as all the Muses put together, and as entertaining as a four-ring circus."

"Oh, Malcolm's all right," answered Kitty. "We're awfully fond of him, but we're not so crazy about him as to think all that. I have a picture of him somewhere in my box of photographs, if you'd like to see it."

Climbing on a chair to reach the box on the top of the wardrobe, she took it down and began rummaging through it. In a moment she tossed a photograph to Gay, who still sat on the floor, Turk fashion.

"STUDYING THE FACE OF THE HANDSOME YOUNG FELLOW WITH INTEREST"

"Here is one he had taken years ago when he and Keith used to play they were two little Knights of Kentucky, and went around trying to set the wrongs of the world to rights."

While Gay was still exclaiming over it, she threw down another. "Here's the one I was looking for. It was taken this summer at Narragansett Pier on his polo pony."

Gay seized it, studying the face of the handsome young fellow with interest. "Why, he's almost grown!" she cried.

"Yes, he's nearly eighteen, and he is even better looking than that picture. And here's Keith, the one I'm so fond of. We always have so much fun when they come out to grandmother's for the holidays."

The box slipped and the entire contents showered over the floor. Gay helped her to put them back into the box, glancing at each one as she did so. One in a cadet uniform attracted her attention.

"Who's this? Now *he's* the one I'd like to know. I suppose it's because I've lived at an army post always that I adore anything military. *He* looks interesting."

Kitty leaned over to look. "Oh, that's my brother Ranald. He's away at military school. Won't he be teased when I tell him what you said? He's dreadfully bashful with girls, though you'd think he oughtn't to be. He was under fire ever so many times with papa in the Philippines when he was a little chap. You know he was the youngest captain in the army, at one time, and was on General Grant's staff when he was still in short trousers."

"Why, of course, I know," cried Gay, enthusiastically. "I heard some officers talking about it one night at dinner just after it happened. Papa toasted 'The Little Captain' in such a pretty speech that the officers who had fought with your father cheered. But I never dreamed then that I'd ever know his sister, or be sitting here holding his picture, talking about him. I'm going to take possession of this," she added, when all the other photographs were back in the box.

"You don't care, do you? I'd like it to add to my collection of heroes. I'll put it in a frame made of brass buttons and crossed guns and all sorts of ornaments that the officers have given me off of their uniforms."

"No, I don't care," answered Kitty. "Allison has one like it, and I can get another any time by writing home for it. I wish you would take it, for that would give me such a fine thing to tease him about. I could worry him nearly distracted."

"I don't care how much you tease him so long as I may keep the picture," laughed Gay. "I'm a thousand times obliged to you."

As she sat looking at it, she exclaimed, suddenly: "Kitty Walton, you're an awfully lucky girl to have such nice boys in your family. I wish I knew them. I haven't a brother or even a forty-second cousin."

"Well, you can know them if you'll come home with me to spend the Christmas vacation. Ranald always brings a boy home with him for the holidays, and mother said Allison and I might bring a friend. I'm sure she'd rather have you than anybody else, she knows your father and mother so well."

The amber lights in Gay's brown eyes deepened. "Oh, I'd *love* to!" she cried. "I'd dearly love to! It's too far to go away back to San Antonio for such a short time, and I hated to think of the holidays, knowing I'd have to stay here at the Hall, with all you girls gone. Are you sure your mother won't object?"

"You wait and see," advised Kitty. "You don't know mammy! You'll not have any doubt of your welcome when her letter comes."

"Oh, it would be too lovely for anything!" exclaimed Gay, listening with a far-away look in her eyes, as Kitty began outlining plans for the coming holidays. Presently, in sheer joy at the prospect, they pulled each other up from the floor, and, springing on to the bed, danced a Highland fling in the middle of it, till a slat fell out with a terrifying crash.

With the coming of December the holiday gaieties began. A spirit of festivity lurked in the very air. A mock Christmas tree was one of the yearly features of the school, when each pupil's pet fad or peculiarity was suggested by appropriate gifts. Preparations for the tree began early in the month, and whispered consultations were carried on in every corner, with much giggling and profound assurances of secrecy.

The practising of Christmas carols went on in the music-rooms, and snatches of them floated down the halls and through the building, till the blithe young hearts were filled to overflowing with the cheer and good-will of the sweet old melodies. Now the usual Monday sightseeing gave way to shopping, and every moment that could be snatched from school work was given to crochet-needles and embroidery-hoops, to the finishing of an endless variety of gifts, and the wrapping of same in mysterious packages.

One Monday Betty did not join the others in their weekly shopping expedition. Her few purchases had been made, and she wanted the day to work on unfinished gifts. She was making most of them with her needle. She was glad afterward that she had decided to stay when a slow winter rain began to fall. It melted the light snow-fall which whitened the ground into a disagreeable compound of slush and mud.

It was almost dark when Kitty and Allison burst into the room, their arms full of bundles, and began displaying their purchases. Lloyd followed more slowly, and, dropping her packages on the floor by the radiator, stood trying to warm her fingers through her wet gloves. Presently, in the midst of the exhibition, with her hat still on, she flung herself across her bed, piled up as it was with strings and crumpled wrapping-paper. "Excuse me if I mash your bargains, Kitty," she said, weakly, closing her eyes. "But I'm as limp as a rag! So ti'ahed—I feel as if I were falling to pieces. We tramped around in the wet so long, and then inside the stores there were such crowds that we were pushed and jammed and stepped on everywhere we turned. It seemed to me we waited hours for our change. Then the car we came out on was so ovah-heated that we almost stifled. I'm suah I caught cold when the icy wind struck us aftah we left the station."

She shivered as she spoke. Betty sprang up and began tugging at her wet wraps.

"Don't lie there that way," she begged. "Let me help you get into some dry clothes, and ask the housekeeper for a glass of hot milk."

At first Lloyd protested that she was too tired to move. Betty could be as persistent as a mosquito at times. She insisted until Lloyd finally allowed her to have her way, and got up wearily to put on the dry skirts and stockings which she brought to her. A hot dinner made her feel somewhat better, but her face was flushed when they went up-stairs for the study hour. Betty saw her wipe her eyes as she took out her Latin grammar, and instantly forgave the petulant way in which Lloyd had answered her several times during the evening.

"Don't try to study, Lloyd," she urged. "I know you don't feel well."

"No," acknowledged the Little Colonel, "every bone in my body aches, and my head is simply splitting."

"Let me run down to the sanitarium and ask Miss Gilmer to come up and see if she can't do something for you," began Betty, but Lloyd interrupted her, stamping her foot with a touch of her old childish imperiousness.

"You sha'n't go! I'm not sick! I've just caught a plain cold."

"But people don't catch just plain colds nowadays," persisted Betty. "They always catch microbes at the same time, that are apt to turn into la grippe and pneumonia and all sorts of dreadful things. 'A stitch in time saves nine,' you know," she added, wisely, quoting from the motto embroidered on her darning-bag, which happened to be hanging on a chair-post in the corner. "'An ounce of prevention is worth a pound of cure' every time."

"Oh, for mercy's sake, Betty," cried Lloyd, impatiently, "let me alone and don't be so preachy. I'm not going to repo't a little thing like a headache and a soah throat to the nurse. She'd put me to bed and keep me there for a week. I'd get behind with my lessons, and lose all the holiday fun. Like as not mothah and Papa Jack would come straight aftah me, and take me home befoah we'd had the mock Christmas tree or any of the things I've been looking forward to so long."

Betty picked up her algebra again without an audible reply, but inwardly she was saying: "I know she is sick, or she wouldn't be so cross."

The next day found Lloyd with such high fever that she was installed at once in the sanitarium. "It is la grippe that she has," the nurse told Betty. "It is the real thing, and not what people always claim to have with an ordinary cold. The worst will probably be over in a few days, but it will leave her so exhausted and so susceptible to other things that I shall keep her with me for a week at least."

Lloyd rebelled at first, but she had to submit as her fever mounted higher, and the world grew, to her blurred fancy, one great, throbbing ache. She was glad to give herself up to Miss Gilmer's soothing touches. Mrs. Sherman did not come, for a letter from the school physician assured her that Lloyd was receiving every care and attention that she could have had at home, and the case was quite a simple one.

Miss Gilmer, the nurse, was a big motherly woman, who seemed to radiate comfort and cheer, as a stove does heat. After the first few days, Lloyd would have enjoyed the time spent with her in the cheerful room assigned her had she not been haunted by the thought that she was falling behind her classes.

"It's a pretty good sawt of a world, aftah all," she said one day, as she sat propped up among the pillows, enjoying a dainty mid-afternoon lunch Madam Chartley had personally prepared and sent in hot from the chafing-dish. Bouillon in the thinnest of fragile china, and a toasted scone which recalled delightfully the little English inn she had visited near Kenilworth ruins. By some oversight, no spoon had been sent in on the tray, and Miss Gilmer supplied the deficiency by bringing one of her own from a little cabinet in the next room.

"It has a history," Miss Gilmer said, and Lloyd looked at it with interest before dipping it into the cup.

"Why, the handle is a May-pole!" she exclaimed, with pleasure. "And the date down among the garlands is the queen's birthday, isn't it? I remembah we were up in the Burns country that day, when we saw the school-children celebrating it."

"To think of an American girl remembering that date!" cried Miss Gilmer, in a pleased tone. "It is a great day on my calendar, for it was then that I met Madam Chartley, for the first time, on the queen's birthday. She has been my good angel ever since. It was she who sent me that May-pole spoon, as a souvenir of that meeting."

"Oh, would you tell me about it?" asked Lloyd. "It sounds so interesting."

Taking up some needlework from a basket on the table, Miss Gilmer leaned back as if to begin a long story.

"There isn't so much to tell, after all," she said, pausing to thread her needle. "It was long ago, when Madam Chartley was Alicia Raeburn, and I was a bashful little English schoolgirl at St. Agnes Hall. Alicia had come from America to visit her uncle, who was proctor of the cathedral. His grounds joined the school premises on the south, and I often used to peep through the hedge and watch her strolling around the garden. She was older than I, and the difference in our ages seemed greater then than now, for I was still wearing short frocks, and she had just put on long ones. I had heard that she was to be presented at court next season. That, and the fact that she was an American, and very beautiful, and that she looked lonely strolling around the old proctor's garden by herself, threw a glamour of romance about her.

"I would have given a fortune to have made her acquaintance, and I spent hours down by the brook dreaming innocent little day-dreams in which I pictured such meetings. Suddenly heliotrope became my favourite flower instead of roses, because she so often wore a bunch of it tucked in the belt of her gray dress. Indeed, because she so often wore it, I grew to regard it as sacred to her alone, and felt that no one else had a right to wear it. Fortunately, at that season of the year it grew only in the proctor's conservatory, so that the schoolgirls could not obtain it. I would have inwardly resented it, if any one of them had taken such a liberty as to wear her flower. She seemed to me the most beautiful and perfect creature I had ever seen, and I worshipped her from afar, and imitated her in every way possible. I don't suppose you can understand such an infatuation."

"Indeed I do undahstand," interrupted Lloyd, eagerly. She was thinking of Ida Shane, and the way she had fallen under the spell of her charming personality. Even yet the odour of violets brought back the same little thrill it had awakened when violets seemed made for Ida's exclusive wearing. Miss Gilmer's feeling for the beautiful Alicia Raeburn was no deeper than hers had been for Ida. She could readily understand about the heliotrope.

"Well, then," Miss Gilmer went on, "you can imagine my state of mind when at last I actually met her. It was on the queen's birthday. At our school, instead of having the May-pole dance on May-day, we waited until the queen's birthday, and on that occasion Alicia was one of the invited guests. It was quite by accident she spoke to me. She dropped her handkerchief, and I sprang to pick it up. But she must have seen the adoration in my poor little embarrassed face, for I went quite red I am sure. I could fairly feel the hot blood surge over me. She said something pleasant to cover my confusion, and then swept her skirts aside for me to share her seat. She wanted to ask some questions about the customs of the school, she said.

"That was the beginning of our acquaintance. Next day she waved her handkerchief over the hedge to me, and the next called me over for a little chat. She was lonely in the great garden. After awhile I plucked up courage to tell her how I had watched her through the hedge, and dreamed about meeting her. I could not put it into words, but she could readily see that the good Victoria and the queen of the May were not the sovereigns who claimed my dearest allegiance. It was the 'Queen Rose of the rosebud garden of girls,' the beautiful Alicia Raeburn.

"She went away that summer, but we had grown to be such friends that she promised to write to me once a year, in order that I might not lose her entirely out of my life. She knew what a lonely little orphan I was, and she never denied me the joy of that yearly letter. They were full of her travels and the interesting experiences of her life, for she married a young English officer and went to India.

"They came back to England once. I saw her then. It was at a great ball given for the Prince of Wales when he honoured the little cathedral town with a visit. She could hardly believe that I was the little schoolgirl who had eyed her so adoringly through the hedge. I had grown so large. But she found from others what a lonely life I had, and, knowing how much her friendship meant, she still gave me the pleasure of that yearly letter, written on the queen's birthday. That she should remember through all her busy years shows one of the finest traits of her character.

"Once she was too ill to write, but the message came just the same. She sent this spoon with the May-pole handle, and on her card was scrawled the one line, 'I keep the tryst.' She had told me the story of their family crest. You don't know how many times in the next few years the sight of that card and the souvenir spoon helped me. Her fidelity to a promise made me rely on her and her friendship when all others failed me. My guardian died and left my property in such shape that I found I would have to support myself, and I began to take training for a professional nurse. When she heard of it, she wrote and told me that she, too, had been obliged by her husband's death to earn her own living, and that she had established this school in her great-grandmother's old mansion. She offered me the position of professional nurse here. I came on the next steamer, and have been here ever since.

"You don't know how many times I've thought how different my life would have been if she had failed in that one little matter of sending a yearly letter. No doubt it was a bore to her oftentimes, but it was the line that kept us in touch and finally drew me to this happy anchorage. Alicia Chartley is a great woman, my dear. She has left her imprint on every girl who has passed through this school, and there'll be a long line of them to rise up and call her blessed. Not so much for the fine ladies she has made of them with her high-bred ways and ideals, but for the example she has set them always in that one thing. No matter in how small a duty, she has never once failed to keep the tryst."

Lloyd would have liked to ask some questions about Madam's girlhood, but some one called Miss Gilmer into the office just then, so, taking the tray with its empty cup and plate, she passed out. Lloyd thumped her pillows and lay looking out of the window at the sparrows on the balcony railing. All the ache was gone, and, with a delightful sense of drowsiness and of well-being, she began slipping into a little doze. Even illness had its bright side, she thought, languidly. She liked Miss Gilmer's reminiscences. They opened into a world so delightfully English. When she came back she would ask for more stories. Down from the distant music-room stole the faint echo of one of the carols. She opened her eyes to listen.

"God rest you, merry Christians,
Let nothing you dismay,
For Christ our Lord and Saviour
Was born on Christmas Day."

Lloyd liked that carol. "'Let nothing you dismay,'" she repeated, softly. "No, it doesn't really make any difference what happens," she thought, closing her eyes again and curling up like a sleepy kitten. "It will all come right in the end, as it did with Miss Gilmer. I'll not worry about missing so many lessons and so many pearls on my rosary. I'll just be thankful for Christmas and all it brings."

Again through her drowsy senses echoed the refrain, and she dropped to sleep, repeating, slowly, "'Let—nothing—you—dismay!'"

CHAPTER VI.

CHRISTMAS CAROLS

"This is the worst time of all the yeah to be sick," fretted the Little Colonel, pausing in her restless journey around the room. She had been pacing from window to fireplace in the nurse's office, and from fireplace to window again, watching the clock and the slowly westering sun, as if watching would hasten the day to its close.

Miss Gilmer, who was placidly knitting, changed needles without looking up. "That is what people always say. I've never yet found one whose calendar had a time when illness would be convenient."

"But now, just befoah the holidays, a thousand things are waiting to be done. I'm behind a whole week with my studies, and my Christmas presents that I'm going to make are scarcely begun. You haven't even let me look at the material. I feel like a caged lion, and I'd like to roah and claw and ramp around till I'd smashed my bah's."

"You'll have your liberty soon," laughed Miss Gilmer. "I think it will be safe to let you go down to the dining-room this evening, and I'll give you your honourable discharge in the morning. But, if I were in your place, I would make no attempt to catch up with the classes this term. I would lock the unfinished presents away in a drawer, and not give any this Christmas. You ought to spend the holidays as quietly as possible, doing nothing but rest."

Lloyd turned toward her with an exclamation of dismay.

"Oh, Miss Gilmer! That's impossible! We've planned for a gayer Christmas vacation than we've evah had befoah. Every day will be full to the brim. And I *must* make up the recitations I have missed. I've had such good repoah'ts all term that I can't beah to spoil everything right at the end. When I was in bed, feeling so bad, I made up my mind I wouldn't worry about them, but now I feel as good as new, only a little weak, and one always feels weak aftah fevah. It's to be expected. You know I wasn't dangerously ill."

"No," admitted Miss Gilmer, "but your little illness has left you with less strength than you think you have. You are like an ice-pond that is just beginning to freeze over. A very light weight will break it through at that stage, but if there is no strain until it has frozen properly, it can bear the weight of the most heavily loaded wagons."

Lloyd slipped into a chair and stared dismally at the fire.

"But I am strongah than you think, Miss Gilmer. Except one time when I had the measles, I'd never been sick in my life till last week. I don't believe it's good for people to coddle themselves and worry all the time for feah they are going to be ill."

"Oh," answered the nurse, "I fully agree with you in that, still I should not be doing my duty if I did not put up a warning signal when I see danger ahead. I do see it now. You are getting on very nicely, but the ice is very thin,—far too thin for any such extra weights as double study hours and holiday dissipations. If you don't walk lightly, there'll be a nervous breakdown."

Some one called Miss Gilmer away before she could finish her warning, and Lloyd sat facing the fire and this unpleasant bit of counsel for nearly half an hour. A verse from her favourite carol came echoing through the halls from the distant music-room, for it was practice hour again, but this time it did not fit her mood, and it brought no cheer. It was all well enough for those girls up-stairs, happy and well and able to do as they pleased, to be singing "Let *nothing* you dismay," but she couldn't help being dismayed at Miss Gilmer's opinion of her condition. She was ready to cry, thinking how all her holidays would be spoiled should she follow the nurse's advice.

With her chin in her hand and her elbow on the arm of the chair, she sat picturing her doleful Christmas if she could have no part in the giving, and must be left out of all the merrymaking they had planned. Tears welled up into her eyes, and her miserable reverie might have ended in a downpour had it not been interrupted by the entrance of Gay and Betty. Having taken a hasty run across the terraces, they had obtained permission to spend the rest of the recreation hour with Lloyd.

"We can't waste a minute now," exclaimed Gay, as she pulled out her knitting-work and began clicking her ivory needles through a rainbow shawl she was making. "I believe Betty sleeps with her embroidery hoops under her pillow, and I know that Allison paints in her sleep."

"What would you do if you were in my place?" mourned Lloyd. She repeated the nurse's dismal warning.

"Boo! She magnifies her office," said Gay, glancing over her shoulder to make sure that they were alone. "I suppose it is perfectly natural that she should. When you're with Miss White, she makes you feel that there's nothing in life to live for but Latin. When you're with Miss Hooker, mathematics is the chief end of man. With Professor Stroebel the violin is the one and only. So of course a professional nurse is in duty bound to make hygiene the first consideration. Don't listen to them, listen to me. I change my mind a dozen times a day, and have a new fad every fortnight, so it stands to reason that my advice is more broad-minded than the advice of a person who rides only one hobby, and rides that in a rut."

Lloyd laughed at Gay's foolishness, but groaned when Betty told her how far the classes had advanced during her absence from recitations.

"I'll have to work like a beavah this next week to catch up. I stah'ted out to have perfect repoah'ts, and I feel that I must stick to it, as Ederyn did when he heard the king's call. It is an obligation that I *must* meet. I must keep tryst or die."

Gay looked at her admiringly. "I knew you were like that," she exclaimed. "If there is anything I envy it is strength of character."

The admiring glance and Gay's remark carried greater weight than all the nurse's warning. There was another reason now for persevering in her determination. Gay expected it of her, and she could not fall below Gay's expectation of what a strong character should accomplish.

Gay, having finished a white stripe across the shawl, opened the sweet-grass Indian basket hanging on her chair-post, and took out several skeins of zephyr of a delicate sea-shell pink.

"Let me hold it while you wind," begged Lloyd. "It's such an exquisite shade, like the heart of a la France rose. It makes me think of the stories mothah used to tell me. Everything in them had to be pink, from the little girl's dress to the bow on her kitten's neck. Her slippahs, parasol, flowahs in the garden, papah on the wall, icing on the cake, everything had to be pink."

"What a funny little creature you must have been," laughed Gay, secretly making note of Lloyd's favourite colour, and resolving to change the names on two packages laid away in her trunk. The blue sachet-bag with the forget-me-nots should go to Betty instead of Lloyd, as she had originally intended. Lloyd should have the one with the garlands of pink rosebuds.

"My room at home is furnished in pink," Lloyd went on. "Oh, Gay, I'm wild for you to see Locust. I'm going to have you and the Walton girls and Katie Mallard, one of our neighbahs, spend two days and nights with us. While I've been cooped up heah getting well, I've planned some of the loveliest things to do that you evah dreamed of. It's going to be the gayest vacation that evah was."

When Miss Gilmer returned at the end of the hour, Lloyd looked so much brighter and better that she gave her an unexpected furlough.

"There, run along to your room with the other girls. I'll expect you back at bedtime, for I want to keep you under my wing one more night, but you're at liberty till then on one condition,—you're not to look into a book."

"I'll promise! Oh, I'll promise!" cried Lloyd, impetuously throwing her arms around the nurse. "You're *such* a deah! Not that I'm anxious to get away from you," she added, fearing that her delight might be misunderstood. "But I just want to get *out!*"

True to her promise, Lloyd opened no books, but, flying to her room, she took out one of the uncompleted Christmas gifts, a pair of bedroom slippers, and worked with feverish haste until dinner was ready. It was good to be at the table again with the other girls after her week of solitary meals in the nursery. Afterward it was a temptation to linger in the library talking with them, but the thought of the many tasks undone sent her hurrying back to her room.

Betty followed presently with the Walton girls, and they all worked steadily on their various gifts until the bell rang for the evening study hour. Then Allison and Kitty reluctantly departed, and Betty took out her algebra. Lloyd crocheted in silence for half an hour longer, her fingers flying faster and faster in her eagerness to complete the task. Finally she laid it down with a sigh of relief.

"There!" she exclaimed aloud. "That's done. They're all ready for the bows. Now, thank fortune, I can check them off my list."

Betty looked up with an absent-minded smile, nodded approvingly at the finished slippers standing on the table, and then went on with her problems. Lloyd opened her bureau-drawer to search for the ribbon which she had bought for the bows. As she rummaged through it, her hand touched the little sandalwood box that held the unfinished rosary. She glanced over her shoulder. Betty was deep in her algebra. So, taking out the string of beads, she passed it slowly through her fingers. Then she held it up, and, looping it around her throat, looked in the mirror.

"I suppose it's mighty childish of me," she said to herself, "but I can't enjoy my vacation if I go home with a single one of this term's pearls missing. I've *got* to make up those lessons, no mattah what the nurse says. I can rest aftahward."

A few minutes later she presented herself at Miss Gilmer's door with the announcement that she would go to bed an hour earlier than usual, in order to get a good start for the next day.

All that week she worked with a restless energy that kept her keyed to the highest pitch of effort. She scarcely ate, and her sleep was broken, but her eyes were so bright and her manner so animated, that Betty wrote home that Lloyd's little spell of illness seemed to have done her good.

By studying before breakfast, and snatching every minute she could spare from other duties, she managed to have perfect recitations in each study, and at the same time to make up the lessons she had missed. Five o'clock Saturday afternoon found her with the last task done. She slipped ten more little Roman pearls over the silken cord; five for the week's advance work, and five for the days she had missed. Then with a sigh of relief she put the sandalwood box into her trunk, already partly packed for home-going, and flung herself wearily across the bed.

The mock Christmas tree had been lighted the evening before, and the gifts distributed. She had not enjoyed it as she had expected to, although some of the jokes were excruciatingly funny, and the girls had laughed until they were limp. She was too tired to laugh much. She was glad that Sunday was coming before the day of leave-taking. She made up her mind that she would skip dinner, and ask Betty just to slip her something from the table.

Then she remembered that this was the night the carols were to be sung in the chapel. She could not miss that. It was the prettiest service of all the year, the old girls said. Some one had told her it was a custom for everybody to wear white to the carol-singing, but it was hard to remember things, maybe she had only dreamed it. She wished that she did not have to remember things, but could lie there without moving, until morning. What was it her mother used to sing to her? "Asleep in the arms of the slow-swinging seas." Oh! The white seal's lullaby. That was what she wanted. How good it would feel to be rocked by the restful motion of the waves, to be caught in that long sleepy sweep of the slow-swinging seas.

When she opened her eyes again it was to find the room lighted, and Betty dressing for the carol service. She had slept an hour.

"It'll never do to miss the carols," Betty assured her, when she suggested skipping dinner. "Come on, I'll help you dress. Just tell me what you want to wear, and I'll lay out your things while you're shaking your wits together. You'll feel better after you've had a hot dinner." So struggling with the weariness which nearly overpowered her, Lloyd forced herself to follow Betty's example, and go down to the dining-room when the bell rang. An hour later she fell into line with the other girls, as, all in white, they filed into the chapel.

"How Christmasey it looks and smells," she whispered to Allison, as the doors swung open and a breath from the pine woods greeted them. The chancel was wreathed and festooned with masses of evergreen. To-night tall white candles furnished the only light. Far down the dim aisles they twinkled like stars against the dark background of cedar and hemlock.

Betty was glad that they had entered early. The deep silence of those moments of waiting, the dim light of the Christmas tapers, and the fragrance of the pine seemed as much a part of the service as anything which followed. In the expectant hush that filled the little chapel, she pictured the three kings riding through the night, until she could almost see the shadowy desert and hear the tread of the camels who bore the wise men on their starlit quest. She saw the hillside of Judea, where the shepherds kept their night-watch by their flocks, and all the mystery and wonder of the first great Christmastide seemed to vibrate through her heart, as the deep organ prelude suddenly filled the air with the jubilant chords of "Joy to the world, the Lord has come."

Presently the music changed, and the girls looked around expectantly. From far down distant halls and corridors came a chorus of girlish voices: "Oh, little town of Bethlehem." So sweet and far away it was, the audience in the chapel involuntarily leaned forward to listen. Across the campus it sounded, gradually drawing nearer and clearer, until, with a triumphant burst of melody, the doors swung open and the white-robed choir swept in.

Only the best voices in the school had been chosen for this choir, and weeks of training preceded the service. One after another they sang the sweet old tunes of the Christmas waits until they reached Lloyd's favourite, "Let nothing you dismay." She listened to it with pleasure now, since her greatest cause for dismay had been removed. She had kept tryst with the term's obligations, as the last pearl on the rosary could testify.

In the hush that followed that carol, an old man, with silvery hair and benign face, rose under the tall candles of the chancel.

"It's the bishop," whispered Gay to Lloyd. "Old Bishop Chartley. He is Madam's uncle, and he always comes down for this service."

Then even her irrepressible tongue grew still, for, in a deep voice that filled the chapel, he began to read the story of the three wise men who followed the star with their gifts of gold and frankincense and myrrh, until it led them to Bethlehem's manger. An old, old story, but it bloomed anew once more, as it has bloomed every year since first the wondering wise men started on their quest.

The bishop closed the Book. "How shall we keep the King's birthday?" he asked. "What gifts shall we bring? To-day in a quaint old tale, beloved in boyhood, I found the answer. It is the story of a strange country called Cathay, and this is the way it runs:

"'The ruler thereof is one Kublan Khan, a mighty warrior. His government is both wise and just, and is administered to rich and poor alike, without fear or favour. On the king's birthday the people observe what is called the White Feast. Then are the king and his court assembled in a great room of the palace, which is all white, the floor of marble and the walls hung with curtains of white silk. All are in white apparel, and they offer unto the king white gifts, to show that their love and loyalty are without a stain. The rich bring to their lord pearls, carvings of ivory, white chargers, and costly broidered garments. The poor present white pigeons and handfuls of rice. Nor doth the great king regard one gift above another, so long as all be white. And so do they keep the king's birthday.'"

Lloyd, leaning forward, listened with such breathless interest that it attracted Gay's attention. "That's just like your pink story," she whispered. Lloyd gave her fingers a responsive squeeze, but never took her eyes from the benign old face. The bishop was applying the story to the audience before him.

"As these pagans of Cathay kept the feast of Kublan Kahn, so we may make of Christmas a White Feast, whose offerings are without stain. We need make no weary pilgrimages across the trackless sands, as did those Eastern sages. 'Inasmuch as ye have done it unto the least of these my brethren' (these are the King's own words), 'ye have done it unto me.' At our very doors we may give to Him, through His poor and needy.

"But there is another way. You are all familiar with the motto of this house, and the legend which gave rise to it. Clad in the white garments of Righteousness, we may keep the tryst as Ederyn kept it, and bring to the King the white pearls of a well-spent life. Days unstained by selfishness, days filled up with duties faithfully performed. It matters not how small and commonplace our efforts seem, the rice and the pigeons of the poor showed Kublan Kahn his subjects' loyalty as fully as the ivory carvings and the costly broidered garment. Nor doth the great King regard one gift of ours above another, so long as all be white. If only on our breasts the tokens Duty gives us spell out the words, '*semper fidelis*,' then ours will be the royal accolade: 'Well done, thou good and faithful servant. Enter thou into the joy of thy Lord.' To give *ourselves*, unstained and gladly, thus may we keep the White Feast on the birthday of the King."

Then the choir stood again, but Lloyd scarcely noticed what it sang. She was thinking of the bishop's story, and her secret hidden away in the sandalwood box. She was so glad now that she had strung the pearls. She had begun it because it pleased her fancy to act out the story of Ederyn, but now the sacred meaning the old bishop gave the story thrilled her through and through. The King's call suddenly seemed very sweet and personal. Henceforth she would string the pearls in answer to that call.

When they all knelt in the closing prayer, she fervently echoed the bishop's petition: "Grant that we make of this Christmastide a White Feast, and that all our days may be worthy of thy acceptance, unstained by selfishness and full of deeds to show our love and loyalty."

The white-robed choir filed slowly out, their music sounding fainter and fainter until it died away across the campus, and the white-robed audience was left kneeling in silence. There were tears in Gay's eyes when she arose. Such music always stirred her to the depths. Kitty went back to her room humming one of the carols, and Betty stole away to write the bishop's sermon in her little white record, while the memory of it was still warm in her heart.

At Miss Gilmer's request, Lloyd waited a moment in the vestibule. At first she wished that Miss Gilmer had not detained her. She wanted to go on with Allison, who had her by the arm. Afterward, however, she was glad of the waiting. It gave her an opportunity to meet the venerable bishop.

"So you are going home to-morrow for the holidays," he said, genially, as he held out his hand. "Godspeed, daughter. May you keep the White Feast with joy."

It seemed to Lloyd that that "Godspeed" followed her like a benediction.

CHAPTER VII.

HOMEWARD BOUND

"O Warwick Hall, dear Warwick Hall,
Thy happy hours we'll oft recall!
No time or change can break thy tie,
Though for awhile we say good-bye—
Good-bye! Good-bye!"

Amid a flutter of handkerchiefs and a babel of parting cries, each 'bus-load of girls departed from the Hall to the station singing the farewell song of the school.

A dozen times on the way home Allison, humming it unconsciously, found the rest of the party joining in. It was an uneventful journey, but a merry one to the five girls, travelling for the first time without a chaperon. For the first few hours they had the observation car to themselves. Even the porter mysteriously disappeared.

"He's curled up asleep somewhere, rest his soul," said Gay, when she had rung for him several times.

"All the better," answered Kitty. "We don't really need the table, and it's nice to have him out of the way. This is as good as travelling in a private car. We can 'stand on our head in our little trundle-bed, and nobody nigh to hinder.' Oh, girls, I'm so crazy glad that we're on our way home that I'm positively obliged to do something to let off steam. I've exhausted my vocabulary trying to express my delight, so there's nothing left but to howl."

"Or to wriggle," suggested Gay. "Why not try facial expression? How is this for transcendent joy?"

The grotesque smile which she turned upon them was so ridiculous that they screamed with laughter.

"Oh, Gay, do stop!" begged Betty. "You're as bad as a comic valentine."

"I'd like to see you do any better," retorted Gay.

"Let's all try," suggested Kitty. "Line up in front of this mirror, girls. Now all look pleasant, please. Now let your smiles express rapture. Now, frenzied delight!"

Fascinated by their own ugliness, the five girls stood in a row distorting their pretty faces with hideous grins and grimaces until they were weak from laughing. The banging of the car door sent them scuttling into their seats. A portly old gentleman passed through the car to the rear platform, and, slamming the door behind him, stood looking down the rapidly vanishing track. Evidently it was too breezy a view-point for the old gentleman, even with his coat-collar turned up and hat pulled down to meet his ears, for in a moment he came in and passed back to his seat in a forward car. The girls sat demurely looking out of the windows until he was gone, then they faced each other, giggling.

"Suppose he had caught us making those idiotic faces," exclaimed Allison. "He would have taken us for a lot of escaped lunatics."

"No, he wouldn't," insisted Gay. "He was a real benevolent-looking old fellow, the kind that understands young people, and he'd know that it was just that Christmas has gone to our heads, and made us a little flighty. I'm sure that his name is James, and that he has six old maid daughters. He lives out West, and he's taking home a trunk full of presents for them."

"Let's guess what he has for them," said Kitty. "I'll say that the oldest one is named Emmaline, and he is taking her a squirrel fur muff."

"And the next one is Agnes Dorothea," said Betty, taking her turn, as if it were a game. "She's the delicate one of the family, and a sort of invalid. So he bought her a lavender shoulder shawl that caught his fatherly eye in a show window, because it was so soft and fluffy. But it will shrink and fade the first time it is washed till Agnes Dorothea will look like a homeless cat if she wears it. Still she will persist in putting it on because dear father brought it to her from Washington."

"He'd certainly think you all were crazy if he could heah yoah remah'ks," laughed Lloyd.

"Speaking of shawls," cried Gay, "that reminds me of that rainbow shawl in my bag. I haven't taken a stitch in it since we started, and I intended to knit all the way home. I simply have to, if I'm to get it done in time."

Taking out the square of linen in which the fleecy zephyr was wrapped, she settled herself by the rear window in a big arm-chair, with her feet drawn up under her, and fell to work with all her might.

"It's so nice and cosy to have the car all to ourselves," sighed Allison, stretching out luxuriously on the sofa. Betty, bending over her embroidery, smiled tenderly at a picture that her memory showed her just then. She was comparing this journey with the first one she had ever taken. And she saw in her thoughts a little brown-eyed girl of eleven, setting forth on her first venture into the wide world, with a sunbonnet tied over her curls, and an old-fashioned covered basket on her arm. What a dread undertaking that journey had been from the Cuckoo's Nest to the House Beautiful. She remembered how frightened she was, and how she had studied the picture of Red Ridinghood, printed in colours on the border of her handkerchief, until she was afraid to speak even to the conductor. She saw a possible wolf in every stranger.

Somehow her thoughts kept going back to that time, even in the midst of Gay's most amusing nonsense, and Kitty's brightest repartee. Even when Allison began to sing "O Warwick Hall," and she chimed in with the others, "Dear Warwick Hall," she was not thinking of school, but of the Cuckoo's Nest, and Davy, and the old weather-beaten meeting-house, in whose window she had passed so many summer afternoons, reading the musty dog-eared books she found in the little red bookcase.

"What are you smiling about, Betty, all to yoahself?" asked Lloyd. "You look as if you are a thousand miles away."

Betty glanced up with a little start. "Oh, I was just thinking about the Cuckoo's Nest, and wishing that I could see Davy's face when they open the Christmas box I sent. There are only trifles in it, but the box will mean a lot to them, for Cousin Hetty never has time to make anything of Christmas."

Lloyd sat up with a sudden exclamation. "Oh, Betty, I *beg* yoah pah'don. There's a lettah for you in my bag from some of them that I forgot to give you. Hawkins came up with it just as we drove off, and there was so much excitement and confusion I nevah thought of it again till this minute. I'm mighty sorry I forgot."

"It doesn't make any difference," Betty assured her. "Good news can afford to wait, and, if it's bad news, it would have spoiled all the first part of this trip."

She tore open the envelope and glanced down the page. Lloyd, looking up, saw a distressed expression cross her face and the brown eyes fill with tears.

"Oh, it's poor little Davy that's in trouble," said Betty, answering Lloyd's anxious question. "He had his leg badly hurt last week, broken in two places. He was riding one of those heavy old farm horses, hurrying home to get out of a storm. Going down a steep, slippery hill, it stumbled and fell on him. He'll have to lie in bed for weeks, with his knee in plaster, and he's so tired of it already, and *so* lonesome. Nobody has any time to sit with him. I know how it is. I was sick myself once at the Cuckoo's Nest. Oh, I'd give anything if I could spend my vacation there with him."

"And give up all your good times at home?" cried Kitty. "He surely couldn't expect such a sacrifice as that."

"But it wouldn't be any sacrifice. Not a mite! I haven't seen him for such a long time, and I'd love to go. He used to be the dearest little fellow, never out of my sight a moment during the day. They used to call him 'Betty's shadow.'"

"Why don't you go if you wish it so much?" was on the tip of Gay's tongue, but she stopped the question just before it slipped off, remembering Betty's dependence on her godmother. Kitty had told her all about it one time. Naturally she wouldn't want to ask for the money, even for such a short journey, when so much was being spent to keep her at school with Lloyd; and naturally she would not want to ask to leave Locust at Christmas, when that was the time of all the year when she could be of service, and in many ways add greatly to the pleasure of the entire household.

The nonsense stopped for a few minutes. No one knew what to say to comfort Betty, although they were genuinely sorry, and glanced from time to time at the brown head turned away from them toward the window. She was looking at the flying landscape through a blur of tears, recalling the way little Davy's dimpled fingers had clung to hers, his chubby feet followed her. Of course he was much larger and older, she told herself, not at all like the little fellow she had left so long ago. He was big enough to stand pain now, and probably the worst of his suffering was over. Still, she saw only a solemn baby face when she pictured him, and heard only the lisping voice, saying as he used to say when stumped toe or bruised finger brought the tears: "It hurth your Davy boy. Tie a wag on it, Betty." How he had loved her stories! What a pleasure they would be to him now in the long days he would be forced to spend in bed.

Suddenly conscious of the silence around her, Betty turned, realizing that her depression had cast a shadow on the spirits of all the rest.

"Don't think about my bad news any more," she said, brightly. "It probably isn't half as bad as I have been picturing it. My imagination always runs away with me. It isn't Davy the baby that's had such an awful accident. It was that thought that hurt me so at first. I keep forgetting that it's five years since I left there. I'm going to drop him a postal card at the next station. I can write to him every day, and make a sort of game of the letters with riddles and suggestions of things for him to do, and that will help the time pass."

"First call to dinnah in the dinah," called a coloured waiter, passing through the car in white jacket and apron.

"Now we'll have to stop all our foolishness," said Allison, sedately, as she rose to lead the way to the dining-car. They followed as decorously as grandmothers, each realizing the responsibility that devolved on her, since they were travelling without a chaperon.

To be sure, Gay choked on an olive when Kitty made some wicked remark about the fussy old woman across the aisle, who wouldn't be pleased with anything the waiter brought her; and it was too much for their gravity when an excessively dignified man at the next table, who had been staring at the wall like a wooden Indian, suddenly sneezed so violently that his eye-glasses dropped into his soup with a splash.

Otherwise they were models of propriety, and more than one head turned to look at the bright girlish faces, and smile at the keen, unspoiled enjoyment which they evidently found in life and in each other.

They did not stay long in the observation-car when they went back to it after dinner. Other people had come in, and it was not so attractive as when they occupied it alone. The lamps had been lighted so early that short December day that it seemed much later than it really was, and they were all tired. At nine o'clock, when they went to their berths in the forward end of the car, they found several sections already made up for the night, and the porter was moving on down toward theirs.

The fussy old woman, who had been so hard to please at the table, came squeezing her way through the valises that blocked the aisle, and took possession of the section opposite Betty and Lloyd.

"Oh, my country!" whispered Lloyd. "I wondah if she's going to keep up that grumbling and scolding all night. I'm glad that I am not that poah henpecked maid of hers. She certainly makes life misahable for her."

It was nearly two hours before Jenkins, the long-suffering maid, succeeded in settling her mistress to her satisfaction behind the curtains of her berth. The girls made no attempt to get into the dressing-room until the little comedy was over. They laughed until they were hysterical over each scene as it occurred. A comedy in three acts, Betty called it—the losing of the cold-cream bottle and the finding of same in madam's overshoe. The unavailing search for a certain black silk handkerchief in which madam was wont to tie her head up in of nights, and the substitution of a towel instead, which the porter obligingly brought.

Next there was a supposed case of poisoning, Jenkins in her trepidation having administered three pink pellets from a bottle instead of two white ones from a box. Five minutes' reign of terror after that mistake brought the poor maid to a witless state that left her almost helpless. Various trips were made to the dressing-room, at which times the old lady's face was massaged, her grizzly hair rolled on crimping-pins, and her shoulders rubbed with an evil-smelling liniment which permeated the whole car. She seemed as oblivious to the presence of the other passengers as if she were on a desert island, and, being somewhat deaf, made Jenkins repeat her timid replies louder and louder until they were almost screaming at each other.

Every one on the car was smiling broadly when at last she subsided behind the curtains. The smiles grew to audible mirth when she confided in a loud voice to Jenkins, stowed away in the berth above her, that she hoped to goodness nobody on board would snore and keep her awake.

Jenkins's answer, floating tremulously down, convulsed the sleepy girls: "Hi 'ope not, ma'am. Hit's a bad 'abit, ma'am, halmost, you might say, han haffliction."

"What?" came in a thunderous voice from the lower berth, and Jenkins, craning her head turtle-wise over the edge of her bed, called back in a tremulous squeak: "Hi honly said as 'ow hit were a bad 'abit, ma'am!"

"Hump!" was the answer. "See that you don't do it yourself. I've got my umbrella here ready to punch you if you do."

A titter ran from seat to seat. The girls, unable to stifle their amusement any longer, seized their bags and hurried down the aisle to the dressing-room, where, under cover of the rattle of the train, they could laugh as freely as they pleased.

When Lloyd and Betty stole back to their berths a few minutes later, they looked at each other with an amused smile. From the opposite section came an unmistakable sound, long-drawn and penetrating as a cross-cut saw. Madam was evidently asleep. Betty giggled, as from Jenkins's perch came a gentle echo.

"'Hi honly said as 'ow hit were a bad 'abit, ma'am,'" whispered Lloyd. "Wouldn't you love to jab the old lady herself with an umbrella?"

Gay, in the dressing-room, was carefully counting over her toilet articles, as she put them back into her bag. "Soap-box, comb, nail-file, tooth-powder—I haven't lost a thing this trip, Allison. I'm beginning to feel proud of myself.

Here's my watch and here's my tickets, buttoned up in this pocket. Mamma had it made on purpose, so in case of a wreck at night I'd have them on me. She patted the pocket sewed securely in the dark blue silk robe she wore, made in loose kimono fashion.

"Now I'm all ready," she added, dropping her shoes into her bag and closing it. In her soft Indian moccasins, beaded like a squaw's, she executed a little heel and toe dance in the narrow passage outside, while she waited for Allison to gather up her clothes and follow. She thought every one else was in bed, and when suddenly the outside door opened and she heard some one coming in from the next car, she flew down the aisle like a frightened rabbit.

It was only a brakeman who stood just inside the door a moment with his lantern, and then went out again. All the lights had been turned down in the car, and Gay stumbled several times over shoes and valises protruding in the aisle. But finally, with a bound, she made her escape, as she supposed, from whoever it was that had caught her dancing in her moccasins in the passage.

She gave a headlong dive into her berth. Just then the car lurched forward, sending her bag banging against the window, but she did not loosen her hold of it, and she was still clinging to it five minutes later.

For, with a scream of terror, she rolled out of the berth far faster than she had rolled in. It was madam's fat body that writhed under her, and her stern voice that yelled "Murder! murder!" in a voice calculated to wake the dead.

"'Elp! 'elp!" screamed Jenkins from the upper berth, afraid to look out between the curtains, but bravely pushing the button of the porter's bell till some one, wakened by the cries and persistent ringing, wildly called "Fire!"

"It's train robbahs!" gasped Lloyd, sitting up. Little cold shivers ran up and down her back, but she was conscious of a pleasant thrill of excitement. Heads were thrust out all up and down the aisle. The bell and the cries of murder and 'elp never stopped until the porter and Pullman conductor came running to the rescue.

But there was nothing for them to see. At the first yell, Gay had tumbled hastily out, still clinging to her bag. Before the old lady had sufficiently recovered from her surprise enough to wonder what sort of a wild beast had pounced in upon her, Gay was safe in her own berth, drawn up in a knot, and trembling behind her closely buttoned curtains. Her heart beat so loud that she thought it would certainly betray her.

"You must have had the nightmare," said the conductor, politely, trying not to smile as the angry face, under its towel turban, glared out at him.

"Nightmare!" blazed the irate old lady. "I'm no fool. Don't you suppose that I know when I'm hit? I tell you somebody was trying to sandbag me. I thought a Saratoga trunk had fallen in on me. It's your business to take care of passengers on this train, and I intend to hold the company responsible. I shall certainly sue the railroad for this shock to my nervous system as soon as I get home. I have a weak heart and I can't stand such performances as this."

It took a long time to pacify her. Gay lay in her berth, shaking first with fright and then with laughter. She could not go to sleep without sharing her secret with the other girls, but she was afraid to trust herself to speak. She had grown almost hysterical over the affair. Finally she crept in beside Lloyd to whisper, brokenly: "*I* am the nightmare that sandbagged the old lady. *I* am the Saratoga trunk that fell on her. Oh, Lloyd, I'll never brag again. I had just told Allison I hadn't lost a single thing this trip, and then I turned around and lost myself. I got into the wrong berth. Oh! oh! It was so funny to see her, all done up in that towel. It'll kill me if I can't stop laughing."

She crept back to her own side of the aisle again, and Lloyd got up to repeat it to Betty and Allison, who passed it on to Kitty. It was nearly half an hour before they stopped giggling over it, and then Kitty started them all afresh by leaning out to say, in a stage whisper, as a certain duet was renewed by Jenkins and her mistress, "'Hi honly said as 'ow hit were a bad 'abit.'"

It was snowing next morning, just a few flakes against the window-pane, as they sat in the dining-car at breakfast, but the landscape grew whiter as they whirled on toward home.

"Just as it ought to be for Christmas," declared Allison. "Oh, The Beeches will look so lovely in the snow, and the big log fire will seem so good, I can hardly wait to get there!"

"I know just how it's all going to be," exclaimed Kitty, wriggling impatiently in her seat. "It will be this way, Gay. They'll all be down at the station to meet us, mother and little Elise and Uncle Harry and his dog. Aunt Allison will probably be there, too, and grandmother, if she feels well enough. And old black fat Butler will be standing by the baggage-room door with his wheelbarrow, waiting to take our trunks. And we'll all talk at once. Everybody along the road will be calling 'Howdy!' to us, and at the post-office Miss Mattie will come out to shake hands with us, and tell us how glad she is to see us back. Then it'll be just a step, past the church and the manse and the Bakewell cottage, and we'll turn in at The Beeches, *and the fun will begin.*"

Betty turned to Gay. "That doesn't sound very exciting or especially interesting to a stranger, but, oh, Gay, the Valley is so *dear* when you once get to know it. And when you go back, you feel almost as if everybody were related to you, they're all so friendly and cordial and glad to welcome you home."

Even to impatient schoolgirls homeward bound, the journey's end comes at last, so by nightfall it all happened just as Kitty had predicted. Such a royal welcome awaited Gay that she felt drawn into the midst of things from the moment she stepped from the car.

"You're right, Betty," she whispered as she left her. "It *is* a dear Valley, and I feel already as if I belong here."

The two groups separated when the checks had been sorted out and the baggage disposed of. Then, still laughing and talking, Kitty led one on its merry way toward The Beeches, and the other whirled rapidly away in the carriage toward the lights of Locust.

CHAPTER VIII.

A PICNIC IN THE SNOW

"What a good gray day this is!" exclaimed Betty next morning, turning from the window to look around the cheerful breakfast-room, all aglow with an open wood-fire. "It's so bleak outside that there is no temptation to go gadding, and so cosy indoors that we'll be glad of the chance to stay at home and finish tying up our Christmas packages."

"Yes," assented Lloyd, who, having finished her breakfast, was standing on the hearth-rug, her back to the fire and her hands clasped behind her. "And for once I intend to have mine all ready the day befoah, so I need not be rushed up to the last minute. For that reason I am glad that mothah had to take the early train to town this mawning, to finish her shopping. If she'd been at home, I should have talked all the time, without accomplishing a thing."

"I think your tissue-paper and ribbon was put into my trunk," said Betty, drumming idly on the window-pane. "I'll go and unpack it in a minute, and have it off my mind, as soon as I see who this is coming up the avenue."

A tall young fellow had turned in at the gate, and was striding along toward the house as if in a great hurry.

"It's Rob Moore!" she exclaimed, in surprise. "I thought he wasn't coming home until Christmas eve."

"So did I," answered Lloyd, crossing the room to look over Betty's shoulder. "I'll beat you to the front doah, Betty."

There was a wild dash through the hall. Both slim figures bounced against the door at the same instant. There was a laughing scuffle over the latch, and then the two girls stood arm in arm between the white pillars of the porch, gaily calling a greeting.

Rob waved a pair of skates in reply, and quickened his stride until he came within speaking distance. One would have thought from his greeting that they had seen each other only the day before. Rob never wasted time on formalities.

"Hurry up, girls! Get your skates. The ice is fine on the creek, and there's a crowd waiting for us down at the depot."

"Who?" demanded Lloyd.

"Oh, the MacIntyre boys and the Walton girls and that little red-headed thing that they brought home from school with them. Kitty's going to have a picnic on the creek bank for her."

"A picnic in Decembah!" ejaculated Lloyd.

"That's what she said," Rob answered, clicking his skates together as he followed the girls into the house. "They telephoned over to me to hustle up here and get you girls. They're on their way to the station now. We're to meet them in the waiting-room."

"They should have let us know soonah," began Lloyd, "so that we could have had a lunch ready. There'll be nothing cooked to take this time of day."

"They didn't know it themselves," he interrupted. "Kitty proposed it at the breakfast-table, and they just grabbed up whatever they could get their hands on and started off."

"We have so much to do to-day," said Betty. "I don't see how we can ever get through if we stop for this."

"Let everything slide!" begged Rob. "Do your work to-morrow. This will be lots of fun. The ice may not last more than a day or so, and the MacIntyre boys are not going to be out here all vacation."

"I suppose we could tie up those packages to-night," said Lloyd, with an inquiring look at Betty.

"Of course," Rob answered for her. "And I'll help you with anything you have to do. Come on."

"Well, then, you run out to the kitchen and ask Aunt Cindy to give you something for a lunch,—anything in sight, and we'll get ready while Mom Beck finds our skates."

Rob rubbed his ears apprehensively. "I'd as soon beard the lion in his den as Aunt Cindy in her kitchen. She's never forgiven my early thefts."

"Go on, goosey," laughed Lloyd. "Don't you know that since you're 'growed up,' as Aunt Cindy says, she swears by you? I heard her tell Mom Beck last night she reckoned she'd have to make a batch of little sugah hah't cakes right away, for Mistah Rob would be coming prowling round her cooky jah."

"Am I growed up?" asked Rob gravely, throwing back his shoulders and looking into the mirror at the tall reflection it showed him.

"You are in inches and ells," laughed Lloyd, "but you're not always six feet tall in yoah actions."

"It's only when I am in your society that I appear so juvenile," retorted Rob. "When I'm away at school with the other fellows, I feel and act as old as Daddy, but when I'm back home, where you all seem to expect me to be a kid, I naturally adjust myself to that role just to be companionable and obliging. You would be afraid of me if I were to turn out my whiskers and stand back on my dignity. You know you would."

"Don't try it, Bobby," advised Lloyd. "It wouldn't be becoming. Trot out to Aunt Cindy and get the lunch. That's a good little man. We'll be ready in just a few minutes."

Even in her baby days, Lloyd had been patronizing at times to her good-natured playmate, ordering him about with a princess-like right that always seemed part of the game. So now he laughingly shrugged his shoulders and started to the kitchen, while Lloyd followed Betty up-stairs to change her slippers for heavy-soled walking-boots.

A few minutes later the three were hurrying down the avenue to the gate, under the bare windswept branches of the locusts.

"Aunt Cindy had disappeared temporarily," said Rob. "There wasn't a soul in the kitchen, so I rummaged around till I found this old basket, and filled it with a little of everything in sight. It is a long way to the creek. We'll be ready to eat nails by the time we tramp over there in this snappy weather."

"It is snappy," agreed Lloyd. "Betty, yoah cheeks are as red as fiah."

The rosy face under the brown tam-o'-shanter smiled back at her. "So are yours. Aren't they, Rob? They are as red as her coat."

"Hello!" exclaimed Rob, noticing for the first time the long red coat that Lloyd wore. "That's something new, isn't it? I thought you looked different, but I couldn't tell exactly what it was. That's a stunner, sure enough, Princess. It sort of livens up the landscape."

"I'm glad you like it," laughed Lloyd, "but I don't believe you would have seen it at all if Betty hadn't called yoah attention to it. You'll nevah get on in society, Bobby, if you don't learn to notice things. You'll miss all the chances most boys take advantage of to pay compliments and make pretty little speeches."

Rob scowled. "You know I don't go in for that sort of stuff."

"But you ought to," persisted Lloyd, who was in a perverse mood. "I considah it my duty to take you in hand and teach you. You may practise on Betty and me. Now we've been talking to Gay all term about our friends in Lloydsboro Valley, and naturally we want everybody to put their best foot foremost and show off their prettiest. Malcolm and Keith will leave a charming impression of themselves, because they will make her feel in such an easy graceful way that she has made that sawt of an impression on them. If she wears an especially pretty dress, or says an especially bright thing, or plays unusually well, they will notice it in some way so that she will know that they noticed it, and that they were pleased. Naturally that will please her, and she will like them bettah for it."

Rob faced her with a whimsical expression. "Look here, Lloyd Sherman, I've played every kind of a game that you've asked me to ever since I learned to walk. I've been your man Friday when you wanted to be Robinson Crusoe, and played B'r Fox to your B'r Rabbit. You've scalped me and buried me and dug me up. You've made me be Pharaoh with the ten plagues of Egypt, or a Christian martyr thrown to the wild beasts, just as it pleased your fancy. I've even played dolls with you week at a time, but I swear I draw the line at this. I'll do anything in reason to help entertain your chum,—ride or dance or skate or get up private theatricals,—but I'll *not* make a ninny of myself trying to be flowery and get off complimentary speeches. It comes natural to some people, but I'm not built that way. I'd be as awkward at it as a fish out of water."

Lloyd turned her head with a despairing gesture. "Oh, Rob, you're hopeless! You don't undahstand at all! Nobody wants you to be flowery, and nobody likes flat-footed, out-and-out compliments. They're not nice at all. I just meant—well—I scarcely know what I *did* mean, but you know how Malcolm does. It isn't that he says a thing in so many words, but he has a way of somehow making you feel that he has noticed nice things about you, and that he is *thinking* compliments."

"Gee whiz!" exclaimed Rob, in a teasing tone. "Say that again, won't you please, and say it slowly, so that I can take it all in. Do I get the thought? To be agreeable one must not say things, but must cultivate an air of having noticed that you are agreeable, and stand off and think compliments so hard that you can actually feel them flying through the air. Is that your idea?"

"Oh, Rob! Stop your teasing."

"Well, that is what you said, or words to that effect. Didn't she, Betty?"

The brown eyes flashed an amused smile at him. They walked along in silence for a few minutes, then he said, humbly, but with a twinkle in his eye which boded mischief: "Well, I'll do the best I can to please you, Lloyd. I'll watch Malcolm till I get the hang of it, then I'll stand off and think compliments about your friend till her ears burn and she is duly impressed. Grandfather is always saying, 'Who does the best his circumstance allows, does nobly. Angels could do no more.'"

"I wish I had never mentioned the subject," pouted Lloyd, as they walked on down the frozen pike. "I simply meant to give you a little advice for yoah own good, and you've gone and made a joke of it. I am suah you'll say or do something befoah the mawning is ovah that will make Gay think you are perfectly dreadful."

Rob only laughed in answer, leaving her to infer that she had good reason for her fears. As they passed the only store which the Valley boasted, Kitty came rushing out, a bright new tin saucepan dangling at her side like a drum. It was tied by a piece of twine, and she was beating a tattoo upon it with a long-handled iron spoon. Keith followed, his overcoat pockets bulging with parcels.

"Are you playing Santa Claus this early?" cried Betty, as he hurried across to shake hands with them.

"No; Kitty decided that no social function in the woods was properly a picnic without a fire and some kind of a mess to cook. So we stopped at the store, and she's loaded me down with stuff for fudge. Malcolm and the girls are on ahead in the waiting-room."

"Where's Ranald?" asked Lloyd, as they crossed the railroad track and walked along the platform toward the door of the station.

"He's gone hunting with John Baylor, the boy he brought home from school with him," answered Kitty. "We can't get him within a stone's throw of Gay. I teased him so unmercifully in my letters about the girl who had asked for his picture to put in her group of heroes that he won't even look in her direction."

As Lloyd greeted Malcolm, whom she had not seen since the close of the summer vacation, and then stood talking with him while Allison introduced Rob to her guest, she was conscious that Rob was watching every motion, and making note of it, to tease her afterward. A few moments later, when they were all discussing a choice of places for the picnic-grounds, he edged over to her.

"Now I understand what you mean," he said, in a low voice. "Malcolm didn't say anything about that red coat. He just gave a sort of quick, pleased glance at it, as if it had hit him hard, and made some gallant speech about a Kentucky cardinal. I tried my best to follow suit. So when I was introduced, I gave the same kind of a glad start when I saw her hair, and was about to make a similar reference to a Texas redbird, when my courage failed me. So I just stood off and fired the name at her in thought till I'm sure she understood."

"You mean thing!" exclaimed Lloyd, under her breath. "Her hair isn't red. It's just a deep, rich, bronzy auburn, and perfectly lovely. I do wish I'd nevah said anything. Now you'll not act natural, and you won't like each othah as I had hoped you would."

A gayer picnic party never started down the pike than the one that went laughing along the road that winter morning, under barbed-wire fences, through pasture gates, across bare woodlands, and over frozen corn-fields. It was a still gray morning, with the chill of snow in the air, and presently the snow began to fall in big feathery flakes.

Gay was delighted. She held up her face to let the cold, star-shaped crystals settle on it. She caught them on her sleeve to marvel over their airy beauty. "It's like frozen thistle-down!" she cried. "I hope it will snow all day and all night until everything is covered. I never saw a white Christmas."

"This will stop the skating," said Allison, "unless we had a broom to sweep the ice as it falls."

Rob offered to go back for one, but they were so far on their way they all protested it would not be worth while.

"How much farthah is it?" asked Lloyd, presently. For the last half-mile she had had nothing to say, and had fallen behind the others.

"I'm so tiahed I can hardly take another step."

Rob looked at her curiously. It seemed strange for Lloyd to admit that she was tired. He had known her to tramp nearly all day after nuts, and then be ready for a horseback ride afterward.

"We'll stop just over this hill," he replied. "There's a good place to camp. Here! Catch hold of my skate-strap, and I'll help pull you up."

"It helps some," she said, clinging to the strap swung over his shoulder, "but I don't believe I'll evah get ovah this hill."

"It looks like a grove of Christmas trees!" cried Gay, as they started down the other side toward the creek. Little cedars from two to five feet high dotted the hillside, and the snow had drifted across them till the branches drooped with the soft white burden. It began blowing faster, and coming down like a thick white sheet between them and the creek.

Rob, who had often picnicked here on his hunting trips, led the way farther down the hill to a cavelike opening under an overhanging ledge of rocks.

"This will keep the wind off your backs," he said. "Huddle down here a few minutes until we build a fire. Then you'll be all right."

Some charred sticks and ashes between two flat rocks, with an old piece of sheet iron laid on top, marked the spot where many meals had been cooked. The boys began at once foraging for firewood. There was plenty of it all around,— dead limbs and broken twigs,—and soon they had a big heap ready to light.

"Now if somebody can donate a piece of paper to start a blaze, we'll have you warm in a jiffy," said Rob.

Keith slapped his pockets. "I haven't a scrap," he declared. "Malcolm, you might be able to spare that bunch of letters you carry around in your pocket. You've read them enough to know them by heart, I should think."

"Oh, keep still, can't you?" muttered Malcolm, in an aside. "Don't get funny now."

"See him get red!" whispered Keith to Betty. "They're from a girl he met at the first college hop last fall. She's older than he is, but he thinks she's the one and only."

Then he turned to Malcolm again. "You might at least spare the envelopes when it's to keep us from freezing. It would be a big sacrifice, but to save your own blood and kin, you know—"

Malcolm stole a quick glance at Lloyd, but she was leaning wearily against the ledge of rocks, paying no attention to Keith's remarks. Kitty solved the difficulty by diving into Keith's pockets after the packages, and emptying the brown sugar and chocolate into the saucepan. She handed the wrapping-paper and bag to Rob, saying if that was not enough she would scratch the label off the can of evaporated cream.

Carefully holding his hat over the pile of twigs to shield it from the wind, Rob applied a match to the paper. It blazed up and caught the wood at once, and in a few moments a comfortable fire was crackling in front of them. Back in the cavelike hollow, under the rocks, the boys found a big, dry log, which other campers had put there for a seat. They rolled it forward toward the fire. Some flat stones were soon heated for the girls to put their feet on, and, warmed and rested, they began to investigate the contents of the baskets.

"Oh, Rob!" groaned Lloyd. "What a lunch you did pick up for a wintah day! These slabs of cold pumpkin pie would freeze the teeth of a polah beah, and there's nothing else but pickles and cheese and apples and raw eggs."

"That's fine!" exclaimed Allison. "We can roast the eggs in the ashes, and I've brought bacon to broil over the fire on switches. And here's crackers and gingersnaps and salmon—"

"And peanuts," added Kitty, "don't forget them. Or the fudge. We will have that ready in a little while."

"Now what could be jollier than this?" cried Gay, as she took the long, pointed switch that Rob cut for her, and held a piece of bacon over the fire to broil. "It's a thousand times nicer than a picnic in the summer, when you get so hot, and the mosquitoes and redbugs and spiders swarm all over you."

Lloyd, with a sigh of relief, saw that Rob was "acting natural" at last, and he and Gay were showing off to mutual advantage. She was enjoying the novel experience so fully that she was in her brightest spirits, and he was talking to her with the familiar ease with which he talked to Lloyd and Betty, even scolding her with brotherly frankness when she dripped bacon grease around too promiscuously.

The eggs were saltless, the bacon smoked and black, because, held in the flame as often as against the embers, nearly every piece caught fire and had to be blown out. Smoke blew in their eyes, and the snow fell thicker and thicker. But, with their feet on the hot stones, their backs to the sheltering ledge of rocks, and the fire crackling in front of them, they sang and laughed and ate with a zest which no summer picnic could have inspired.

No one had remembered to bring a pail for water, and rather than tramp over another hill to a distant spring, they quenched their thirst with handfuls of snow. The fudge boiled over, and more than half of it was lost in the ashes.

"It's a good thing that it did," Allison declared, tossing the empty salmon box and a bag of peanut shells into the fire. "Ugh! The mixture we've already eaten is enough to kill us! I think we ought to start back home now. I'm sure that I heard the one o'clock train whistle."

But Kitty protested. They hadn't been out half long enough, she said. If the ice on the creek had been free from snow, they would have skated for hours, and she thought as long as that sport had been spoiled, they ought to do something to make up for it. Gay had never gathered any mistletoe. She thought it would be fun for them all to go around by Stone Hollow, and get some off the big trees that grew in the surrounding pastures.

Lloyd listened to the ready assent of the others with a sinking heart. She had been leaning back against the rocks for some time, taking no part in the conversation. She had grown so tired that she dreaded the long tramp home, and had been vainly wishing that Tarbaby could suddenly appear on the scene, or some one with a conveyance. Even a wheelbarrow or a go-cart would have been welcome. She could not remember that she had ever felt so exhausted before in all her life.

"But I won't be the one to hang back and spoil every one's fun," she said to herself, "They wouldn't let me go home the shorter way by myself. It would only break up the pah'ty if I proposed it. But I do not see how I can evah drag myself all the way around by Stone Hollow."

At another time they might have noticed that she lagged behind, that she had little to say, and that she looked white and tired. But Gay, her spirits rising in the wintry air, was in her most rollicking mood. Even Kitty had never known her to say so many funny things or to tell so many amusing experiences. She followed on behind with Lloyd, watching admiringly as Gay's bright face was turned first toward Malcolm, then toward Rob, jubilant to see that her guest was captivating them as she did every one else who fell under the charm of her vivacious manner.

Betty and Allison were on ahead with Keith, keeping a sharp lookout for mistletoe. Lloyd scarcely heard what any one said. She plodded along like one in a dream. It was an effort just to lift her feet. Only one thing in life seemed desirable just then, that was her warm soft bed at home. If she could only creep into that and shut her tired eyes and lie there, she wouldn't care if she didn't waken for a month. She felt that it would be bliss to sleep through Christmas and the entire vacation.

The long walk came to an end at last. The roundabout route through Stone Hollow led them near Locust, and, with their arms full of mistletoe, the merry picnickers parted from Lloyd and Betty at the gate. Gay exclaimed enthusiastically over the beautiful old avenue, leading under the snow-covered locusts to the house, but to Lloyd's relief her invitation to come in was refused. There were a dozen reasons why they could not stop, but they promised to be over early next morning.

"It has been the very loveliest picnic I ever went to in my whole life," declared Gay, as they turned away. "I'd like to turn around and do it all over again."

"So would I," echoed Betty, warmly. "I'm not at all tired."

Lloyd looked at her in vague wonder as they plodded up the avenue. "I don't know what's the mattah with me," she said, "that I couldn't keep up with you all, unless it's true what Miss Gilmer said. The ice is too thin for holiday dissipations, and this picnic was too great a weight for it."

Betty glanced at her white face anxiously. "Go and lie down the rest of the afternoon," she said. "I'll tie up your packages."

"Oh, if you only would!" exclaimed Lloyd, gratefully. "But it seems too much to ask of any one. Don't tell mothah that I got so woh'n out. I'll be all right by evening."

"She hasn't come home yet," said Betty, looking ahead of them at the smooth expanse of newly fallen snow. "There isn't a track either of foot or wheel."

"Then maybe I'll have time for a nap, and be all rested when she comes," said Lloyd. "I don't want her to get any of Miss Gilmer's notions about me."

CHAPTER IX.

A PROGRESSIVE CHRISTMAS PARTY

Lloyd stood at the window in the falling twilight and looked out across the snow. It had been an ideal Christmas Day. She could feel the chill of the white winter world outside as she leaned against the frosty pane, but in her scarlet dress, with the holly berries at her belt and in her hair, she looked the embodiment of Christmas warmth and cheer, and as if no cold could touch her.

The candles had not yet been lighted, but the room was filled with the ruddy glow of the big wood fire. It shone warmly on the frames of the portraits and the tall gilded harp with its shining strings, and gave a burnishing touch to Betty's brown hair, as she stood by the piano, fingering for the hundredth time the presents she had received that day. Her dress of soft white wool suggested, like Lloyd's, the Yule-tide season, for in the belt and shoulder-knots of dull green velvet were caught clusters of mistletoe, the tiny waxen berries gleaming like pearls.

"Everything is *so* lovely!" she sighed, happily, picking up her camera to admire it once more. It was her godmother's gift, and the thing she had most longed to own.

She focussed it on Lloyd, who, in her scarlet dress, stood vividly outlined by the firelight against the curtains. "I took three pictures this morning while Rob was here, all snow scenes. The house, the locust avenue, and a group of little darkies running after your grandfather, calling out, 'Chris'mus gif', Colonel!' I think I'd better carry my things all up to my room," she added, presently. "There'll be so many people here soon, and so much moving around when the hunt begins, that they'll be in the way."

"You'll need a wheelbarrow to take them in," answered Lloyd, turning from the window to watch her gather them up. "You'd bettah call Walkah to help you."

"Santa Claus certainly was good to me," answered Betty, picking up Mr. Sherman's gift, a beautiful mother-of-pearl opera-glass. It was like the one he had given Lloyd, except for the difference in monograms. She rubbed it lovingly with her handkerchief, and laid it beside the camera to be carried up-stairs. There were books from the old Colonel, an ivory photograph-frame exquisitely carved from Lloyd. Dozens of little articles from the girls at school, and remembrances from nearly every friend in the Valley. There was more than her arms could hold, and, bringing a large tray from the dining-room, she made two trips up and down stairs with it before her treasures were all lodged safely in her room.

Left alone for the first time that busy day, Lloyd stood a moment longer peering out into the snowy twilight, and then crossed the room to the table where her gifts were spread out. There had never been so many for her since her days of dolls and dishes and woolly lambs. The opera-glasses like Betty's were what she had wished for all year. The purse her grandfather had slipped into the toe of her stocking was the prettiest little affair of gray suède and silver she had ever seen. She had thought of a dozen delightful ways to spend the gold eagle which it held.

The book-rack which Betty had burnt for her, with her initials on each end, was already nearly filled with the books that different friends had sent her. Rob's gift had been a book. So had Miss Allison's and Mrs. MacIntyre's and the old family doctor's. Malcolm had sent a great bunch of American Beauties. She drew the vase toward her and buried her face a moment in the delicious fragrance. Then she nibbled a caramel from Keith's box of candy. The rosebud sachet-bag which Gay made lay in the box of handkerchiefs that good old Mom Beck had given her.

She patted the thick letter from Joyce that told so much of interest about Ware's Wigwam. She intended to have the water-colour sketch of Squaw's Peak framed to take back to school with her. Mary's fat little fingers had braided the Indian basket which came with Joyce's picture, and Jack himself had killed the wildcat, whose skin he sent to make a rug for her room. Lloyd was proud of that skin. As she stood smoothing the tawny fur, the diamond on her finger flashed like fire, and she stood turning her hand this way and that, that the glow of the flames might fall on her new ring.

It was a beautifully cut stone in an old-fashioned setting, with the word *"Amanthis"* engraved inside; but not for a fortune would Lloyd have had the little circlet changed to a modern setting. For just so had it been slipped on her grandmother's finger at her fifteenth Christmas. She had worn it until her daughter's fifteenth Christmas, and now she, in turn, had given it to Lloyd. All day it had been a constant joy to her. Aside from the pleasure of possessing such a beautiful ring, she had a feeling that in its flashing heart was crystallized a triple happiness,—the joy of three Christmas days: hers, her mother's, and the beautiful young girl with the June rose in her hair, who smiled down at her from the portrait over the mantel.

She smiled up at it now in the same confiding way she had done as a child, saying, in a low tone: "And when you played on the harp, it flashed on yoah hand just as it does on mine." Pleased by the fancy, she crossed the room and struck a few chords on the harp, watching the firelight flash on the ring as she did so.

"'Sing me the songs that to me were so deah,
Long, long ago, long ago!'"

There was a step in the hall, and the portières were pushed aside as the old Colonel came in. She did not stop, for she knew he loved the old song, and that she was helping to bring back his happy past, when he threw himself into a chair before the fire, and sat looking up at Amanthis.

When she had finished the song, she perched herself on the arm of his chair, and began ruffling up his white hair with the little hand which wore the diamond.

"Well, has it been a happy day for grandpa's little Colonel?" he asked, fondly, passing his arm around her.

"Oh, yes, grandfathah! Brim full and running ovah with all sawts of lovely surprises. I'm mighty glad I'm living. And the best of it is, although the day is neahly ovah, the fun isn't. There's still so much to come."

"What kind of a performance is this one on the programme for to-night?" he asked. "Betty said I had to go the whole round, but I haven't been able to gather a very good idea of what's expected of me."

"It's just a progressive Christmas pah'ty, grandfathah," she explained, tweaking his ear as she talked. "We couldn't agree about the celebration this yeah. Judge Moore wanted us all to go to Oaklea. Mrs. Walton thought they had the best right on account of their guests, so we arranged it for everybody to take a turn at entahtaining. At five o'clock they're all to come heah for a Christmas hunt. They ought to be coming now, for it's neahly that time. At half-past six we'll have dinnah at Oaklea. At half-past eight we'll go to The Beeches and finish the evening with a general jollification. Then we'll come home by moonlight."

"What is a Christmas hunt?" asked the Colonel. "You'll have to enlighten my ignorance."

"It's a game that mothah and Betty thought of. Betty has worked like a dawg to get the rhymes ready. She scarcely took time to eat yestahday, and she gave up going to the charade pah'ty that Miss Allison gave for Gay in the aftahnoon. It's this way. We've hidden little gifts all ovah the house, from attic to cellah. When the guests come, each one will be given a card with a rhyme on it, like this."

Slipping from the arm of the chair, she went out into the hall a moment, and came back with a Christmas stocking, trimmed with holly and hung with tiny sleigh-bells. "Little Elise Walton is to distribute the cards from this. Heah is a sample. Miss Allison happens to be on top."

Adjusting his eye-glasses the Colonel turned so that the firelight shone on the card, and read aloud:

"Seek where bygone summers
Have dropped their roses fair.
A little Christmas package
Is waiting for you there."

"Now where would you look if that cah'd were for you?" she demanded.

"In the conservatory?" he replied, inquiringly.

"That is what Miss Allison will do, probably," answered Lloyd, her cheeks dimpling at the thought. "But aftah awhile she will remembah the old dragon that mothah always keeps full of rose-leaves just as Grandmothah Amanthis did. See?"

She lifted the lid of a rare old cloisonné rose-jar that had stood on the end of the mantel for a longer time than Lloyd's memory could reach, and took out a small box. Taking off the cover, she disclosed what appeared to be a ripe cherry with a bee clinging to its side.

"Take the bee in yoah thumb and fingah and pull," she ordered. "See? It's a cunning little tape-measuah for her work-basket."

A sound of sleigh-bells jingling rapidly toward the house made her clap the lid on the box and drop it hastily back into the rose-jar.

"There they come!" she cried, "and the candles haven't been lighted. Hurry, grandfathah! We can't wait to call Walkah! Throw open the front doah!"

Flying to the hall closet for the long taper kept for the purpose, she held it an instant toward the blazing logs, and then darting around the room, passed from one candelabrum to another, till every waxen candle was tipped with its star of light. In her scarlet dress and the holly berries, her cheeks glowing and the taper held above her head as she tiptoed to reach the highest one, she looked like some radiant acolyte of Joy.

Betty, rushing breathlessly down-stairs at the sound of the sleigh-bells, paused an instant between the portières at sight of her. "Oh, Lloyd!" she cried, clasping her hands. "You've given me the loveliest idea! I've only got it by the tail feathers now, but I'll find words for it all some day." Then, without waiting to explain, she ran out to the porch, where, between the tall pillars, the old Colonel waited with elaborate courtesy to receive the coming guests.

As the sleighs glided nearer, Betty looked back through the door swung hospitably open to its widest, and saw Lloyd hastily thrusting the taper back into the closet.

"She lighted it at the Christmas fire," thought Betty, struggling with the tail feathers of her lovely idea, in an effort to grasp all that Lloyd's act suggested. "And red is the emblem of joy. It might go this way: 'She touched the Christmas tapers with the Yule log's heart of flame.' No, it ought to start,—

"Lighting the candles of Christmas joy,
With a spark from the Yule log's fire."

But there was no time for making poetry, with so many voices calling "Merry Christmas," and so many outstretched hands grasping hers. In another instant the house seemed filled to overflowing, and the dim old mirrors were flashing back from every side one of the gayest scenes the hospitable old mansion had ever known.

The hunt began almost immediately. As soon as Elise had emptied the stocking of its contents, up-stairs and down-stairs and in my lady's chamber went old and young at the bidding of the rhymes.

"I feel like a 'goosey gander,' sure enough," said Allison presently. "For I've been all over the house, and there's no place left to wander. Where would you go if you had this card?"

She thrust hers out toward Gay, who read:

"Standing with reluctant feet
Where Brooks and Little Rivers meet."

Gay puzzled over it a moment, and then suggested that she try the library. "I have," answered Allison. "Keith found his package in there, behind the picture of a Holland windmill and canal, but there is nothing else in the room that suggests water that I have been able to find."

"Who wrote 'Little Rivers'?"

Allison stood thinking a moment, and then cried out: "Well, of course! Why didn't I think to look among the books?" Flying down-stairs, she began glancing along the library shelves until she found the book she sought and Brooks's sermons standing side by side. Between them was wedged a thin package which proved to contain a picture which she had long wanted, a photograph of Murillo's painting of the Madonna.

To Betty's surprise the Christmas stocking held a card for her. She had supposed her part of the game would be only making the rhymes and helping to hide the gifts. There was no rhyme on her card, simply the statement, "Some little men are keeping it for you."

Remembering Allison's experience, she ran up-stairs to Lloyd's room, where in a low bookcase were all the juvenile stories that her childhood had held dear. A set of Miss Alcott's books stood first, and, taking out the well-thumbed copy of "Little Men," she shook it gently, fluttering the leaves, and turning it upside down. But the volume held nothing except a four-leaf clover, which Lloyd had left there to mark the place one summer day. Betty turned away, as puzzled as any of the others whom she had helped to mystify.

Then she remembered two little wooden gnomes carved on the Swiss match-box and ash-tray in the Colonel's den. She dashed in there, but the gnomes kept guard over nothing but a few burnt matches. Nearly half an hour went by of bewildered wandering from place to place, until she happened to stray into Mr. Sherman's room. She stood by the desk, letting her eyes glance slowly over its handsome furnishings. Then, with a start of surprise that she had not thought of it before, she bent over a paper-weight. It was a crystal ball supported by two miniature bronze figures. The tiny Grecian athletes were evidently the little men who were keeping something for her, for the toy suit-case standing between them bore a tag on which was printed her initials.

The suit-case was not more than two inches long. She supposed it contained bonbons. One of the girls had used a dozen like them for place cards at a farewell luncheon just before they went away to school. It did not open at the first pull, and when, at the second, it came forcibly apart, there was no shower of pink and white candies, as she had expected. Only a bit of folded paper fell out. Smoothing it on the desk, Betty read:

"Dear little girl, you have helped all the rest
To a happy time with your patient hands.
Now fly for a week to the Cuckoo's Nest,
With godmother's love, for she understands."

Then Betty was glad that she was all alone in the room when she found the suit-case, for the tears began to brim up into her eyes and spill over on to the paper that had a crisp new greenback pinned to it. The tears were all happy ones, but she hardly knew what they were for. Whether she was happier because her heart's desire was granted, and she could spend her vacation with Davy, or whether it was because of that last line, "With godmother's love, *for she understands.*"

"Lloyd must have told her what I said that day on the train," she thought. It was the crowning happiness of the day for Betty. She was singing under her breath when she danced out into the hall to join the others.

Some of the articles were so cleverly hidden that she had to give an occasional hint to the bewildered seekers. In the seats of chairs, over the deer's antlers in the hall, high up in the candelabra, strapped inside of umbrellas, poked into glove fingers, all of them were in unexpected places. Yet the directions of the verses seemed so plain when once understood that the hunters laughed at their own stupidity.

Even Judge Moore and the old Colonel were swept into the game, and Mrs. MacIntyre's silvery hair bent just as eagerly as Elise's dark curls over each suspected spot and out-of-the-way corner until she found the volume of essays that had been hidden for her.

By quarter-past six every one's search had been successful except Rob's. "It would take a Christopher Columbus to find this place," he said, scowling at his verse. "And I'd be willing to bet anything that it isn't the bank that Shakespeare had in mind. Give me a hint, Lloyd." He held out the card:

"I know a bank where the wild thyme grows.
Unseen it lies, unsung by bard.
Something keeps watch there, no man knows,
And over your gift it's standing guard."

"I haven't the faintest idea what it is," she said. "Betty wrote so many of them yestahday aftahnoon while I was at the pah'ty, and she wouldn't tell me this one. She said she thought you'd suahly guess it, but she didn't want you to have a hint from any one. Come ovah to-morrow, and we'll find it if we have to turn the house upside down."

The sleighs had made one trip to Oaklea and returned for another load, when Rob finally gave up the search. Lloyd and Gay climbed into the same seat, and, as they cuddled down among the warm robes, Gay caught Lloyd's hand in an impetuous squeeze.

"Oh, I'm having such a good time!" she exclaimed. "I've been in a dizzy whirl ever since five o'clock this morning. I never had a sleigh-ride before to-day. I don't wonder that Betty calls this the House Beautiful. Look back at it now. It's fairy-land!" A light was streaming from every window, and the snow sparkled like diamonds in the moonlight.

The drive to Oaklea was so short that the Judge and Mrs. Moore were welcoming them at the door before Gay had fairly begun her account of the day's happening. Dinner was announced almost immediately, and she was ushered into one of the largest dining-rooms she had ever seen, and seated at the long table. Such a large Christmas tree formed the centrepiece that she could catch only an occasional glimpse through its branches of Lloyd, seated on the other side between Malcolm and John Baylor.

Gay was between Ranald and Rob. While she kept up a lively chatter, first with one and then the other, a sentence floating across the table now and then made her long to hear what was being said on the other side of the Christmas tree. She heard Malcolm say, in a surprised tone: "Maud Minor! No, indeed, I didn't! Why, I scarcely mentioned you. Don't you believe—"

A general laugh at one of the old Colonel's stories drowned the rest of the sentence, and left Gay wondering which one of Maud's many tales was not to be believed.

"I'll ask her after dinner," thought Gay. But it was a long time till all the courses that followed the turkey gave way in slow succession to plum pudding and the trifles on the Christmas tree. Then Gay had no opportunity to ask her question, for Malcolm still stayed by Lloyd's side when the company broke up into little groups in the hall and the adjoining parlours.

"The children are growing up, Jack," said the old Judge, laying his hand on Mr. Sherman's shoulder, as several couples passed on their way to the music-room. "There's Rob, now, the young rascal, taller than his father; and it seems only yesterday that he was riding pickaback on my shoulders, and tooting his first Christmas trumpet in my ears. And young MacIntyre there is nearly a full-fledged man. He'll soon be eighteen, he tells me. Why, at his age—"

The Judge rambled off into a series of reminiscences which would have been very entertaining to the younger man had his eyes not been following Lloyd. He did not like to think that she was growing up. He wanted to keep her a child. In his fond eyes she was always beautiful, but he had never seen her look as well as she did to-night. The scarlet dress and the holly berries gave her unusual colour. He fancied that there was a deeper flush on her face when Malcolm leaned over her chair to say something to her. Then he told himself that it was only fancy. Looking up, Lloyd caught sight of her father in the doorway, and flashed him a smile so open and reassuring that he turned away, thinking, "My honest little Hildegarde! She asked for her yardstick, and I can surely trust her to use it as she promised."

Presently Malcolm, hunting through his pockets for a programme he was talking about, took out a bunch of letters. As he hastily turned them over, several unmounted photographs fluttered out and fell at Lloyd's feet. An amused smile dimpled her mouth as her hasty glance showed her that they were all of the same girl,—evidently kodak shots he had taken himself. Probably that was the girl and these were the letters that Keith had teased him about at the picnic.

Neither spoke, and he reddened uncomfortably at her amused smile, as he put them back into his pocket. At that moment, Rob turned toward them, holding his new watch in his hand.

"I have just been showing Ranald the present Daddy gave me," he said to Lloyd. "It reminded me that I hadn't told you,—I've put that same old four-leaf clover into the back of this watch that I had in my silver one. I wouldn't lose my luck by losing your hoodoo charm for anything in the world."

At the sight of the clover Lloyd blushed violently. But it was not the little dried leaf that deepened the quick colour in her cheeks. It was the thought of the last time he had shown it to her, and the scene it recalled at the churchyard stile, when Malcolm had begged for the tip of a curl to carry with him always as a talisman; as a token that he was really her knight, as he had been in the princess play, and that he would come to her on some glad morrow.

"He'll have a pocket full of such talismans by the time he's through college," she thought, recalling the kodak pictures she had just seen. "I'm *mighty* glad that I didn't give him one."

Over at The Beeches, Elise and her little friends had arranged to give a Christmas play, so promptly at the hour agreed upon the party "progressed" in Mrs. Walton's wake. There they found the third royal welcome, and the gayest of entertainments. It had been an exciting day for all of them, and, as Kitty expressed it, they were all wound up like alarm-clocks. They would go off pretty soon with a br-r-r and a bang, and then run down.

The play passed off without a hitch in the performance, and ended in a blaze of spangles and red light, when the fairy queen, trailing off the stage, went through the audience showering on her guests Christmas roses, supposed to have been called to life by her magic wand, and distributed as souvenirs of her skill.

Then somebody came up to Gay with her violin. With Allison to play her accompaniments, she chose her sweetest pieces, and threw her whole soul into the rendering of them. She was so grateful to these dear people who had taken her in like one of themselves, and given her such a happy, happy holiday-time that she did her best, and Gay's best on the violin was a treat even to the musical critics in the company. Kitty was so proud of her she could not help expressing her pleasure aloud, much to Gay's embarrassment. To hide her confusion, she started a merry jig tune, so rollicking and irresistible that hands and feet all through the rooms began to pat the time. Keith seized his Aunt Allison around the waist and waltzed her out into the floor.

"Come on, everybody!" he cried.

Lloyd was standing in the doorway, talking to Doctor Shelby, the white-haired physician of the village, one of her oldest and dearest friends.

"Go on, Miss Holly-berry," he said. "If I wasn't such a stiff old graybeard, I'd be at it myself. There's Ranald wanting to ask you."

Lloyd waltzed off with Ranald, as light on her feet as a bit of thistle-down, and the old doctor's eyes followed her fondly.

"She's like Amanthis," he said to himself. "And she will grow more like her as the years go by, so spirited and high-strung. But they'll have to watch her, or she'll wear herself out."

Presently he missed the flash of the scarlet dress, in and out among the others, and he did not see it again until the music had stopped and the revel was ending with the chimes, rung softly on the Bells of Luzon. As he stepped back to allow several guests to pass him on the way up to the dressing-room, he caught sight of Lloyd in an alcove in the back hall. She was attempting to draw a glass of ice-water from the cooler. Her hands shook, and her face was so pale that it startled him. "What's the matter, child?" he exclaimed.

"Nothing," she answered, trying to force a little laugh. "It's just that I felt for a minute as if I might faint. I nevah did, you know. I reckon it's as Kitty said. We've been wound up all day, and we've run so hah'd we've about run down, and we have to stop whethah we want to or not."

He looked at her keenly and began counting her pulse. "You are not to get wound up this way any more this winter, young lady," he said, sternly. "Go straight home and go to bed, and stay there until day after to-morrow. The rest cure is what you need."

"And miss Katie Mallard's pah'ty?" she cried. "Why, I couldn't do it even for you, you bad old ogah."

She made a saucy mouth at him, and then, with her most winning smile, held out her hand to say good night, for the guests were beginning to take their departure. "*Please*, Mistah *My*-Doctah,"—it was the pet name she had given him years ago when she used to ride on his shoulder,—"please don't go to putting any notions into Papa Jack's head or mothah's. I'm just ti'ahed. That's all. I'll be all right in the mawning."

"Come, Lloyd," called Mrs. Sherman. "We're ready to start now." She saw with a sigh of relief that her mother was bringing her coat toward her, so she would not have to climb the stairs for it. She was tired, dreadfully tired, she admitted to herself. But it had been such a happy day it was worth the fatigue.

As she drove homeward in the sleigh, she slipped her hand out of her muff, and turned it in the moonlight to watch the sparkle of the new ring. She wondered if the two girls who had worn it in turn before her had had half as happy a fifteenth Christmas as she.

CHAPTER X.

THE DUNGEON OF DISAPPOINTMENT

It was nearly noon when Lloyd wakened next morning. Her head ached, and she wondered dully how anybody could feel lively enough to sing as Aunt Cindy was doing, somewhere back in the servants' quarters. The sound of a squeaking wheelbarrow had wakened her. Alec was trundling it around the house, with the parrot perched on it. The parrot loved to ride, and its silly laugh at every jolt of the squeaking barrow usually amused Lloyd, but to-day its harsh chatter annoyed her.

"Oh, deah!" she groaned, sitting up in bed and yawning. "I feel as if I could sleep for a week. I wouldn't get up at all if it wasn't for Katie Mallard's pah'ty. I hate this day-aftah-Christmas feeling, as if the bottom had dropped out of everything."

She dressed slowly and went down-stairs. "Where's mothah, Mom Beck?" she asked, pausing in the dining-room door. The old coloured woman was arranging flowers for the lunch-table.

"She's done gone ovah to Rollington, honey, with the old Cun'l. Walkah's mothah is sick, and sent for 'em. I'm lookin' for 'em to come home any minute now. Come right along in, honey. I've kep' yoah breakfus' good and hot."

"I don't want anything to eat. I'm not hungry now. I'd rathah wait till lunch. Where's Betty, Mom Beck?"

"Now listen to that!" ejaculated the old woman, sharply. "Don't you remembah? She went off on the early train this mawning to that place you all calls the Cuckoo's Nest. I packed her satchel befoah daylight."

"I had forgotten she was going," exclaimed Lloyd, turning to the window with a discontented expression, which only the snowbirds on the lawn could see. She had come down-stairs expecting to talk over all the happenings of the previous day with Betty, and to find her gone gave her a vague sense of injury. She knew the feeling was unreasonable, but she could not shake it off.

The flash of the new ring gave her a momentary pleasure, but she was in a mood that nothing could please her long. When she strolled into the drawing-room, everything was in spotless order, and so quiet that the stillness was oppressive. Even the fire burned with a steady, noiseless glow, without the usual crackle, and the ashes fell on the hearth with velvety softness.

Some of her new books lay on a side table. She picked them up and glanced through them, catching at a paragraph here and there. But one after another she laid them down. She was not in a mood for reading. Then she took a candied date from the bonbon dish, but it seemed to lack its usual flavour. After nibbling each end, she threw it into the fire. Slipping her new opera-glass from its case, she went to the window and turned the lens on the distant entrance gate. The road in each direction seemed deserted. So she put the glass back in its case, and, after strolling restlessly around the room, walked over to the harp and struck a few chords.

"It's all out of tune!" she exclaimed, fretfully, thrumming the faulty string with impatient fingers. "Everything seems out of tune this mawning!"

As she spoke, the string broke with a sudden harsh twang that made her jump. She was so startled that the tears came to her eyes, and so nervous that she flung herself face downward on the pillows of the long-Persian divan, and began sobbing hysterically. The strain of the last few weeks had been too much for her. Miss Gilmer's prophecy had come true. The ice had given away under the extra weight put upon it.

She was sobbing so hard that she did not hear the sound of carriage wheels rolling softly up the avenue through the snow, and when the front door banged shut she started again, and began trembling as she had done when the harp-string broke. She was crying convulsively now, so hard that she could not stop, although she clenched her fists and bit her lips in a strong effort to regain self-control.

Mrs. Sherman, her face all aglow from the cold drive, and looking almost girlishly fair in her big hat with the plumes, and her dark furs, hurried in to the fire. The Colonel, throwing back his scarlet lined cape, pushed aside the portière for her to enter. He was the first to catch sight of the shaking form on the divan.

"Why, Lloyd, child, what's the matter?" he demanded, anxiously. "What's the matter with grandpa's little girl?"

Mrs. Sherman, with a frightened expression, hurried to her, and, bending over her, tried to get a glimpse of the tear-swollen face buried so persistently in the cushions.

"Nothing's happened! No, I'm not sick," came in smothered tones from the depths of the pillows. "It's j-just crying itself, and I—I—I c-can't stop-p-p!"

A long shiver passed over her, and Mrs. Sherman, stroking her forehead with a soothing hand, waited for her to grow quiet before plying her with questions. But the old Colonel paced impatiently back and forth.

"The child *must* be sick," he declared. "She'll be coming down with a fever or something if we don't take vigorous measures to prevent it. I shall telephone for Dick Shelby this minute."

He started toward the hall, but a wild wail from Lloyd stopped him.

"I won't have the doctah! I'm not sick, and you sha'n't send for him! I j-just cried because the harp-string b-broke so suddenly that it s-scared me!"

The Colonel paused and looked at her in amazement. Not since the time when she, a five-year-old child, had flung a handful of mud over his white clothes had she spoken to him in such a defiant tone. He answered soothingly, as if she were still that little child, to be coaxed into good behaviour. "Oh, yes, you won't mind the doctor's coming if grandpa wants him to. He'll keep you from getting down sick, and spoiling all the rest of your vacation. I'll just ask him to step up and look at you."

"No, don't!" demanded Lloyd, as he started again toward the hall. "No, you sha'n't!" she insisted, springing up and stamping her foot. "I won't have the old doctah, and I won't take any of his nasty old medicine! He'll make me stay home from Katie's pah'ty this aftahnoon and from the matinée to-morrow—and there's nothing the mattah, only I'm cross and nervous, and the moah you bothah me the hah'dah it is to stop crying!"

Then ashamed of her petulant outburst, she threw her arms around his neck, and sobbed on his shoulder. In the end she had her own way, for the glass of hot milk which her mother sent for, as soon as she found Lloyd had eaten no breakfast, soothed her overstrung nerves. A brisk walk to the post-office in the bracing December air gave her an appetite for luncheon. Then she slept again until time to dress for Katie's party, so that when the old Colonel watched her start off, she looked so bright and was in such buoyant spirits that he wondered vaguely if her crying spell could have been the remnant of some childish tantrum instead of the forerunner of an illness.

He banished the thought instantly from his loyal old heart, ashamed of having applied such a word as tantrum to anything Lloyd might choose to do. Of course she had felt ill, he told himself. So wretched that she hadn't known what she was saying when she stormed at him so angrily. He resolved to watch her closely, and take matters in his own hands if she showed any more alarming symptoms.

There was a matinée next day in Louisville, to which Mrs. Sherman took all the girls in the neighbourhood. That was the end of the Christmas gaieties for Lloyd. Doctor Shelby was at Locust on her return. He came out of the old Colonel's den, where he had been sitting for several hours, deep in a game of chess, and found her shivering in front of the fire with a nervous chill, sobbing hysterically.

She stormed at him almost as she had done at her grandfather, protesting that she was only tired and nervous, and that she would be all right as soon as she had had her cry out. But she submitted meekly when he ordered her mother to put her to bed. The old doctor had always indulged her, but there was a sternness in his manner now that made her obey him.

He called to see her the next day, and the next. But his visits did not seem like professional ones. There was nothing said about medicine or symptoms. He only asked her about school and the good times she had been having, and the extra studying she had been doing. Then he sat and joked and talked with her and her mother, as had been his habit ever since Lloyd could remember. The third afternoon she was down in the drawing-room when he came.

"We'll soon be having Miss Holly-berry back again," he said, playfully pinching her pale cheek.

"And without taking any nasty old medicine," she answered. "I don't mind doctahs when they can cure people without giving them pills and powdahs."

The Colonel looked up sharply. "What's that?" he asked. "Haven't you been giving her anything, Dick? It seems to me the child would get along faster if she had a good tonic."

"I am going to prescribe one this morning," the doctor answered. "That's what I came up for." He laughed at the look of disgust on Lloyd's face.

"It isn't bad," he assured her, with an indulgent smile. "Why, I know dozens of girls who would say that the tonic I am going to prescribe is the most agreeable that could be given. I've even had them beg for it. This is it, simply to lengthen your Christmas vacation. Didn't I hear a certain young lady wishing the other night that she could stretch hers out indefinitely?"

Lloyd's dimples deepened. "How much longah will you make it? A week? If I stay out much longah than that, it will be such hah'd work to catch up with my classes that the game won't be worth the candle."

"But I would make it so long that there would be no necessity of having to catch up, as you call it. You could simply make a fresh start in a new class."

Lloyd looked up in alarm. "When?" she demanded.

"Um—well, next fall, let us say," he answered, deliberately. "Yes, surely by that time you'll be well and sound as a new dollar."

"Next fall!" she gasped, her face growing white and her eyes strangely big and dark. "You don't mean—you *couldn't* mean that I must leave school."

"Yes, that's exactly what I mean. You are overtaxing yourself and must stop—"

"Oh, I can't!" interrupted Lloyd, speaking very fast. "I *won't!* It's cruel to ask it when I've worked so hard to keep from falling behind Betty and the girls. Oh, you don't *know* what it means to me!"

The old doctor looked up in amazement at this unexpected outburst.

"No," he answered, slowly, after a moment's silence. "I don't suppose I do. I had no idea it would be a disappointment to you. I would gladly save you from it if I could. But listen to me, my little girl, and try to be reasonable. You are on the verge of a nervous breakdown. Nothing can mean as much to you as your health. What will keeping up with the other girls amount to if the strain and the overtaxing makes an invalid of you for life, perhaps?

"Mind you, I am not saying that the work itself is too great a tax. Madam Chartley's is one of the best regulated schools I have ever inquired into. Ordinarily a girl ought to be able to take the course with perfect ease. But you see that little spell of la grippe left you weak and unfit for any extra strain, and, instead of easing up a bit, you went on piling on all that extra load of lessons and Christmas preparations and vacation dissipations. It was like trying to walk on a broken foot. The more you tried, the worse it got. The mischief is done now, and there is no remedy but to stop short off."

Lloyd sat very still for a moment, staring out of the window in a dazed, unseeing way, as if not fully understanding all he said. Then she turned with a piteous appeal in her face to Mrs. Sherman.

"Mothah, it isn't so, is it? I won't have to give up school now! You wouldn't make me, would you, when you know how I love it? Oh, it will neahly *kill* me if you do! Please say no, mothah! *Please!*"

Mrs. Sherman's eyes were full of tears. "My poor little girl," she exclaimed as Lloyd threw herself into her arms. "I'm afraid we must do as the doctor says. He would not ask such a sacrifice if it were not necessary. You know how dearly he has always loved you."

Without waiting to hear any more, Lloyd sprang up and ran out of the room. Rushing up-stairs, she bolted her door behind her, and threw herself across the bed.

"It is the first great disappointment she has ever had in her life," said her mother, looking after her with a troubled face. "Couldn't you make the sentence a little easier, doctor? Couldn't she go back and take one study, just to be with the girls?"

He shook his head. "No, Elizabeth. She is too ambitious and high-strung for that. One study wouldn't satisfy her. She'd chafe at not being able to keep up in everything. She has nothing serious the matter with her now, but it would not take long to make a wreck of her health at the gait she has been going. There must be no more parties, no more regular school work, and even no more music lessons this winter. She must have the simplest kind of a life. Keep her out-of-doors all you can. A little prevention now will be worth pounds of cure after awhile."

"I suppose you are right, Dick," said the old Colonel, huskily, "but I swear I'd give the only arm the Yankees left me to save her from this disappointment."

Lying across the bed up-stairs, Lloyd cried and sobbed until she was exhausted. The handkerchief clutched in her hand in a damp little ball had wiped away the bitterest tears she had ever shed. In her inmost heart she knew that the doctor was right. It had been weeks since she had felt strong and well. She remembered the way she had lagged behind at the picnic, and what an effort it had been to talk and make herself agreeable lately. Recalling the last few weeks, it seemed to her that she had been in tears half the time. She admitted to herself that she would rather be dead than to be an invalid for life like her great-aunt Jane. To sit always in a darkened room that smelled of camphor, and to talk in a weak, complaining voice that made everybody tired. Of course if there was danger of her growing to be like *her*, she would rather leave school than run such a risk. But why, oh, *why* was she forced to make such a choice? The other girls didn't have to. She had done no more than they to bring about such a state of affairs.

They could go back to dear old Warwick Hall, but she would have to stay behind. And she would always be behind, for, even if she went back with them another year, it couldn't be the same. They would have done so much in the meantime,—gone on so far ahead, made new friends and found new interests, and she would have to drop back in the class below, and never, never stand on the same footing with them again. It was so hard, so cruel, that she should have to face a blighted life at only fifteen.

She unlocked the door presently at her mother's knock, but she didn't want to be comforted. Nothing anybody could say could change things, she sobbed, or make the disappointment any easier to bear. So Mrs. Sherman wisely withdrew, and left her to fight it out alone.

The next time she peeped into the room, Lloyd was asleep, worn out with the violence of her grief, so she tiptoed down-stairs, leaving the door ajar behind her. The Colonel was pacing up and down the library.

"I declare I can't think of anything but that child's disappointment!" he exclaimed, as she came in. "I can't read! I can't settle down to anything. I have been trying to think of some pleasure we could give her to make up for it in a way. A winter in Florida, maybe. Poor baby! if I could only bear it for her, how glad I would be to do it!"

Mrs. Sherman picked up a bit of needlework from the table where she had left it, and, sitting down by the window, began to hemstitch.

"I don't know, papa," she said, slowly, "but I'm beginning to fear that we have done too much of that for Lloyd; smoothed the difficulties out of her way too much; made things too easy. We've fairly held our arms around her to shield her not only from harmful things, but from even trifling unpleasantness. Maybe if she had had to face the smaller disappointments that most children have to bear, the greater ones would not seem so overwhelming. She could have met this more bravely."

The Colonel sniffed impatiently. "All foolishness, Elizabeth! All foolishness! That may be the case with ordinary children, but not with such a sweet, unspoiled nature as Lloyd's."

It was nearly dark when Lloyd wakened. She heard Kitty's voice down in the hall, asking to see her, and Gay's exclamation of surprise and regret at something her mother said in a low voice. She knew that she was telling them the doctor's decision. Then Mom Beck tapped at the door to ask if she would see the girls awhile, but she sent her away with a mournful shake of the head. She was too miserable even to speak.

The low murmur of voices went on for some time. It grew loud enough for her to distinguish the words when the girls came out into the hall again to take their departure. Lloyd raised herself on her elbow to listen. Kitty was telling something that had happened that afternoon at the candy-pull from which they were just returning. A wan smile flitted across Lloyd's face, in sympathy with the merry laugh that floated up the stairs. But it faded the next instant as she whispered, bitterly: "That's the way it will always be. They will go on having good times without me, and they'll get so they'll nevah even miss me. I'll be left out of everything. There's nothing left to look forward to any moah. Oh, it's all so dah'k and gloomy—I know now how Ederyn felt, for I'm just like he was, walled up in a dreadful Dungeon of Disappointment."

The fancy pleased her so that she went on making herself miserable with it long after the door closed behind Kitty and Gay. Over and over she pictured Warwick Hall, which just then seemed the most desirable place in all the world. She could see the shining river, as she had watched it so many times from her window, flowing past the stately terraces between its willow-fringed banks. She could hear the breezy summons of the hunter's horn, calling the girls to rambles over the wooded hills or through the quaint old garden. She could see the sun streaming into the south windows of the English room, with the class gathered around Miss Chilton, eager and interested. All the dear, delightful round of inspiring work and play would go on day after day for the others, but it would go on without her. Henceforth she would be left out of everything pleasant and worth while.

She would not go down to dinner. She could not take such a puffed, tear-swollen face to the table to make everybody else unhappy, and she couldn't throw off her despondent mood. Maybe in a few days, she thought, she might be able to hide her feelings sufficiently to appear in public, but it would always be with a secret sorrow gnawing at her heart. Just now she shrank from sympathy, and she didn't want any one to cheer her up. It did not seem possible that she could ever smile again, and she wasn't sure that she wanted to.

Mom Beck brought up the daintiest of dinners on a tray, but carried it back almost untasted. As soon as she was gone, Lloyd undressed and crept into bed.

Sleep was far from her, however, and she lay with her eyes wide open. The room was full of soft shadows and the flicker of firelight on the furniture. She could think of only one thing, and she brooded over that until it seemed to her feverish, disordered fancy that her disappointment was the greatest that any one had ever been forced to bear.

"Why couldn't it have happened to some girl who didn't care?" she thought, bitterly. "Some girl like Maud Minor, who doesn't like school, anyhow. It doesn't seem fair when I've tried my best to do exactly right, to leave a road of the loving hah't in everybody's memory, to keep the tryst—"

That thought brought a fresh reason for grief. There was the string of pearls. Now she could not finish her little white rosary. The fire flared up and shone brilliantly for a few moments, lighting a group of pictures over her bed. They were the photographs she had taken in Arizona. There was Ware's Wigwam. The firelight was not bright enough to enable her to read the lines Joyce had written under it, but she knew the inscription was the Ware family's motto, taken from the "Vicar of Wakefield": "Let us be inflexible, and fortune will at last change in our favour." A shadow of a smile actually came to her lips as she remembered Mary Ware gravely explaining it.

"Why, even Norman knows that if you'll swallow your sobs and *stiffen* when you bump your head or anything, it doesn't hurt half as bad as if you just let loose and howl."

And there was the photograph of old Camelback Mountain, bringing back the story of Shapur, left helpless on the sands of the Desert of Waiting, while the caravan passed on without him to the City of his Desire. She remembered that when she hung it over her bed she had thought, "If ever *I* come to such a place, this will help me to bear it patiently."

Then she thought of Joyce, how bravely and uncomplainingly she had met her disappointment. Not only had she left school and given up her ambition to be an artist, but she had had to give up the old home she loved, all her friends, and everything that made her girlhood bright, to go out into the lonely desert and work like a squaw.

The thought of Joyce brought back all the lessons she had learned in the School of the Bees. But she sighed presently: "Oh, deah, all those things sounded so nice and comforting when they seemed meant for othah people. They don't seem so comforting now that I'm in trouble myself. It's like the poultice Aunt Cindy made for Walkah's toothache. She was disgusted because he didn't stop complaining right away, and said it ought to have cured him if it didn't. But it wasn't such a powahful remedy when she had the toothache herself. She grumbled moah than Walkah. It's all well enough to say that I'll seal up my troubles as the bees seal up the things that get into the cells to spoil their honey, but now the time is heah, I simply can't!"

Nevertheless, what the School of the Bees taught did help. So did the sight of the patient old Camelback Mountain, that had inspired the legend of Shapur. And more than all the little group in front of the Wigwam helped, as she remembered how bravely they had met their troubles.

One by one her happy Arizona days came back to her. After all, it was something to have lived fifteen beautiful years untouched by trouble. She was thankful for that much, even if the future held nothing more for her. If she couldn't be happy, she could at least take Mary's advice and "not let loose and howl" about it any more. If she couldn't be bright and cheerful, she could "swallow her sobs and stiffen." With the resolution to try Mary's remedy for her woes in the morning, she lay drowsily watching the firelight flicker across the picture of the Wigwam.

CHAPTER XI.

IN THE ATTIC

If the sun had been shining next morning, it would have been easier for Lloyd to keep her resolution, and face the family bravely at breakfast. But the rain was pouring against the windows: a slow, monotonous rain that ran in little rivers over the lawn, melting the snow, and turning the white landscape into a dreary scene of mud and bare branches.

Twice on the way down-stairs she paused, thinking that she could not possibly sit through the meal without crying, and that it would be better to go back and breakfast alone in her room than to be a damper on the spirits of the family. Even so slight a thing as the tone of sympathy in her grandfather's "good morning" made the tears spring to her eyes, but she winked them back, and answered almost cheerfully his question as to how she felt.

"Oh, just like the weathah, grandfathah. All gray and drippy; but I'll clean up aftah awhile."

She could not smile as she said it, but the effort she made to be cheerful made the next attempt easier, and presently she acknowledged to herself that Mary was right. It did help, to swallow one's sobs.

After breakfast she stood at the window, watching her father drive away to the station in the rain. As the carriage disappeared and there was nothing more to watch, she wondered dully how she could spend the long morning.

"Some one wants you at the telephone, Lloyd," called the Colonel, on his way to his den.

"Oh, good! I hope it is Kitty," she exclaimed, anticipating a long visit over the wire.

But it was Malcolm MacIntyre who had rung her up, to bid her good-bye. He and Keith were about to start home. They had intended to go up to Locust, he told her, for a short call before train time, but it was raining too hard. Would she please make their adieus to her mother and the rest of the family. He had heard that she was not going back to school. Was it true? She was in luck. No? She was disappointed? Well, that was too bad. He was awfully sorry. But she mustn't worry over missing a few months of school. It wouldn't amount to much in the long run. For his part, if he were a girl and didn't have to fit himself for a profession, he would be glad to have such a postscript added to his Christmas vacation. He'd noticed that usually the postscript to a girl's letter had more in it than the letter itself. Possibly it would be that way with her vacation. He hoped so.

Although it was in the most cordial tone that he expressed his regret at her disappointment, and bade Princess Winsome good-bye until the "good old summer-time," it was with a vague feeling of disappointment that Lloyd hung up the receiver and turned away from the telephone.

"He doesn't undahstand at all!" she thought. "He hasn't the faintest idea how much it means to me to give up school. He thinks that, because I'm a girl, I haven't any ambition, and that it doesn't hurt me as it would him. Maybe it wouldn't have sounded quite the same if I could have seen him say it, but ovah the telephone, somehow—although he was mighty nice and polite—it sounded sawt of patronizing."

She went into the library to deliver Malcolm's farewell messages to her mother. "He seems so much moah grown up this time than he evah has befoah," she added. "I don't like him half as much that way as the way he used to be."

Mrs. Sherman was busy about the house all morning, so Lloyd found entertainment following her from room to room, as she inspected the linen

closet, superintended the weekly cleaning of the pantry, and rearranged some of
the library shelves to make room for the Christmas books. But in the afternoon
she had a number of letters to write, acknowledging the gifts which had been
sent her by distant friends, and Lloyd was left to her own amusement.

"ONE OF THE BOYS HAD
DARED HIM TO CARRY IT."

The doctor did not want her to read long at a time. The rain was pouring too
hard for her to venture out-of-doors, and about the middle of the afternoon the
silence and loneliness of the big house seemed more than she could endure.

"I could scream, I'm so nervous and ti'ahed of being by myself," she
exclaimed. "If just a piece of a day is so hah'd to drag through as this has been,
how can I stand all the rest of the wintah?"

She was counting up the weeks ahead of her on the big library calendar, when,
through the window, she caught sight of Rob coming toward the house. The rain

was running in streams from the bottom of his mackintosh, and from a huge umbrella that spread over him like a tent. It was an enormous advertising umbrella, taken from one of the delivery wagons at the store. One of the boys had dared him to carry it. "*Groceries, Dry Goods, Boots and*" appeared in black letters on the yellow side turned toward Lloyd. "*Shoes. Jayne's Emporium,*" she called, supplying the rest of the familiar advertisement from memory.

"What on earth are you doing with that wagon-top ovah you?" she asked from the front door, where she stood watching his approach. He was striding along whistling as cheerily as if it were a midsummer day. He looked up and smiled in response to her call, and twirled the umbrella till the rain-drops flew in every direction in a fine spray. Lloyd felt as if the sun had suddenly come out from behind the clouds.

"I've come to finish my Christmas hunt," he said, as he stepped up on the porch and shook himself like a great water-spaniel.

"Oh," cried Lloyd, "I intended to ask Betty befoah she went away where she had hidden yoah present, and she left next mawning so early that I was still asleep. Maybe mothah knows."

But Mrs. Sherman, busy with her letters, shook her head. "I haven't the faintest idea," she answered. "But I remember she said something about Rob's being the hardest one of all to find, so you'll probably be kept busy the rest of the day. Don't you children bother either Mom Beck or Cindy to help you hunt," she called after them. "They have all they can attend to to-day."

"Let's see that verse again, Rob," said Lloyd, as they went out of the library into the drawing-room. He fumbled in several pockets and finally produced the card.

"I know a bank where the wild thyme grows.
Unseen it lies, unsung by bard.
Something keeps watch there, no man knows,
And over your gift it's standing guard."

As on Christmas Day, the only bank the verse suggested was in the conservatory, a long, narrow ledge of ferns and maidenhair, green with overhanging vines and graceful fronds. For nearly half an hour they poked around in it, lifting the ferns from the warm, moist earth to see if anything lay hidden at their roots. It was like April in the conservatory, steamy and warm, and the fragrance of hyacinths and white violets made it a delightful place in which to linger.

"Bank—bank—" repeated Lloyd, puzzling over the verse again, when they had given up the search in the conservatory and gone back to the drawing-room. "It might mean a savings-bank, but there hasn't been one in the house since that little red tin one of mine that you dropped into the well with my three precious dimes in it. I've felt all these yeahs that you owed me thirty cents."

"Now, Lloyd Sherman, there's no use in bringing up that old quarrel again," he laughed. "You know we were playing that robbers were coming, and we had to lower our gold and jewels into the well, and you tied the fishing-line around the bank your own self. So I am not to blame if the knot came untied at the very first jerk. We've wasted enough breath arguing that point to start a small cyclone."

They laughed again over the recollection of their old quarrel, then Rob read the verse once more. Presently he stopped drumming on the table with his thumbs, and said, slowly, as if trying to recall something long forgotten: "Don't you remember,—it seems ages before we dropped your red bank in the well,— that I had a remarkable penny savings-bank? It was some sort of a slot machine in the shape of a little iron dog. Daddy brought it to me from New York. There was some kind of an indicator on the side of it that looked like the face of a watch. That was my introduction to puns, for Daddy said it was a *watch* dog, made to guard my pennies. Surely you haven't forgotten old Watch, for after the indicator was broken I brought the safe over here, and we kept it on the door-mat in front of your playhouse, to guard the premises."

"I should say I do remembah!" answered Lloyd. "Probably it's up in the attic now. But what has that to do with the rhyme?"

"Don't you see? That must be the 'bank' where the wild thyme grows. I don't know whether Betty refers to the wild time we used to have playing in the attic, or the wild time that the watch kept. But I'm certain that that is the bank she means."

"Come on, then," cried Lloyd. "Let's go up to the attic and hunt for it. I haven't been up there for ovah a yeah."

Rob led the way to the upper hall, and then up the attic stairs, taking the steep steps two at a time in long leaps.

"That isn't the way you used to climb these stairs," laughed Lloyd. "Don't you know you had to weah little long-sleeved aprons when you came ovah to play with me, to keep yoahself clean? You always stepped on the front of them and stumbled going up these steps."

A headless and tailless hobby-horse of Rob's, on which they had ridden many imaginary miles, stood in one corner, and he crossed over to examine it, with an amused smile.

"It certainly didn't take much to amuse us in those days," he said, touching the rockers with his foot, and starting the disabled beast to bobbing back and forth. "How long has it been since we used to ride this thing? Is my hair white? I declare I never had anything make me feel so ancient as the sight of this old hobby-horse. I feel older than grandfather."

Lloyd had opened a dilapidated hair-covered trunk, and was bending over a family of dolls stowed away inside. "Heah is old Belinda!" she exclaimed. "And Carrie Belle May, and Rosalie, the Prairie Flowah! 'And, oh, Rob! Look at poah Nelly Bly, all wah-paint and feathahs, just as you fixed her up for a squaw that day we had an Indian massacre in the grape arbour. I had forgotten that we left her in such a fix!"

"I'll never forget that day," answered Rob. "Don't you remember how sore I made my arm, trying to tattoo an anchor on it with a darning-needle and clothes bluing? What else have you buried in that old trunk?"

Despite his six feet and seventeen years, Rob dropped down on a roll of carpet beside the trunk, and watched with interest as Lloyd lifted out one article after another over which they had quarrelled, or in whose pleasure they had shared in what now seemed a dim and far-away playtime. Don't you remember this? Don't you remember that? they asked each other, finding so many things to laugh over and recall that they quite forgot the object of their search.

Lloyd was sitting with her back against the warm chimney, which ran up through the middle of the attic, but presently she began to feel chilly, and sent Rob over to a chest, away back under the eaves, for something to put around her. It was packed full of old finery they had used on various occasions for tableaux and plays. The first thing he pulled out was a gorgeous red velvet cloak covered with spangles.

"That will do," she said, as he held it up inquiringly. "It's good and warm."

He pushed the chest back into place. Then, straightening up, his glance fell on the discarded playhouse, standing back in a dim corner. With a whoop he pounced upon it.

"Here's old Watch!" he exclaimed, holding up the little iron dog. "And he is the bank where the wild time grows, for here is the gift he is standing guard over." Throwing the spangled cloak over Lloyd's shoulders, he seated himself again on the roll of carpet, and began to untie the little package fastened to the dog's neck with a bit of ribbon. Inside many layers of tissue-paper, he came at last to a memorandum-book, small enough to fit in his vest-pocket. It was bound in soft gray kid, and on the back Betty had burned in old English letters, with her pyrography-needle, the motto of Warwick Hall: "I keep the tryst." Over it was the crest, a heart, out of which rose a mailed arm, grasping a spear.

"Betty did that," said Lloyd. "She traced the letters on first with tracing-papah, and then burnt them. I remembah now, she made it a few days befoah we came home. She thought we would have our usual tree, and she intended to hang this on it for you. Then when we had the hunt instead of a tree, she took this way of giving it to you. That is an appropriate motto for a memorandum-book, isn't it? You'll appreciate it moah when she tells you the story about it. Miss Chilton read it to the English class one day, and had us write it from memory for the next lesson."

"Then what's the matter with your telling it to me?" asked Rob, eying the mailed hand and the spear with interest. "I'll be gone before Betty gets back. Go on and tell it. This is an ideal time and place for story-telling."

He leaned comfortably back against the warm chimney and half-closed his eyes. The patter of the rain on the roof made him drowsy.

"Well," assented Lloyd, "I can't tell it with as many frills and flourishes as Betty could, but I remembah it bettah than most stories, because I had to write it from memory." Drawing the glittering cloak closer around her, she began as if she were reading it, in the very words of the green and gold volume:

"'Now there was a troubadour in the kingdom of Arthur, who, strolling through the land with only his minstrelsy to win him a way, found in every baron's hall and cotter's hut a ready welcome.'"

Here and there she stumbled over some part of it, or told it hesitatingly in her own words, but at last she ended it as well as Betty herself could have done:

"So Ederyn won his sovereign's favour, and, by his sovereign's grace permitted, went back to woo the maiden and win her for his bride. Then henceforth blazoned on his shield and helmet he bore the crest, a heart with hand that grasped a spear, and, underneath, the words, 'I keep the tryst.'"

"That's a corking good motto," said Rob as she paused. "I like that story, Lloyd, and I'll remember it when I keep the engagements that I put down in this little book."

He sat a moment, flipping the leaves and whistling a bar from "The Old Oaken Bucket."

"Stop!" commanded Lloyd, suddenly, clapping her hands over her ears, and making a wry face. "You're off the key. Haven't I told you a thousand times that it doesn't go that way? This is it."

Puckering up her lips, she whistled the tune correctly, and he joined in. At the end of the chorus he looked at his watch.

"It's been like old times this afternoon," he said. "I'll tell you what, Lloyd, let's come up here once a year after this, just to keep tryst with our old playtimes. I'll put that down as the first engagement in my memorandum-book. A year from to-day we'll take another look at these things."

"All right," assented Lloyd, cheerfully. Then a wistful expression crept into her eyes as she peered through the tiny attic window. Twilight was falling early on account of the rain. A deep gloom began to settle over her spirits also.

"Rob," she said, slowly, "I haven't told you yet. I didn't want to spoil our aftahnoon by thinking about it any moah than I could help, and you made me almost forget it for a little while. I couldn't talk about it when you first came without crying,—this yeah is going to be *such* a long, hah'd one. They aren't going to let me go back to school aftah the holidays. The doctah says I am not strong enough, and it is such an awful Dungeon of Disappointment that it just breaks my hah't to think about it."

To Rob's consternation she laid her head down on old Belinda, who still lay limply across her lap, and began to sob. He sat in embarrassed silence for a moment, scarcely knowing her for the same little companion whom he had taught to meet hurts like a boy. He remembered the many times she had winked back the tears over the bruises and bumps and cuts she had encountered in following his lead. He was bewildered by the unfamiliar mood, and it hurt him to see her so grieved.

"There! there! Don't cry, Lloyd!" he begged, hurt by the sight of the fair head bowed so dismally over the old doll. "I know how it would knock me out to have to stop now, just when I've got into the swing of things, so I know just how you feel. I'm mighty sorry."

Then, as the sobs continued: "I'd go off and whip somebody if it would do any good, but it won't. You'll have to brace up as Ederyn did, and you'll get out of your dungeon all right."

There was no answer. School was so very dear, and the disappointment so very bitter. It had all surged over her again in a great wave. He tried again.

"It's tough, I know, but it will be easier if you take it as all the Lloyds have taken their troubles, with your teeth set and your head up. Somehow, that's the way I've always thought you would take things. Don't cry, Lloyd. Don't! It breaks me all up to see you this way, when you've always been so game."

She straightened up and wiped her eyes, announcing suddenly: "And I'm going to be game now. If there's one thing I nevah could beah, it was for you to think I was a coward, and I can't have you thinking it now. It's a sawt of tryst I've kept all these yeahs, unconsciously, I suppose. Ever since I was a little thing, if I thought 'Bobby expects it of me,' I'd do it, no mattah what it was, from jumping a fence to climbing on the chimney. I've lived up to yoah expectations many a time at the risk of killing myself."

"Indeed you have," he answered, in a tone of hearty admiration. There was a tender light in his gray eyes which she did not see, she was so busy wiping her own.

"I'm done crying now," she announced, springing to her feet and thrusting Belinda back into the trunk. "Come on, let's go down and pop some cawn ovah the library fiah. Put this cloak away first."

He pushed the chest back to its place under the eaves and started after her, pulling out his handkerchief as he went, to wipe away a stray cobweb into which he had thrust his hand. It reminded him of the story.

"You know," he suggested, consolingly, "there's bound to be some way out of your dungeon. I'll spend all the rest of the vacation helping you twist cobwebs for your rope, if you like."

She made no answer then to his offer of assistance. She felt that she could not steady her voice if she tried to speak her appreciation of his sympathy.

So she called out, as she dashed past him: "As Joyce used to say at the house pah'ty, 'the last one down is a jibbering Ornithorhynchus!'"

Away they went in a mad race, whose noisy clatter made it seem to the old Colonel in his den that the rafters were falling in. But on the landing she paused an instant.

"It—it helps a lot, Rob," she said, wistfully, "to have you undahstand,—to know that you know how it hurts."

"I wish I could really help you," he answered, earnestly. "You're a game little chum!"

She flashed back a grateful smile from under her wet eyelashes, and led the race on down the next flight of stairs.

CHAPTER XII.

HUMDRUM DAYS

All through the rest of that week, and through New Year's Day, Lloyd managed to keep her resolution bravely. Even when the time came for the girls to go back to school without her, she went through the farewells like a little Spartan, driving down to the station with tearful Betty, who grieved over Lloyd's disappointment as if it had been her own.

When the train pulled out, with the four girls on the rear platform, she stood waving her handkerchief cheerily as long as she could see an answering flutter. Then she turned away, catching her breath in a deep indrawn sob, that might have been followed by others if Rob had not been with her. He saw her clench her hands and set her teeth together hard, and knew what a fight she was making to choke back the tears, but he wisely gave no sign that he saw and sympathized. He only proposed a walk over to the blacksmith shop to see the red fox that Billy Kerr had trapped and caged. But a little later, when she had regained her self-control and was poking a stick between the slats of the coop where the fox was confined, to make it stretch itself, he said, suddenly:

"By cricky, you were game, Lloyd! If it had been me, I couldn't have gone to the station and watched the fellows go off without me, and joke about it the way you did."

Lloyd went on rattling the stick between the slats and made no answer, but Rob's approval brightened her spirits wonderfully. It was not until the next day, when he, too, went back to school, that she fully realized how lonely her winter was going to be. She strolled into her mother's room, and threw herself listlessly into a chair by the window.

"What can I do, mothah? I mustn't read long, I mustn't study, Tarbaby is lame, so I can't ride, and I've walked as far as I care to this mawning."

"What would you like to do?" asked Mrs. Sherman, who was dressing to go out.

"Nothing but things that I can't do," was the fretful answer. "It would be lots of fun if I could go out in the kitchen and beat eggs, and make custah'd pies and biscuits and things. I'd love to cook. I haven't had a chance since I was at Ware's Wigwam. But Aunt Cindy scolds and grumbles if anybody so much as looks into the kitchen. She says she won't have me messing around in her way."

"I know," sighed Mrs. Sherman. "Cindy is getting more fussy and exacting every year. But she has cooked for the family so long that she seems to think the kitchen is hers. If she were not such a superior cook, I wouldn't put up with her whims, but in these days, when everybody is having so much trouble with servants, we'll have to humour her. She's a faithful old creature. You might cook on the chafing-dish in the dining-room. There are all sorts of things you could make on that."

Lloyd shrugged her shoulders impatiently. "But not bread and pies and things you do with a rolling-pin. That's the pah't I like."

She sat a moment, swinging her foot in silence, and then broke out:

"If I were a girl in a story-book, this disappointment would turn me into such a saintly, helpful creatuah that I'd be called 'The Angel of the Home.' I've read about such girls. They keep things in ordah, and mend and dust and put flowahs about, and make the house so bright and cheerful that people wondah how they evah got along without them. Every time they turn around, there are lovely, helpful things for them to do. But what can *I* do in a big house like this moah than I've always tried to do? I've tried to be considerate of everybody's comfo't evah since I stah'ted out to build a road of the loving hah't in everybody's memory. The servants do everything heah, and don't want to be interfered with. I wish we were dead poah, and lived in a plain little cottage and did our own work. Then I wouldn't have time to get lonesome. I'd be lots happiah.

"One day, when Miss Gilmer and I were talking about Ederyn in his Dungeon of Disappointment, she said that we could always get out of our troubles the same way that he did; that the cobwebs he twisted into ropes were disagreeable to touch. Nobody likes to put their hands into dusty cobwebs, and that they represent the disagreeable little tasks that lie in wait for everybody. She said that, if we'll just grapple the things that we dislike most to do, the little homely every-day duties, and busy ourselves with them, they'll help us to rise above our discontent. I've been trying all mawning to think of some such cobwebs for me to take hold of, and there isn't a single one."

Mrs. Sherman smiled at the wobegone face turned toward her. "Fancy any one being miserable over such a state of affairs as that!" she laughed. "Actually complaining because there's nothing disagreeable for her to do! Well, we'll have to look for some cobwebs to occupy you. Maybe if you can't find them at home, you can do like the old woman who was tossed up in a basket, seventy times as high as the moon. Don't you remember how Mom Beck used to sing it to you?

"'Old woman! Old woman! Old woman, said I,
O whither, O whither, O whither so high?
To sweep the cobwebs out of the sky,
But I'll be back again, by and by.'"

She trilled it gaily as she fastened her belt, and took out her hat and gloves.

"Fate must have given her just such a cobwebless home as you have, and she had to soar high to rise above her troubles. Come on, little girl, get your hat and coat, and we'll go in search of something disagreeable for you to do; but I hope your quest won't take you seventy times as high as the moon."

They drove down to the store to attend to the day's marketing. While Mrs. Sherman was ordering her groceries, Lloyd went to the back of the store, where one of the clerks was teaching tricks to a bright little fox-terrier. She was so interested in the performance that she did not know when Miss Allison came in, or how long she and her mother stood discussing her.

"Yes," said Mrs. Sherman, "she has been brave about it. She never complained but once, and that to me this morning. But we know how unhappy she is. Jack and papa worry about her all the time. They want me to take her to Florida. They think she must be given some pleasure that will compensate in a way for this disappointment. But it is not at all convenient for me to leave home now, and I feel that for her own good she should learn to meet such things for herself. It would be far easier, I acknowledge, if there was anything at home to occupy her, but I cannot allow her to interfere with Mom Beck's work, or Cindy's. They resent her doing anything." She repeated the conversation they had had that morning.

"Loan her to me for the rest of the day," said Miss Allison. "I can show her plenty of cobwebs, the kind she is pining for."

So it happened that a little later, when Miss Allison crossed the road to the post-office, and started up the path toward home, Lloyd was with her, smiling happily over the prospect of spending the day with the patron saint of all the Valley's merrymakings. From Lloyd's earliest recollection, Miss Allison had been the life of every party and picnic in the neighbourhood. She was everybody's confidante. Like Shapur, who gathered something from the heart of every rose to fill his crystal vase, so she had distilled from all these disclosures the precious attar of sympathy, whose sweetness won for her a way, and gained for her a welcome, wherever she went.

As they turned in at the gate, Lloyd looked wistfully across at The Beeches, and her eyes filled with tears. Miss Allison slipped her arm around her and drew her close with a sympathetic clasp, as they walked around the circle of the driveway leading to the house.

"I know just how you feel, dear. Like the little lame boy in that story of the 'Pied Piper of Hamelin.' Because he couldn't keep up with the others when they followed the piper's tune, he had to sit and watch them dance away without him, and disappear into the mountainside. He was the only child left in the whole town of Hamelin. It *is* lonely for you, I know, with all the boys and girls of your own age away at school. But think how much lonelier Hamelin would have been without that child. You'll find out that old people can play, too, though, if you'll take a hand in their games. I want to teach you one after awhile, which I used to enjoy very much, and still take pleasure in."

Miss Allison led the way up-stairs to her own room. As they passed the door leading to the north wing, Lloyd exclaimed: "I'll nevah forget that time, the night of the Valentine pah'ty, when Gingah and I went into the blue room, and the beah that Malcolm and Keith had tied to the bed-post rose up out of the dah'k and frightened us neahly to death."

"We had some lively times that winter with Virginia and the boys," answered Miss Allison. "I kept a record of some of their sorriest mishaps. Wait a minute until I speak to the housemaid, and I'll see if I can find it."

Miss Allison had been wondering how she could best entertain Lloyd, but the problem was solved when she found the journal, in which she had written the history of the eventful winter when her sister's little daughter Virginia and her brother's two boys had been left in her charge. Lloyd had taken part in many of the mischievous adventures, and she sat smiling over the novelty of hearing herself described with all the imperious ways, naughty temper, and winning charm that had been hers at the age of eight.

"It is like looking at an old photograph of oneself," she said, after awhile. "It seems so strange to be one of the characters in a book, and listen to stories about oneself."

"That reminds me of the game I spoke of," said Miss Allison. "I invented it when I was about your age. I had just read 'Cranford,' and the story of life in that simple little village seemed so charming to me that I wished with all my heart I could step into the book and be one of the characters, and meet all the people that lived between its covers. Then I heard some one say that there were more interesting happenings and queer characters in Lloydsboro Valley than in Cranford. So I began to look around for them. I pretended that I was the heroine of a book called 'Lloydsboro Valley,' and all that summer I looked upon the people I met as characters in the same story.

"It happened that all my young friends were away that summer, and it would have been very lonely but for my new game. The organist went away, and, although I was only fifteen, I took her place and played the little cabinet organ we used then in church and Sunday school. That threw me much with the older people, for I had to go to choir-practice to play the organ, and also attend the missionary teas. Gradually they drew me into a sewing-circle that was in existence then, and a reading club. I found it was true that my own little village really had far more interesting people in it than any I had read about, and I learned to love all the dear, cranky, gossipy old characters in it, because I studied them so closely that I found how good at heart they were despite their peculiarities and foibles.

"That's what I want you to do this winter, Lloyd. Join the little choir, and meet with the King's Daughters, and learn to know these interesting neighbours of yours. And," she added, smiling, "I promise you that you'll find all the cobwebs you need to help haul you out of your dungeon."

"Oh, Miss Allison!" exclaimed Lloyd, looking horrified at the thought. "*I* couldn't sing in the choir and join the King's Daughtahs and all that. They're all at least twice as old as I am, and some of them even moah."

"Yes, you can," insisted Miss Allison. "We need your voice in the choir, and you need the new interest these things would bring into your life. So don't say no until after you've given my game a trial. The King's Daughters' Circle is to meet here this afternoon, and I want you to help me. I'm going to serve hot chocolate and wafers, and, as long as it is such a cold, blowy day, I believe I'll add some nut sandwiches to make the refreshments a little more substantial."

Privately, Lloyd looked forward to the afternoon as something stupid which she must face cheerfully for Miss Allison's sake, but she found her interest aroused with the first arrival. It was Libbie Simms, whom she had known all her life, in a way, for she could scarcely recall a Sabbath when she had not looked across at the dull, homely face in the opposite pew, and pitied her because of her queer nose and mouse-coloured hair. In the same way she had known Miss McGill, who came with Libbie. She had simply been one of the congregation who had claimed her attention for a moment each week, as she minced down the aisle like an animated rainbow. All she knew about Miss McGill was that she usually wore so many shades of purple and pink and blue that the clashing colours set one's teeth on edge.

But in five minutes Lloyd had forgotten their peculiarities of feature and dress, and was listening with interest to their account of a call they had just made in Rollington. They had been to see a poor washerwoman who had five children to support. The youngest, a baby who had fits, was very ill, about to die. At the mention of Mrs. Crisp, Lloyd recalled the forlorn little woman in a wispy crêpe veil, who had enlisted her sympathy to such an extent one Thanksgiving Day that she and Betty had walked over to Rollington from the Seminary to carry the greater part of the turkey and fruit that had been sent them in their box of Thanksgiving goodies.

There was so little poverty in the Valley that, when any real case of suffering was discovered, it was taken up with enthusiasm. Lloyd wondered how she could have thought Libbie Simms so hopelessly ugly, when she saw her face light up with unselfish interest in her poor neighbours, and heard her suggestions for their relief. And her conscience pricked her for making fun of Miss McGill's taste when she saw how generous she was, and listened to her humourous description of several things that had happened in the Valley. She was certainly entertaining, and looked at life through spectacles as rose-coloured as her necktie.

The library filled rapidly, and soon a score of needles were at work on the flannel garments intended for the Crisp family. Lloyd, on a stool between Katherine Marks and Mrs. Walton, sewed industriously, interested in the buzz of conversation all around her.

"This is not malicious gossip," explained Mrs. Walton, in an amused undertone, smiling with Lloyd and Katherine at a remark which unintentionally reached their ears. "But in a little community like this, where little happens, and our interests are bound so closely together, the smallest details of our neighbours' affairs necessarily entertain us. It *is* interesting to know that Mr. Rawles and his great-aunt are not on speaking terms, and it is positively exciting to hear that Mr. Wolf and Mrs. Cayne quarrelled over the leaflets used in Sunday school, and that she told him to his face that he was a hypocrite and no better than an infidel. It doesn't make us love these good people any the less to know that they are human like ourselves, and have their tempers and their spites and feuds. We know their good side, too. Wait till calamity or sickness touches some one of us, and, see how kind and sympathetic and tender they all are; every one of them."

'I NEARLY FAINTED WHEN I HAPPENED TO LOOK UP'"

"You'll hear more gossip here in one afternoon than at all the Cranford tea-tables put together," said Katherine Marks. "But it is a mild sort, like the kind going on behind us."

Miss McGill, with her head close to Abby Carter's, was saying: "Oh, but, my dear, he gets more suspicious and foxy every day of his life. I don't see how Emma Belle puts up with such a cranky old father."

"I know," responded Abby. "They say he drives the cook nearly distracted, going into the kitchen every day and lifting the lids off all the pots and pans to smell what's cooking for dinner. Then he makes a fuss if it's not to his liking."

"Yes," responded Miss McGill, "but that isn't a circumstance to some of his ways. I ran in there last night a few minutes, to show Emma Belle a pattern she wanted. He got it into his head we were hiding something from him, and he actually climbed up on the dining-room table and peeped through the transom at us. I nearly fainted when I happened to look up and saw that old monkey-like face, with its dense, gloomy whiskers, looking down at me. I just screamed and sat jibbering and pointing at the transom. I couldn't help it. He gave me such a turn, I didn't get over it all night. Emma Belle was so mortified she didn't know what to do. It isn't as if he was crazy. He's just mean. That girl has the patience of a saint."

Before the afternoon was over, Lloyd decided that Miss Allison was right. The Valley held a number of interesting characters, whose acquaintance was well worth cultivating if she wanted to be entertained. Part of the time, while the needles were flying, Mrs. MacIntyre read aloud. Miss Allison called Lloyd into the dining-room when it was time to serve the refreshments.

"I'm going to ask a favour of you, dear," she said. "I want you to sing for us presently. No, wait a minute," she added, hurriedly, as Lloyd drew back with an exclamation of dismay. "Don't refuse till you have heard why I ask it. It is on account of Agnes Waring. These meetings are the great social events of the winter to her. She never gets to go anywhere else except to church. She's passionately fond of music, and I always make it a point to prepare a regular programme when the Circle meets here. But all my musicians failed me this time, and I cannot bear to disappoint her. I know you are timid about singing before older people, but this is one of the cobwebs I promised to find for you. It will be disagreeable, but I have a good reason for thinking that you will find it the first strand of the rope that is to lift you out of your dungeon. I'll tell you some things about Agnes after awhile that will make you glad you have had such an opportunity."

When Lloyd went back to the library, bearing a pile of snowy napkins, she stole several glances at Agnes Waring in her journey around the room to distribute them. All that she knew of her was that she was the youngest of three sisters who sewed for their living. She was almost as slim and girlish in figure as Lloyd, although she was nearly twice as old. She had kept the timid, shrinking manner that she had when a child. That and her appealing big blue eyes, and almost babyish complexion, made her seem much younger than she was. It was a sensitive, refined face that Lloyd kept glancing at, one that would have been remarkably pretty had it not been so sad.

Lloyd had sung in public several times, but always in some play, when the costume which she wore seemed to change her to the character she personated. That made it easier. It was one of the hardest things she had ever done, to stand up before these twenty ladies who had been exchanging criticisms so freely all afternoon, on every subject mentioned, and sing the songs which Miss Allison chose for her from the Princess play: The Dove Song, with its high, sweet trills of "Flutter and fly," and the one beginning:

"My godmother bids me spin,
That my heart may not be sad.
Sing and spin for my brother's sake,
And the spinning makes me glad."

It was with a very red face that she slipped into her seat after it was over, surprised and pleased by the applause she received. They were all so cordial in their appreciation, that presently she was persuaded into doing what Miss Allison had suggested. When the circle broke up she had consented to join the choir, and to meet with them the next Friday night, when they went to the Mallards' to practise.

The carriage came for her soon after the last guest departed, and Miss Allison stepped in beside her to take the finished garments over to Rollington. It was the quaintest of little villages, settled entirely by Irish families. Only one lone street straggled over the hill, but it was a long one with little whitewashed cabins and cottages thickly set along each side. Mrs. Crisp's was the first one on the street, after they left the Lloydsboro pike. It was clean, but not half so large or comfortable as the negro servants' quarters at Locust.

It was so late that Miss Allison did not go in, only stopped at the door to leave the bundle and inquire about the baby, promising to come again next morning. Lloyd had a glimpse of the two children next in age to the baby. They were playing on the floor with a doll made of a corn-cob wrapped in a towel, and a box of empty spools.

"Just think!" she exclaimed as she climbed into the carriage again. "A cawn-cob doll! And the attic at home is full of toys that I don't care for! I'm going to pick out a basketful to-morrow and bring them down to these children. And did you see that poah little Minnie Crisp? Only eight yeahs old, and doing the work of a grown woman. She was getting suppah while her mothah tended to the sick baby. Oh, I wondah," she cried, her face lighting up with the thought. "I wondah if Mrs. Crisp would mind if I'd come down to-morrow and cook dinnah for them. That's what I've been crazy to do,—to cook. I could bring eggs and sugah and all the materials, and make lemon pie and oystah soup and potato croquettes. I know how to make lots of things. Oh, do you suppose she would be offended?"

"Not in the least," responded Miss Allison, heartily. "She is a very sensible little woman who is nearly worn out in her struggle with poverty and sickness. She has been too proud and brave to accept help before, when she was able to stagger along under her own burden, but now she will be very grateful. And the children will look upon you as a wonderful mixture of Santa Claus, fairy godmother, and Aladdin's lamp."

Then she turned to peer into the happy face beside her.

"Here are your cobwebs!" she exclaimed, gaily. "A whole skyful, and you can sweep away to your heart's content. You need have no more humdrum days unless you choose."

Lloyd looked back at the cottage where four towheads at the window watched the departing carriage. Then with a smile she leaned out and waved her hand.

CHAPTER XIII.

IN THE FOOTSTEPS OF AMANTHIS

Lloyd hurried down the road to the post-office, her cheeks almost as red as her coat from her brisk walk in the wintry air. It was too cold to saunter, or she would have made the errand last as long as possible. There would be nothing to do after she had called for the mail. The day before she had had her visit to Mrs. Crisp to fill the morning. It brought a pleasant thrill now to think of the little woman's gratitude and the children's pleasure in the dinner she had cooked in the clean bare kitchen. She wished she could go every day and repeat the performance, but her family would not allow it. They said it was just as injurious for her to waste her strength in charity as it was in study, and she must be more temperate in her enthusiasms.

She wished that Miss Mattie would invite her into the tiny office behind the rows of pigeonholes and letter-boxes, and let her sit by the window awhile. Just watching people pass would be some amusement, more than she could find at home.

She was passing the Bisbee place as she made the wish. It was a white frame house standing near the road, and commanding a view of both station and store, as well as the approach to the post-office. To her surprise, some one tapped on the pane of an up-stairs window. Then the sash flew up, and Mrs. Bisbee called in her thin, fluttering voice: "Lloyd! Lloyd Sherman! If you're going to the post-office, I wish you'd ask if there is anything for me. I don't dare set foot out-of-doors this cold weather."

Then, fearful of draughts, she banged the window down without waiting for a reply. Lloyd smiled and nodded, glad of an opportunity to be of service. As she hurried on, she remembered that Miss Allison had spoken of this gentle little old lady, with her fluttering voice and placid smile, as one of the most interesting and "Cranfordy" characters in the Valley, and that, while she never went out in the winter, and seldom in the summer, except to church, she kept such a sharp eye on the neighbourhood happenings from the watch-tower of her window that Mrs. Walton laughingly called it the "Window in Thrums."

It was with the feeling that she was stepping into a story that Lloyd opened the gate five minutes later and started up the path. A vigorous tapping on the window above, and a beckoning hand motioned her to come up-stairs. Hesitating an instant on the porch, she opened the front door and stepped into the hall.

"Do come up!" called the old lady, plaintively, from the head of the stairs. "I've been wishing so hard for company that I believe my wishing must have drawn you. Now that daughter is married and gone, I get so lonesome, with Mr. Bisbee in town all day, that I often find myself talking to myself just for the sake of sociability. Not a soul has been in for the last two days, and usually I have callers from morning till night. This is such a good dropping-in place, you know. So central that I see and hear everything."

She ushered Lloyd into a room, gay with big-flowered chintz curtains, and quaint with old-fashioned carved furniture. There was a high four-poster bed in one corner, with a chintz valance around it, and pink silk quilled into the tester. The only modern thing in the room was a tiled grate, piled full of blazing coals. It threw out such a summer-like heat that Lloyd almost gasped. She was glad to accept Mrs. Bisbee's invitation to take off her coat and gloves. She moved her chair back as far as possible into the bay-window.

"I reckon you feel it's pretty warm in here," said Mrs. Bisbee. "I have to keep it that way so that I can sit over here against the window without catching cold. I couldn't afford to miss all that's going on in the street. It's my only amusement."

She drew her work-basket toward her and picked up the quilt pieces she had laid down when she went to welcome Lloyd. She was making a silk quilt of the tea-chest pattern, and the basket was full of bright silk scraps and pieces of ribbon.

"It's like a panorama, I tell Mr. Bisbee. Oh, by the way, I've been aching to find out. Where did you all go that day just before Christmas when you started off, a whole party of you, traipsing down the road with a new saucepan and baskets and things? I heard you had a picnic in the snow. Is that so?"

Lloyd really gasped this time, but not from the heat. She was so surprised that Mrs. Bisbee should have taken such an interest in her affairs, or in any of the unimportant doings of their set, as to remember them longer than the passing moment. Mrs. Bisbee was associated in Lloyd's mind with solemn churchly things, like the Gothic-backed pulpit chairs or the sombre brown pews. Lloyd had never seen her before, except when she was singing hymns, or sitting with meekly folded hands through sermon-time. It was almost as surprising to find that she was inquisitive and interested in human happenings as it would have been to discover that the ivy-covered belfry kept an eye on her.

In the midst of her description of the picnic, Mrs. Bisbee leaned forward and peered eagerly out of the window over her spectacles.

"I don't want to interrupt you," she said; "I just wanted to make sure that that was Caleb Coburn out again. He has been house-bound with rheumatism ever since Thanksgiving."

Lloyd looked out in time to see a tall, stoop-shouldered man with a bushy beard go slowly across the road. He was buttoned up in a heavy overcoat, and limped along with the aid of two canes.

"He's the queerest old fellow," commented Mrs. Bisbee, looking after him, with a gentle shake of the head. "Lately he has taken to knitting, to pass the time."

"To knitting!" echoed Lloyd, in amazement. "That big man?"

"Yes. He calls it hooking. He has a needle made out of a ham bone. Fancy now! Daughter said it was the funniest thing in life to see him propped up in bed with a striped skull-cap on, hooking his wife a shawl."

Lloyd laughed, but she followed the stooped figure with a glance of sympathy. She knew from experience how hard it was to spend the time in enforced idleness. Old Mr. Coburn had always been a familiar figure to her. She recognized him on the road as she did the trees and the houses which she passed daily, but he had never aroused her interest any more than they. Now the knowledge that he was lonely like herself, so lonely that, big, bearded man as he was, he had learned to knit in order to occupy the dull days, seemed to put them on a common footing.

Lloyd took a long step forward out of her childhood that morning when she wakened to the fact that some things are as hard to bear at fifty as at fifteen. With a dawning interest she watched the people of the Valley go by, one by one,—people whom she had passed heretofore as she had passed the fence-posts on the road. It could never be so again, for henceforth she would see them in a new light,—the light of understanding and sympathy shed on them by Mrs. Bisbee's choice bits of gossip or scraps of personal history.

She had watched the procession for nearly an hour, when Agnes Waring suddenly turned the corner, and went into the store with a bundle in her arms. Mrs. Bisbee, pausing in the act of threading a needle, looked out again over her spectacles.

"There goes a girl I'm certainly sorry for. She is a born lady, and comes of as good a family as anybody in the Valley, but she has to work harder than any darkey in Lloydsboro. She's up at four o'clock these winter mornings, milks the cow, chops wood, gets breakfast, and maybe walks two or three miles with a big bundle like that, taking home sewing, or going out to fit a dress for somebody."

Miss Allison had already awakened Lloyd's interest in Agnes, and she leaned forward to watch her, while Mrs. Bisbee went on.

"She's never had any of the pleasures that most girls have. To my certain knowledge she's never had a beau or been to a big party or travelled farther than Louisville. I suppose you could count on the fingers of one hand the times she has been on a train. She's wild about music, but she's never had any advantages. By the way, she was in here the day after the King's Daughters met at Allison MacIntyre's, to fit a wrapper on me. Knowing how few outings she has, I encouraged her to talk it all over, as I knew she was glad to do. I declare she made as much of it as if it had been the governor's ball. She told me how much she enjoyed your singing. She said that, if there was any one person in the world whom she envied more than another, it was Lloyd Sherman. Not for your looks or the handsome things you have (for the Valley is full of pretty girls, and many of them are wealthy), but for the advantages you have had in the way of music and travel.

"They have an old piano, about all that was saved out of the wreck when their father lost his fortune. She'd give her eyes to be able to play on it. But she wasn't much more than a baby when her father died, so she missed the advantages the older girls had. You see she is twenty years younger than Marietta, and nearly twenty-five years younger than Sarah. Poor Agnes! I suppose she will never know anything but work and poverty. It's too bad,—such a sweet, refined girl, and as proud as she is poor."

Lloyd echoed Mrs. Bisbee's sympathetic sigh, as she looked after the hurrying figure in its worn jacket and shabby shoes. She was just coming out of the store again.

"I feel so sorry for her sistahs, too," she ventured. "I nevah knew till the othah day that Miss Marietta has been an invalid so long. Miss Allison told me she had been in bed for fifteen yeahs! It's awful! Why, that is as long as my whole lifetime has been."

"She was to have been married," began Mrs. Bisbee, pouring out the romance at which Miss Allison had only hinted. "She was engaged to Murray Cathright, one of the finest young lawyers I ever knew, steady as a meeting-house. He had the respect and confidence of everybody. Well, Marietta had her trousseau all ready, and a beautiful one it was. Her father had sent to Paris for the wedding-gown, and all her linen was hand-embroidered by the nuns in some French convent.

"They certainly had all that heart could wish in those days. It is a pity that Agnes was too young to enjoy her share of luxuries. Well, just a week before the time set for the wedding, Murray Cathright mysteriously disappeared. He had gone away on a short business trip. His family traced him to a hotel in Pittsburg, and then lost all clue, except that just before leaving the hotel he had asked the clerk for the time-tables of an Eastern railroad. There was a terrible wreck on that road that same night. The entire train went through a bridge into the river, and they thought he must have been swept away with the unidentified dead. But it was months before Marietta would believe it.

"She acted as if her mind were a little touched all that summer. Used to dress up every evening in the clothes he had liked best, with a flower in her hair, and go down to the honeysuckle arbour to wait for him. She'd sit there and wait and wait all alone, until her father'd go down and lead her in. The next day she'd go through the same performance. It ended in a spell of brain fever. She came out of that with her mind all right, but she never was strong again. After all the rest of their troubles came, she had a stroke of paralysis. It's left her so she can't walk. But she can lie there and make buttonholes and pull basting threads. She's a perfect marvel, she's so patient and cheerful. People like to go there just on that account. You'd never know she had a trouble to hear her talk. But I know what she's suffered, and I know that she still keeps the wedding-gown. It's laid away in rose leaves for her to be buried in."

Mrs. Bisbee paused and spread out the finished quilt-piece on her knee, patting it approvingly before choosing the scraps for another block. Then she wiped her spectacles. "Sometimes I don't know which I'm the sorriest for, Marietta, who had such a good man for a lover as Murray Cathright was, and lost him, or Agnes, who's never had anything."

"Why don't people invite her out and give her a good time?" asked Lloyd. "Her being a seamstress oughtn't to make any difference to old family friends, when she's such a lady."

"It doesn't," answered Mrs. Bisbee. "People used to be nice to those girls, and they were always invited everywhere at first. But after awhile there was Marietta always in bed, and Agnes a mere baby, and poor Miss Sarah with the burden of their support. She had only her needle to keep the wolf from the door. She couldn't accept invitations then. There was no time. Gradually people stopped asking her. She dropped out of the social life of the Valley so completely that Agnes grew up without any knowledge of it. All she has known has been hard work. Miss Allison has tried to draw her into things, but the older sisters are proud, as I said. Agnes cannot dress suitably, and they can make no return of hospitalities, so she has never ventured into anything more than the King's Daughters' Circle."

"There's Alec with the carriage!" exclaimed Lloyd. "He's stopping at the stoah. If I hurry, I can ride back home. I've stayed so long that mothah will wondah what has become of me."

"Don't go!" begged Mrs. Bisbee, as Lloyd began drawing on her coat. "I don't know when I've enjoyed a morning so much. Since daughter's married and gone I miss her young friends so much. She used to have the house full of them from morning till night. Now I fairly pine for the sight of a fresh young face sometimes. You've livened me up more than you can know. *Do* come again!"

Lloyd went away highly pleased by her cordial reception. She had enjoyed being talked to as if she were grown, and these glimpses into the lives of her neighbours were more interesting than any her books could give her. When she passed the lane leading up to the house where the three sisters lived, she wished that she could turn over a leaf and read more about them. She wondered if Miss Marietta ever took out the beautiful wedding-dress that was to be her shroud. She mused over the newly discovered romance all the way home.

If it had not been for that morning's call, and the interest it aroused in her neighbours, several things might not have happened, which afterward followed each other like links in a chain. Probably Miss Sarah would have walked up to Locust just the same, to take home a wrapper she had finished, and not finding Mrs. Sherman at home would have stepped inside the door a moment to warm by the dining-room fire; and Lloyd, with the courtesy that never failed her, would have been as graciously polite as her mother could have been. But if it had not been for the interest in her that Mrs. Bisbee's story gave, several other happenings might not have followed.

As Lloyd looked at the gray-haired woman on whom toil and poverty and care had left their marks, and remembered there had been a time when Miss Sarah had been as tenderly cared for as herself, a sudden pity surged up into her heart. She longed to lighten her load in some way, and to give back to her for a moment at least the comforts she had lost. With a quick gesture she motioned her away from the dining-room door. "No, come in heah!" she exclaimed, leading the way into the drawing-room, and pushing a big armchair toward the fire.

Blue and cold from her long walk against the wind, Miss Sarah sank down among the soft cushions and leaned back luxuriously.

"It's so ti'ahsome walking against the wind," exclaimed the Little Colonel. "When I came in awhile ago, I was puffing and blowing. I'm going to make you a cup of hot tea. That's what mothah always takes. No! It won't be any *trouble,*" she exclaimed, as Miss Sarah protested. "It will be the biggest kind of a pleasuah. It will give me a chance to use mothah's little tea-ball. I deahly love to wiggle it around in the cup and see the watah po'ah out of all the little holes. I've been wishing somebody would come, or that I had something to do. Now you have granted both wishes. I can have a regulah little tea-pah'ty. Excuse me just a minute, please."

Left to herself, Miss Sarah sat looking around at the handsome furnishings: the thick Persian rugs, the old portraits, the tall, burnished harp in the corner, the bowl of hothouse violets on the table at her elbow, until Lloyd returned, bearing a toasting fork and a plate of thinly sliced bread. Miss Sarah turned toward her with wistful eyes.

"I have always loved this old room," she said. "This is the first time I have been in it for twenty years. It is an old friend. I have spent many happy hours here in your grandmother's day. She was always entertaining the young people of the Valley. Sometimes that time seems so far away that I wonder if it was not all a dream. It was a very beautiful dream, at any rate. I often wish Agnes could have had a share in it. She has missed so much in not having *her* friendship."

She nodded toward the portrait over the mantel. "Amanthis Lloyd was my ideal woman when I was a young girl like yourself," she added, softly, with her eyes on the beautiful features above her.

"I have missed so much, too," said Lloyd, following Miss Sarah's gaze. "And yet it seems to me I must have known her. The portrait has always seemed alive to me. I used to talk to it sometimes when I was a little thing, and I nevah could beah to look at it when I had been naughty. I wish you would tell me about her."

She knelt on the hearth-rug as she spoke, and held the long toasting-fork toward the fire. "Mothah and grandfathah often talk about her, but they don't tell the same things that one outside of the family might."

By the time the toast was delicately browned and buttered, Mom Beck came in with the tea-tray, and placed it on the table beside the bowl of violets.

"Good!" exclaimed Lloyd, seating herself on the other side of the table as the old woman left the room. "I didn't think to tell her to bring cold turkey and strawberry preserves and fruit cake, but she remembered that I didn't eat much lunch, and she is always trying to tempt my appetite. She's the best old soul that evah was. Oh, Miss Sarah, I'm so glad you came. I haven't had a pah'ty like this for ages. Heah! I'll let you wiggle the tea-ball in yoah own cup, so that you can make it as strong as you like, because you're company."

The dimples deepened playfully in her cheeks as she passed the tea-ball across the table. Miss Sarah smiled, although her eyes felt misty. "You dear child!" she exclaimed. "That was Amanthis Lloyd all over again. She never reached out and gave pleasure to other people as if she were bestowing a favour. She always made it seem as if it were only her own pleasure which you were enhancing by sharing. You don't know what an interest I have taken in you for her sake, as I've watched you growing up here in the Valley. I used to hear remarks about your temper and your imperious ways, and day after day, as I've watched you ride past the house beside your grandfather, sitting up in the same straight, haughty way, I've thought she's well named. She's the Colonel over again.

"But to-day, in this old room, you are startlingly like her in some way, I can hardly tell what." She glanced up again at the portrait. "Your eyes look at me in the same understanding sort of way. They almost unseal the silence of twenty years. I have never said this to any one else. But I used to look at her sometimes and think that George Eliot must have meant her when she wrote in her 'Choir Invisible' of one who could 'be to other souls the cup of strength in some great agony.' She was that to me. People always used to go to her with their troubles."

Lloyd bent over her cup, her face flushing. "Then I'm so glad you think I'm even a little bit like her," she said, softly. "Nobody evah told me that befoah. I've always wanted to be."

The thought gave her a glow of pleasure all through the meal. Long after Miss Sarah went away, warmed and quickened in heart as well as body, it lingered with her. Afterward it prompted her to pause before the portrait with a questioning glance into the clear eyes above her.

"'The cup of strength to other souls in some great agony,'" she repeated. "And you were that! Oh, I would love to be, too, if I didn't have to suffer too much first to learn how to sympathize and comfort. Maybe that is what I am to learn from this wintah's disappointment,—a way to help othah people beah their disappointments. If I could do that," she whispered, looking wistfully at the face above her, "if only one person in the world could remembah me as Miss Sarah remembahs *you*, you beautiful Grandmothah Amanthis, it would be worth all the misahable time I have had."

Then she turned suddenly and went into the library to look for the poem Miss Sarah had quoted. She had never taken the volume from the shelves before. She did not care for poetry as Betty did, and it took her some time to find the lines she was looking for. But when she found them, she took the book back to the drawing-room, and read the page again and again, with a quick bounding of the pulses as she realized that here in words was the ambition which she had often felt vaguely stirring within her. Even if she could not reach the highest ones, and be "the cup of strength," or "make undying music in the world," she could at least attempt the other aims it held forth. She could at least try "to ease the burden of the world." She could live "in scorn for miserable aims that end with self."

With the book open on her lap, and her hands clasped around her knees, she sat looking steadily into the fire. She did not know what a long, long step she was taking out of childhood that afternoon, nor that the sweet seriousness of her new purpose shone in her upturned face. But when the old Colonel came into the room and found her sitting there in the firelight, he paused and then glanced up at the portrait. He was almost startled by the striking resemblance,—a likeness of expression that he had never noticed before.

CHAPTER XIV.

"CINDERELLA"

Lloyd sat on the window-seat of the stair-landing, looking out on the bare February landscape. She was thinking of the poem she had learned three weeks before, on the afternoon of Miss Sarah's visit, and it made her dissatisfied. When one was all a-tingle, as she had been, with a high purpose to help ease the burden of the world and make undying music in it, and when one longed to do big, heroic deeds and had ambitions high enough to reach the stars, it was hard to be content with the commonplace opportunities that came her way.

The things she had been doing seemed so paltry. To carry a glass of jelly to the Crisps, a pot of pink hyacinths to Miss Marietta, to write a letter for Aunt Cindy, to sit for an hour with Mrs. Bisbee,—these all were so trivial and pitifully small that she felt a sense of disgust with herself and her efforts. Yawning and swinging her foot, she sat in the window-seat several minutes longer, then started aimlessly up-stairs to her room. In the upper hall the door leading into the attic stairway stood open, and for no reason save that she had nothing else to do, she began to mount the steps. She had not been up in the attic since Christmas week, when she and Rob had gone to finish his Christmas hunt.

She stood looking around her an instant, then, moved by some unaccountable impulse, drew out the chest containing the fancy-dress costumes they had used in so many plays and tableaux. One by one she shook them out and hung them over Rob's headless hobby-horse, when she had finished examining them. There were the velvet knickerbockers and blouse she had worn as Little Boy Blue at the Hallowe'en party at the Seminary. There was Betty's Dresden Shepherdess dress, and the godmother's gown, and the long trailing robe of the Princess Winsome. Even the little tulle dress she had worn as the Queen of Hearts at Ginger's Valentine party, years ago, came out of the chest as she dived deeper into its contents, and a star-spangled costume of red, white, and blue, in which she had fluttered as the Goddess of Liberty one Fourth of July.

Slippers and buckles and plumes, fans and gloves and artificial flowers, were piled up all around her. The hobby-horse was hidden under a drapery of velvet and lace and silk. Still the chest held a number of old party gowns that had never been cut down to fit their childish revels.

As Lloyd shook them out, thinking of the gay scenes they had been a part of, the picture of Agnes Waring in her worn jacket and shabby shoes flashed across her mind, followed by Mrs. Bisbee's remark: "She's never had any of the pleasures that most girls have. Twenty-five years old, and to my certain knowledge she's never had a beau or been to a big party, or travelled farther than Louisville."

Lloyd pressed her lips together and stood staring at the old finery around her, thinking hard. A sudden vision had come to her of this modern Cinderella, and of herself as the fairy godmother. Her eyes shone and her cheeks grew pink as she stood pondering. If she could only make an occasion, it would be easy enough to provide the coach and the costume, even the glass slippers. There lay a pair of white satin ones, beaded in tiny crystal beads that shone like dewdrops. Suppose she should play godmother and send Agnes to a ball. Suppose the shy, timid girl should look so fine in her fine feathers that people would stare at her and wonder who that beautiful creature was. Suppose a prince should be there who never would have noticed her but for the magic glass slippers, and then suppose—

Lloyd did not put the rest of the delightful daydream into words, but just stood thinking about it a long time, until her expression grew very sweet and tender over a little romance which she dreamed might grow out of her plan to give Agnes pleasure.

"If I only had thought of it in time to have had a Valentine pah'ty," she exclaimed aloud, "that would have been the very thing. But it is too late now. This is the seventeenth." Then she clasped her hands delightedly as that date suggested another. "It is five days till Washington's Birthday. Maybe there will be time to get up a Martha Washington affair. I'll ask Miss Allison about it this very night at choir practice. She always has so many new ideas."

Tumbling the costumes back into the trunk, helter-skelter, she danced down the stairs, impatient to tell her mother about it. But there were guests in the library who had been invited to spend the afternoon and stay to dinner, and Lloyd had no opportunity to speak of the subject that was uppermost in her thoughts. Immediately after dinner she excused herself, to slip into her red coat and furs, while Mom Beck lighted the lantern they were to carry.

It was only a short distance to the Mallard place, where the choir was to meet that week, so they did not need Alec's escort this time. The wind flared their lantern as they went along the quiet country road. They could see other lights bobbing along toward them, and, as they neared the gate, Lloyd recognized Mrs. Walton's voice. She and Miss Allison were coming up with their brother Harry.

"Is that you, Lloyd?" called Mrs. Walton, as they drew nearer. "I hoped you would come early, for I have a letter from the girls that I know you will want to read. They are full of preparations for a grand affair to be given on the twenty-second,—a Martha Washington reception. As usual, Kitty wants to depart from the accustomed order of things, and have a costume in George's honour, instead of Martha's. She says why not, as long as it is his birthday. She's painted a picture of the dress she has concocted for the occasion. It is green tarlatan dotted all over with little silver paper hatchets, and trimmed with garlands and bunches of artificial cherries."

"Oh, I'm so glad you brought the pictuah with you to-night!" exclaimed Lloyd. "And I'm wild to see the lettah. Kitty always writes such funny ones. And I'm glad I met you out heah befoah the choir practice begins. I want to ask you about a celebration I have been planning. It's for Agnes Waring," she explained, catching step with them as they turned in at the gate. "So of co'se I can't talk about it befoah all the othah people.

"I happened to be looking ovah a chest of old costumes to-day, thinking of all the fun we'd had in them, when I remembahed her and what Mrs. Bisbee had told me about her nevah having good times like othah girls. She said she'd nevah had any attention, and nevah been to a big pah'ty. I thought I'd like to give her one on the twenty-second, because I could offah her a costume then without hurting her feelings. I was suah that you and Miss Allison could suggest something moah than I had thought of. I don't know exactly how to begin. People will think it strange, and Agnes might, too, if I gave a pah'ty just for her, when all her friends whom I would want to invite are so much oldah than I."

Miss Allison and her sister exchanged glances in the lantern-light, then Mrs. Walton said, hesitatingly: "Why—I don't know—I'm sorry, Lloyd, that we didn't know before. We've already made plans which I am afraid will interfere with yours. The King's Daughters' Circle has arranged to have an oyster supper at my house on the afternoon and evening of the twenty-second. Most of the people you would want to ask will be busy there, for everybody in the Valley lends a hand at these entertainments."

They could not see the disappointment that shadowed Lloyd's face as she listened to this announcement in silence. But Miss Allison knew it was there, and, as they walked on up the path together, she slipped her arm around Lloyd's waist.

"Never mind, dear," she said. "You shall not have your beautiful plan spoiled by the old oyster supper. We'll combine forces. As Agnes is a member of the Circle, maybe you can bring about what you want more naturally and easily this way than in any other. The girls who are to wait on the table are to powder their hair and wear white kerchiefs and Martha Washington caps. But we had intended to ask you to take charge of the fancy-work table, as you have more time for getting up elaborate costumes. We wanted to ask you to dress in as handsome a costume of that period as you could find. We remember what lovely brocade gowns and quilted petticoats and old-fashioned fol-de-rols used to be laid away in your grandmother's attic that belonged to *her* grandmother. If you like, you may give your place to Agnes, and let her be the belle of the ball."

Lloyd returned the pressure of the arm about her with an impulsive hug. "Oh, I *knew* you'd think of something perfectly lovely," she cried. "That would be much the best way, for she is so timid and quiet you couldn't keep her from being a wall-flowah at an ordinary pah'ty. But this way she will have something to do, and she'll have to talk when people come to buy things. I wish it were not so long till to-morrow! I want to tell her about it this minute."

Usually the choir practice was a bore to Lloyd. She was one of the few members who sang by note, and Mrs. Walton, the leader, had to take them through the simple anthems over and over again, until they caught the tune by ear. Lloyd, knowing that her strong young voice was needed, sang dutifully through the tiresome repetitions, but sometimes she wanted to put her fingers in her ears to shut out the sound. To-night she did not chafe inwardly at the false starts and the monotonous chant, "Oh, be thankful! Oh, be thankful!" which had to be sung over numberless times in order that the bass and alto singers might learn to come in at the proper places with their responsive refrain. She was so absorbed in thinking of the pleasure in store for Agnes, and imagining what she would say, that she sang the three measures over and over, unheeding how long the choir stuck there, or uncaring how many times they seesawed up and down on the same tiresome notes.

The excitement began for Agnes next day, when Lloyd delivered Miss Allison's invitation, and bore her away in the carriage to search through the attic for a costume. She had never been farther than the door at Locust. Her journeys thither had been to carry home some finished garment. But many an hour of patient sewing had been brightened by her sisters' tales of the place. Both Miss Sarah and Miss Marietta remembered it affectionately, for the sake of the woman who had welcomed them there on so many happy occasions in the past.

Agnes thought she knew just how the interior of Locust would look, especially the stately old drawing-room, with its portraits and candles, its harp and the faint odour of rose-leaves; and really there was something familiar to her in its appearance as she caught a glimpse of it on her way up-stairs to Lloyd's room. But she had never imagined such a dainty rose of a room as the pink and white bower Lloyd led her into. There might have been a throb of resentment that all such beauty and luxury had been left out of her life, if there had been time for her to look around and compare it with her own scantily furnished room at home.

Lloyd hurried over to the bed, eager to display a gorgeous brocade gown of rose and silver laid out there, which Mrs. Sherman had brought down from the attic in her absence, and from which Mom Beck had pressed all the wrinkles.

"It's as good as new," said Lloyd. "I'm glad that mothah wouldn't let us cut it up last yeah, when we wanted to make it fit Katie. There are pink slippahs to match, but I hoped you'd rathah weah these. They make me think of Cinderella's glass ones, and they're twice as pretty."

She tossed the crystal beaded slippers over to Agnes for her inspection. "Try them on," she urged. "I want to see how you'll look."

In a few moments the shabby shoes and the old brown dress lay in a heap on the floor like a discarded chrysalis, and Agnes stepped out, a dazzled butterfly, in her gorgeous robes of rose and silver.

Lloyd clasped her hands ecstatically. "Oh, Agnes, it's *lovely!* And it's almost a perfect fit. If Miss Sarah can just take it up a little on the shouldahs, and change the collah a tiny bit, it will look as if it were made for you. When yoah hair is powdahed and you have this little bunch of plumes in it, you'll be simply perfect. It doesn't mattah if the slippahs do pinch a little. They look so pretty you can stand a little thing like that for one evening."

Lloyd walked around and around her, till she had admired her to her heart's content, and then led her away to show to Mrs. Sherman. "You ought to carry yoah head that way all the time," she said. "It's becoming to you to 'walk proud,' as old Mammy Easter used to say."

It was with the air of a duchess that Agnes sailed into the drawing-room, and with the feeling that at last she had come into her own. On every side the dim old mirrors flashed back the reflection of the slender figure with its head proudly high. She looked at it curiously, scarcely recognizing the delicate, high-bred features for her own. There was colour in her face for one thing. The dull browns and grays, which she wore for economy's sake, were apt to make her look sallow. But this wonderful rose-pink lent a glow to her cheeks, and pleasure and expectancy brightened her eyes, and left her a-tingle with these new sensations.

"You'll be the feature of the occasion," Mrs. Sherman assured her. "Come up to lunch with us Thursday. We'll powder your hair and help you dress, and take you down in the carriage with us. Tell your sisters that we'll see that you get home safely that night."

So to the other pleasures of the twenty-second was added the undreamed-of delight of being invited out to lunch, and forgetting for awhile that there were such tiresome things in the world as sewing-machines and endless ruffling for other people. Although she wore her old brown dress, darned at the elbows, and, with her usual timidity, scarcely ventured a remark at the table unless directly questioned, she was all aglow with the new experience.

Afterward it was easy to talk and laugh with Lloyd, as they went through the conservatory cutting the flowers which were to decorate the tables at The Beeches. Hyacinths and lilies-of-the-valley made a spring-time of their own under the sheltering skylight. Agnes bent over them with a cry of delight. "They make you forget the calendar, don't they?" she said, looking shyly up at Lloyd. She wanted to add, "And so do you. You make me forget that I am ten years older than you. It seems only pussy-willow time by my feelings to-day." But their friendship was too new as yet for such personal speeches.

As they went back to the drawing-room with a basket piled full of hothouse blooms, Mrs. Sherman called to Lloyd that she needed her up-stairs a few moments. Hastily excusing herself, she left Agnes with a new magazine for her entertainment. When she came down later, the magazine was lying uncut on the table, and Agnes, seated in front of the piano, was fingering the keys with light touches which made no sound, they pressed the ivory so gently. She started guiltily as Lloyd came in.

"I couldn't help it!" she stammered. "It drew me over here like a magnet. It has been the dream of my life to know how to play, but it is all such a mystery. I've puzzled over the music in the hymn-book many a time, the little notes flying up and down like birds through a fence, and then watched Miss Allison's fingers on the organ keys, going up and down the same way."

"It is just as easy as reading the alphabet," said Lloyd. "I'll show you. Wait till I find my old music primer. It is somewhere in this cabinet."

Hastily turning over the exercise books and worn sheets of music that filled one of the lower shelves, she dragged out an old dog-eared instruction book, which she propped up on the rack in front of Agnes.

"Heah," she said, pointing to a note. "When one of those little birds, as you call them, perches on this place on the fence, then you're to strike the A key on the piano. If it lights on the line just above it, then you strike the next key, B. See?" She ran her fingers lightly up the octavo and began again with A. Agnes leaned hungrily over the page, reading the printed directions below each simple measure, where the fingering was plainly marked.

"Oh, I could learn to do it by studying this!" she cried, her face all alight. "I am sure I could. I don't mean that I could ever learn to play as you do, or Miss Allison, but I could learn simple things and the accompaniments to old songs that Marietta loves. It would be almost as great a joy to her and sister Sarah as it would to me, for my learning to play has always been one of our favourite air-castles. If you could loan me this instruction book for awhile—" She hesitated.

"Of co'se!" cried Lloyd, thrilled by the eagerness of the eyes which met hers. "I'll give you a lesson right now, if you like. I'll teach you a set of chords you can use for an accompaniment. They are so easy you can learn them befoah you go home, and you can surprise Miss Marietta by singing and playing for her. They fit evah so many of the ballads."

Turning the leaves of the instructor, she found the simple chords of "Annie Laurie," and wrote beside each note the letters that would enable Agnes to find them on the keyboard. "This isn't the right way to begin," she said, with a laugh, "but we'll take this short cut just to surprise Miss Marietta. You can come back aftahward and learn about time and all the othah things that ought to come first. I'll give you a lesson every week for awhile, if you like."

The eyes that met hers now were brimming with happy tears.

"If I like," Agnes repeated, with a tremulous catch of the voice. "As if I wouldn't jump at the chance to have the key to paradise put into my hands. It's the happiest thing that ever happened to me."

With her heart as well as her whole attention given to the effort, it was not long before Agnes found her fingers falling naturally into place, and she played the chords over and over, humming the tune softly, with a pleasure that was pathetic to Lloyd.

"Oh, I could keep on all day and all night!" exclaimed Agnes, when Mrs. Sherman called to them that it was time to dress. "I've never been so happy in all my life! You don't know what it means to me!" she cried, turning a radiant face to Lloyd's. "You've lifted me clear off the earth. I wish I could run home before the reception begins and play this for Marietta. I want to see her face when I open the old piano."

Lloyd followed her up the stairs, wondering at the girl's uplifted mood. She did not see how such a trifle could bring about such a transformation in any one's spirits, not realizing that this bit of knowledge which Agnes had picked up was to her a veritable key which would open the door she had longed for years to enter.

When Agnes swept into the house at The Beeches, she was in such high spirits that people looked twice to be sure that they knew the radiant girl presiding so gaily over the fancy-work table.

"She is actually talking," Miss McGill whispered to Libbie Simms. "Talking and laughing and making jokes like other girls. Somebody has surely worked a hoodoo charm on her."

But happiness was the only hoodoo, and, under its expanding influence, she fairly bloomed that night. Lloyd, hovering near her, jubilant over the success of her popular Cinderella, beamed and dimpled with pleasure, and stored away the many compliments she overheard, to repeat to Agnes next day. Once she darted into the butler's pantry, where Miss Allison was slicing cake, to announce, in an excited whisper: "Agnes has actually had three invitations to suppah. She's gone in now with Mistah John Bond. I must run back and take charge of the sales, but I just had to tell you. Do peep in and see her there at the cawnah table, eating ice-cream and talking away as if she'd been used to such attentions all her life. Isn't it great? Now people can't shake their heads and say poah girl, she's nevah had any attentions like othah girls. Nobody takes any interest in her."

Miss Allison turned to give Lloyd's cheek a playful pinch. "You dear little fairy godmother! All Cranford will take an interest in her, now that she has blossomed out so unexpectedly. Even old Mr. Wade, who never says nice things about any one, asked me who our distinguished-looking guest was, and, when I told him Agnes Waring, he fairly gasped and dropped his eye-glasses. Then he gave his usual contemptuous sniff that always makes me want to shake him, and walked away, saying: 'Who'd have thought it! Well, well, fine feathers certainly do make fine birds!'"

Lloyd hurried back to her place behind the fancy-work table. Nearly every one was out in the room where supper was being served, and except for an occasional question from some one who strolled by to ask the price of a laundry-bag or a hemstitched centrepiece, no one disturbed her. To the music of mandolin, guitar, and piano, played softly behind the palms in one corner, she went on with her pleasing day-dreams for Agnes. She would make other opportunities for her next week, take her in town to a concert or a matinée. She wished she could offer her clothes, but she dared not take that step. There would be the Waring pride to reckon with if she did.

In the midst of this reverie, Agnes came up all a-flutter, saying, shyly: "Lloyd, would you mind if I didn't go back in the carriage with you? Your mother wouldn't think it strange, would she? It was because I had no other way to get home that she invited me. But Mr. Bond has asked to take me home behind his new team. He wants me to see what fine travellers his horses are."

"Of co'se mothah wouldn't think it strange!" exclaimed Lloyd. "Especially if it is Mistah Bond who wants to take you. She and Papa Jack are so fond of him."

"He wants me to join the choir," Agnes went on, in a lower tone, as a group of people crowded around the table. "Mrs. Walton and Mrs. Mallard and Miss Flora Marks have asked me also. I've pinched myself black and blue this evening, trying to make sure that I am awake. Oh, Lloyd, you'll never, never know how I have enjoyed it all."

There was no time for further conversation then. People were beginning to leave, and were crowding around the table to claim the articles they had purchased earlier in the evening. But it was not necessary for Agnes to repeat that she was radiantly happy. It showed in every word and laugh and gesture. Lloyd went home that night nearer to the Castle of Content than she had been for many weeks.

CHAPTER XV.

A HARD-EARNED PEARL

The reaction came next day, however, when a budget of letters from the girls turned her thoughts back to all that she was missing. Betty was rooming with Juliet Lynn now, and they were writing a play together in spare minutes. Allison had had honourable mention three times in the Studio Bulletin, and a number of her sketches had been chosen for display on the studio walls. Kitty had surprised them all by the interest she had suddenly taken in French, and had translated a poem so cleverly that Monsieur Blanc had sent it home for publication in a Paris paper. The work was so interesting now, Betty wrote, and the time so full, Warwick Hall grew daily more inspiring and more dear.

The old ache came back to Lloyd as she read. She felt that she had fallen hopelessly behind the others. She was so utterly left out of all their successes. The little efforts she had made to fill her days with things worth while suddenly shrivelled into nothing, and she sat with the letters in her lap, staring moodily into vacancy.

"What's the use?" she sobbed. "All that I can do heah doesn't amount to a row of pins. I am out of it."

Thinking of Warwick Hall and the girls and all that she was missing, she sat pitying herself until the tears began to come. She let them trickle slowly down her face without attempting to wipe them away or fight them back. Nobody was there to see, and she could be as miserable as she chose. In the midst of her gloomy reverie she heard the door-bell ring.

Dabbing her handkerchief over her eyes, she started across the room to make her escape up-stairs before Mom Beck could open the front door. But she was too late. As she pushed aside the portières, she heard Agnes Waring ask if she were at home, and Mom Beck immediately ushered her in.

"I came to bring the costume back," she began, hurriedly. "No, I must not sit down, thank you. I am on my way to Mrs. Moore's to fit a lining. But I just had to stop by and tell you what a lovely time I had yesterday and last night. You should have seen Marietta's face this morning when I opened the piano and played and sang for her. The tears just rolled down her face, but it was because we were so happy.

"She said she had been afraid that I would grow morose and bitter because I had so few pleasures, and she is so glad about the music lessons and my joining the choir. Mr. Bond is going to come by for me next Friday night. Sister Sarah said she had no idea that colours could make such a difference in one till she saw me in that costume. She has been looking over the silk quilt pieces your mother sent Marietta, and she recognized two pieces that are parts of dresses your grandmother used to wear. One is a deep rich red,—a regular garnet colour, and the other is sapphire blue. She said that if they had belonged to any one else but Amanthis Lloyd she couldn't do it,—but instead of cutting them up into quilt pieces she—she is going to make them into shirt-waists for me."

The colour deepened in Agnes's face as she made the confession, with an unconscious lifting of the head that made Lloyd remember Mrs. Bisbee's remark about the Waring pride. She hastened to say something to cover the awkward pause that followed.

"Grandmothah Amanthis and Miss Sarah were such good friends, even if there was so much difference in their ages. I know she would be glad for you to use the silk that way. Looking pretty in it and having good times in it seems a bettah way to use it as a remembrance of her than putting it into a quilt, doesn't it?"

Then, to change the subject, which disconcerted her more than it did Agnes, she held up the package of letters.

"I heard from the girls to-day, and they are all getting on so beautifully, and making such good records, that it neahly breaks my hah't to think I can't be with them." She laughed nervously. "I suppose you wondahed what made my eyes so red, when you came in. I've been regularly howling. I couldn't help it. I sat heah thinking about deah old Warwick Hall, and all that I had to give up, till I was so misahable I *had* to cry."

Agnes, turning toward the window so that her face could not be seen, looked out at the bare branches of the locusts.

"I wonder," she began, slowly, "if it would make any difference to you—if it would make your disappointment any easier to bear—to know how much your being in the Valley this winter has meant to me. Fifty years from now one term more or less in your studies won't amount to much. It will not count much then that you've solved a few more problems in algebra, or learned a little more French, or fallen behind the others in a few credit marks, but it will make all the difference in the world to me that you were here to open a door for me.

"If you've done nothing more than give me that one music lesson, it has showed me the possibility of all that I may accomplish, and started me on the road to my heart's desire. If you've done no more than prove to me that I can conquer my timidity and be like other girls, and accept the little pleasures just at hand for the taking, don't you see that you have opened up a way for me that I never could have found alone? And to do that for any one, why, it's like teaching him a song that he will teach to some one else, and that one will go on repeating, and the next and the next, until you've started something that never stops. If I were making up the accounts in the Hereafter, I am very sure I'd count it more to your credit,—the unselfish way you are helping people than all the lessons you could learn in a term at school. I am not saying half what I feel. I couldn't. It is too deep down. But, oh, I do want you to know that your disappointment has not all been in vain."

The voice that uttered the last sentence was tremulous with feeling. Tears were very near the surface now. Before Lloyd could think of any reply to her impetuous speech, she had started toward the door.

"Mrs. Moore will wonder what is keeping me," she said, as she turned the knob. "Good-bye!"

With a lighter heart than Lloyd could have believed possible half an hour earlier, she went up to her room. Dropping the damp little ball of a handkerchief into her laundry-bag, she opened a drawer for a fresh one. By mistake she drew out, not her handkerchief-box, but one that in some previous haste had been pushed into its place,—the sandalwood box containing the pearl beads. She took up the uncompleted rosary and began slipping the beads back and forth over the string,—the string that would have been two-thirds full by this time if she could have gone on with school work. Suddenly she looked at it with widening eyes.

"I wondah," she said aloud, "I wondah if I couldn't slip one moah on for yestahday. She said herself that it ought to count for moah than school work. In a way she said it was like making 'undying music in the world.' And what was it old Bishop Chartley said at the carol service?" She stood with a little pucker on her forehead, trying to recall his words about keeping the White Feast.

"So may we offer our pearls, days unstained by selfishness." That was it. She could go on with her rosary then, and, instead of perfect lessons at school, she could fill the string in token of days spent unselfishly at home. Days not stained by regrets and tears and idle repining for what could not be helped.

With a deep sigh of satisfaction, she slipped one more pearl bead down the string, and laid it back in the box.

"That is for yestahday. I can't count to-day, for I sat for an houah thinking about my troubles and pitying myself and making myself just as misahable as possible."

So the little string began to grow again, and, though she was half-ashamed of the childish pleasure it gave her, it did help when she could see every night a visible token that she had tried to live that 'day through unselfishly and well,— that she had kept tryst with the duty of cheerfulness which we all owe the world.

But not all her pearls were earned as easily as the one that marked her efforts for Agnes. One day, when she rode over to Rollington with some illustrated magazines for the Crisp children, she was met by an announcement from Minnie, the oldest one, who had charge of the family in her mother's absence.

"Mis' Perkins said I was to tell you she didn't see why folks passed her by when she liked wine jelly and good things just as well as some other people she knew."

"Who is Mrs. Perkins?" asked Lloyd, astonished by such a message.

Minnie nodded her towhead toward a weather-beaten house of two rooms across the street. "She lives over there. She's sick most of the time. She saw you cooking in our kitchen that day that you came and got dinner, and ma sent her over a piece of the pie you made, and she's been sort of sniffy ever since, because nobody does such things for her."

Minnie seemed so anxious that Lloyd should include Mrs. Perkins in her visit that finally Lloyd agreed to be escorted over to see her. Wrapping the baby in a shawl, and staggering along under its weight, Minnie ordered the other children to stay where they were, and led the way across the street.

The tilt of Lloyd's dainty nose, as she went in, said more plainly than words, "Poah white trash!" For the house had a stuffy smell of liniment and bacon grease. An old woman came forward to meet them in her stocking feet and a dirty woollen wrapper. Her uncombed gray hair straggled around her ears, and her wrinkled face was unwashed and grimy. Lloyd was thankful that she did not offer to shake hands. She sat down on the edge of a chair, breathing the stuffy air as sparingly as possible.

She had always been taught that old age must be respected, no matter how unlovely, and as Mrs. Perkins counted her aches and pains in a weak, whining voice, pity got the better of Lloyd's disgust. She began to feel sorry for this poor old creature, for whom no one else seemed to have any sympathy. She complained bitterly of her neighbours and the church-members who professed to be so charitable, but who left her to suffer.

Then she praised the lemon pie that Lloyd had made, until Lloyd gladly promised to make one for her. "I'll bring it down the last of the week," she promised, later, when she rose to go, and Mrs. Perkins introduced the subject again. But that was not what the old woman wanted.

"Why can't you come down here and make it in my kitchen?" she whined, "same as you did in Mrs. Crisp's. I get dreadful lonesome setting here, and it would be so much company to see you whisking around beating eggs and rolling out the crust. Then I could smell it baking, and eat it hot out of the oven. It's been many a long day since I've done a thing like that. It makes my mouth water, just thinking of it."

"Certainly I could do it heah, if you would like it bettah," promised Lloyd, rashly. "Is there anything I can do for you befoah I go?"

"Yes, there is," was the ready answer. "I didn't eat much dinner, and I'm that weak and faint I'd like if you'd make me a cup of tea."

"Certainly," answered Lloyd again. "If you'll just tell me where to find things."

"I'll be going on," said Minnie Crisp, beginning to wrap the baby up in its shawl again. "Those kids will be turning the house upside down if I'm not there to watch them."

Nobody paid any attention to her departure, for Lloyd, hanging her coat over the back of a dusty chair, had gone into the kitchen before Minnie finished making a woollen mummy of the baby.

"The tea is in a paper bag in the corner cupboard," called Mrs. Perkins. "Mrs. Moore sent it to me. It's green tea, and I never did care for any kind but black. I'd pretty nigh as soon have none as green. You might poach me an egg, too, if you feel like it, and make a bit of toast."

With a shiver of disgust, Lloyd looked around her. Everything was dirty. She wished she dared run across the street and prepare the lunch in Mrs. Crisp's immaculate kitchen. There everything shone from repeated scrubbings with soft soap and sand. She enjoyed cooking over there. As she opened the cupboard door a roach ran out, and she jumped aside with another shiver of disgust. She wanted a pan in which to poach the egg, but nothing looked clean enough to use. Finally she chose a battered saucepan, but dropped it when she discovered that a spider had woven a web inside.

Spiders had always been an abomination to Lloyd. It made her feel cold and creepy to touch a cobweb. But the story of Ederyn flashed through her thoughts, and she grasped the pan, determined to use it or die in the effort. She had started and she would not turn back. It was plainly her duty to minister to the wants of this complaining old invalid whom others neglected, and she would keep tryst at any cost. With many an inward shudder she went on with her task. As the water in the kettle was already steaming, it was not long before the lunch was ready, and she carried it in.

"It's simply impossible for me to come and make the pie in this dirty kitchen," thought Lloyd, "and I can't tell her so. Maybe I could ask Mrs. Crisp to invite her ovah and she could see it done there."

While she worried over the problem of introducing the subject tactfully, Mrs. Perkins herself opened the way. She hadn't been well enough to do any cleaning for several weeks, she said. If she could get a little stronger, she intended to do two things: to slick up the place a bit, and to go on a visit to Jane O'Grady's up near the black bridge. She had been wanting to spend the day with Jane all winter, but didn't have any way to get there. It was too far to walk. Lloyd saw her opportunity and seized it.

"Why, mothah will send the carriage for you, Mrs. Perkins, any day you set. She'd be glad to. Alec can drive you ovah early in the mawning, when he is out for the marketing, and go for you befoah dah'k."

"Then you may send to-morrow," said Mrs. Perkins, ungraciously. "I don't want to risk putting it off. Folks usually forget such promises overnight. So I'd best make sure of it."

Lloyd flushed angrily, but the next instant excused the old woman's rudeness on the score of her ill health. She had a plan that she was anxious to carry out, and she hurried home to begin, all a-tingle with her charitable impulses. She was surprised that her mother should treat it so lightly.

"Of course you can have the carriage," said Mrs. Sherman. "But, my good little Samaritan, I must warn you. That old woman is a pauper in spirit. She hasn't a particle of proper pride. People have done too much for her. She'll take all she can get, and grumble because it isn't more. So you mustn't be disappointed if, instead of thanks, you get only criticism."

But Lloyd, full of the zeal of a true reformer, danced down to the servants' quarters to find May Lily, one of the cook's grandchildren. May Lily, a neat-looking coloured girl of seventeen, had been one of Lloyd's most loyal followers since they made mud pies together on the Colonel's white door-steps, and the readiness to serve her now was prompted not so much by the promised dollar as the desire to still follow her lead. So next morning, soon after Mrs. Perkins's departure in the Sherman carriage, a mighty revolution began in the house she left behind her.

May Lily, strong and willing, went to work like a small cyclone. Under Lloyd's direction, she swept and scrubbed and scoured. The bed was aired, the stove was blacked, the windows washed, the tins polished till they shone like new. By four o'clock not a cobweb or a speck of dust was to be seen in either room. Lloyd sat down to wait for Mrs. Perkins's return. She felt that it was safe to breathe now, and she did not have to sit gingerly on the edge of the chair. Every piece of furniture had been washed and rubbed. She could keep her promise about the pie very comfortably now. Everything smelled so clean and wholesome to her that she was sure that Mrs. Perkins would notice the change at once and be pleased.

Mrs. Perkins did notice the change the moment she entered the door, but it was with a displeased face. "Hm! Hm!" she sniffed. "Smells mightily of soft soap in here. What have you been doing? I never could bear the smell of soft soap or lye. Hm! Hm!"

Then she turned accusingly on Lloyd. "Didn't you know better than to put stove-blacking on that stove? When it gets het up, it will smoke to fare-ye-well, and start my asthma to going again full tilt. Some folks are mighty thoughtless, never have no consideration for other people."

Lloyd shrank back, almost overcome by such a reception. It was like a dash of cold water in her face. She was angry and indignant.

"Well," continued Mrs. Perkins, still sniffing around the room, as she put her bonnet and shawl away. "Now you're here I'd like it if you would put on the teakettle and make me a good strong cup of coffee. Jane O'Grady gave me a pound, all parched and ground. I haven't had any before to-day for weeks. I'm plumb tuckered out with the visit."

Lloyd hurried to build up the fire, thankful that May Lily had spent much time scouring the old coffee-pot. Otherwise she could not have brought herself to touch it. It shone like new now. As she poured the water into it, three tiny streams spurted out of the side, hissing and sputtering over the stove.

"Now just see what you done!" scolded Mrs. Perkins. "You hadn't ought to have scoured that coffee-pot so. You'd ought to have let well enough be, for you might have known you'd rub holes in it and make it leak."

"I'll get you a new one in place of it at once," said Lloyd, stiffly, her indignation rising till she could hardly speak calmly. "I'll go this minute."

There was a small grocery store farther up the hill, where a little of everything was kept in stock, and Lloyd dashed out bareheaded, glad of an excuse to cool her temper. By the time she had made the coffee in the new pot, Alec drove up to the door for her.

"You'll come again to-morrow to make that lemon pie, won't you?" asked Mrs. Perkins, anxiously.

"No, I can't come till the day aftah."

"What? Thursday?" was the impatient answer. "Time drags awful slow for a body that can only sit and wait."

"I have an engagement to-morrow," said Lloyd, stiffly, remembering it was the day for Agnes Waring's music lesson. "But you can depend on me Thursday."

Mrs. Sherman only laughed when Lloyd repeated her day's adventure at home, but the old Colonel fairly snorted with indignation.

"Poor white trash!" he exclaimed. "Don't go near her again!"

"But I promised," answered Lloyd, dolefully. "I must keep my promise."

"Then tell Cindy to make a pie, and let Alec take it down," he suggested.

"No, she said she wanted to smell it cooking, and to eat it hot out of the oven, and I promised her she might."

The Colonel glared savagely at the fire. "Beggars shouldn't be choosers," he muttered, then turned to Mrs. Sherman. "Little daughter, are you going to let that poor child of yours be imposed on by that creature?"

"I can't interfere with her promise, papa," she answered. "It may be a disagreeable experience, but it will not hurt her any more than it hurt the old woman to sweep the cobwebs out of the sky. Hers was a thankless job, too, but no doubt she was better for the exercise, and she must have learned a great deal on such a trip."

It was in the same spirit in which Ederyn cried, "Oh, heart and hand of mine, keep tryst! Keep tryst or die!" that Lloyd gathered up the necessary materials and started off on Thursday to Mrs. Perkins's cottage. This time there was no admiring audience of little towheads tiptoeing around the table, as there had been at Mrs. Crisp's. But everything was clean, and, with her recipe spread out before her, Lloyd followed directions to the letter.

Mrs. Perkins, watching the beating of eggs and stirring of the golden filling, the deft mixing of pastry, grew cheerful and entertaining. She forgot to complain of her neighbours, and was surprised into the telling of some of her girlish experiences that actually brought an amused twinkle to her sharp old eyes. Lloyd was vastly entertained. She had, too, a virtuous feeling that in keeping her promise she had given pleasure to one who rarely met kindness. It gave her a warm inward glow of satisfaction.

To her mortification, when she finally drew the pie from the oven, the meringue, which had been like a snowdrift a moment before, and which should have come out with just a golden glow on it from its short contact with the heat, was all shrivelled and brown.

"The nasty little oven was too hot!" cried Lloyd, in disgust.

"Just my luck," whined Mrs. Perkins. "I might have known that I'd never get anything I set my heart on. But you can scrape off the meringue, and I'll try and make out with the plain pie."

Although she ate generously, she ate grumblingly, disappointed because of the scorched meringue, and it wasn't as sweet as she liked.

That night, Lloyd, mortified over her failure, stood long with the white rosary in her hand. "Maybe I ought to count the poah pie as I would an imperfect lesson," she thought, hesitating, with a bead in her fingers. Then she said, defiantly: "But I did my best, and the day has certainly been disagreeable enough to deserve two pearls."

After another moment of conscientious weighing of the matter, she slipped the bead slowly down the string. "There!" she exclaimed. "I suahly went through the black watahs of Kilgore to get that one."

Next day when she stopped in Rollington to pay for the coffee-pot, and drove by the Crisps' to ask about the baby, Minnie Crisp told her several things. Mrs. Perkins was sick all night, and had told her ma that it was the lemon pie that was the cause of the trouble; that it would have made a dog sick. "Them was her words," said Minnie, solemnly.

"I don't wondah!" cried Lloyd. "The greedy old thing! There was enough for foah people, and it was very rich, and she ate it all."

"And she didn't like it because you had May Lily scrub and clean while she was gone," added Minnie, with childlike lack of tact. "She talked about you dreadful after you went away. Didn't she, ma?"

"Shoo, Minnie!" answered Mrs. Crisp, with a wave of her apron. "Don't tell all you know."

"I didn't," answered the child. "I didn't say a word about the names she called her,—meddlesome Matty, and all that."

Lloyd took her leave presently, with a flushed face and a sore heart. On the way home she stopped at The Beeches, and Mrs. Walton, who saw at a glance that something was wrong, soon drew out the story of her grievance.

"Don't pay any attention to that old creature," she said, laughing heartily, "and forgive my laughing. Everybody in the Valley has had a similar experience. The King's Daughters long ago gave her up in disgust. She's one of those people who doesn't want to be reformed and won't stay helped. Her house will be just as dirty next week as when you first went there."

"I didn't suppose there were such people in the world," said Lloyd, in disgust.

"You'll find out all sorts of disagreeable things as you get older," sighed Mrs. Walton. "It is one of the penalties of growing up. But still it is good to have such experiences, for the wiser we grow the better we know how to 'ease the burden of the world,' and that is what we are here for."

Lloyd's eyes widened with surprise. Here was another person quoting from the poem she had learned. She was glad now that she had committed it to memory, since on three occasions it had made people's meaning clearer to her.

"Yes," she answered, the dimples stealing into her smile. "But the next time I'll find out first if they really want their burden eased, and if that burden is dirt, like Mrs. Perkins's, I'll suahly let it alone."

CHAPTER XVI.

"SWEET SIXTEEN"

The red coat Lloyd wore that winter was long remembered in the Valley, for wherever it went it carried a bright face above it, a cheery greeting, and some pleasant word that made the day seem better for its passing.

Mrs. Bisbee and the little Crisps were not the only ones who learned to watch for it. As all the lonely town of Hamelin must have felt toward the one child left to it after the Pied Piper had passed through its streets, so all the Valley turned with tender regard to the young girl left in its midst. Mothers, whose daughters were away at school, stopped to talk to her with affectionate interest. The old ladies whom she regularly visited welcomed her as if she were a part of their vanished youth. The young ladies took her under their wing, glad to have her in the choir and the King's Daughters' Circle, for she was bubbling over with girlish enthusiasm and a sincere desire to help.

So she found the cobwebs in the neighbourhood sky, and disagreeable enough they were at times, even more disagreeable than her experience with Mrs. Perkins. But she swept away with praiseworthy energy, till gradually she found that the accumulation of outside interests, like the cobweb strands which Ederyn twisted, made a rope strong enough to lift her out of herself and her dungeon of disappointment.

After the novelty of giving music lessons had worn off, it grew to be a bore. Not the lessons themselves, for Agnes's delight in them never flagged. It was the tied-up feeling it gave her to remember that those afternoons were not her own. It happened so often that the afternoons devoted to Agnes were the ones which of all the week she wanted to have free, and she had to give up many small pleasures on account of them.

It grew to be a bore, also, calling on some of the people who claimed a weekly visit. She never tired of Mrs. Bisbee's lively comments on her neighbours and her interesting tales about them. But there was old Mr. and Mrs. Apwall, who, with nothing to do but sit on opposite sides of the fire and look at each other, were said to quarrel like cat and dog. It mortified Lloyd dreadfully to have them quarrel in her presence, and have them pour out their grievances for her to decide which was in the wrong.

She always rose to go at that juncture, flushed and embarrassed, and vowing inwardly she would never visit them again. But they always managed to extract a promise before she got to the door that she would drop in again the next time she was passing.

"Somehow you seem to get husband's mind off himself," Mrs. Apwall would whisper at parting. "He isn't half so touchy when you've cheered him up a spell."

And Mr. Apwall would follow her out through the chilly hall to open the front door, and say, huskily: "Come again, daughter. Come again. Your visits seem to do the madam a world of good. They give her something to talk about beside my fancied failings."

So inwardly groaning, Lloyd would go again, painfully alert to keep the conversation away from subjects that invariably led to disputes. And inwardly groaning, she went dutifully to the Coburns' at their repeated requests. The first few times the garrulous old couple were interesting, but the most thrilling tale grows tiresome when one has heard it a dozen times. She could scarcely keep from fidgeting in her chair when the inevitable story of their feud with the Cayn family was begun. They never left out a single petty detail.

No one will ever know how often the thought of the little rosary in the sandalwood box helped Lloyd to listen patiently, and to keep tryst with the expectations of those about her, so that at nightfall there might be another pearl to slip on the silken cord, in token of another day unstained by selfishness.

There was rarely time for envying the girls at school now. The days were too full. Almost before it seemed possible, the locusts were in bloom and it was mid-May by the calendar. In that time perfect health had come back to her. There were no more crying spells now, no more hours of nervous exhaustion, of fretful impatience over trifles. She went singing about the house, with a colour in her cheeks that rivalled the pink of the apple blossoms.

"Spring has come indoors as well as out," said Mrs. Sherman one morning. "I think that we may safely count that your Christmas vacation is over, and you may go back to your music lessons whenever you choose."

The night before her birthday, Lloyd sat with her elbows on her dressing-table, peering into the mirror with a very serious face.

"You'll be sixteen yeahs old in the mawning, Lloyd Sherman," she told the girl in the glass. "'Sweet sixteen!' You've come to the end of lots of things, and to-morrow it will be like going through a gate that you've seen ahead of you for a long, long time. A big, wide gate that you have looked forward to for yeahs, and things are bound to be different on the othah side."

Next morning, just in fun, she trailed down to breakfast in one of her mother's white dresses, with her hair piled on the top of her head. It was very becoming so, but it made her look so tall and womanly that she was sure her grandfather would object to it.

"He'll nevah let me grow up if he can help it," she said, half-pouting, as she gave a final glance over her shoulder at the mirror, vastly pleased with her young ladylike appearance. "He'll say, 'Tut, tut! That's not grandpa's Little Colonel.' But I can't stay his Little Colonel always."

She was standing by the window looking down the locust avenue when he came in to breakfast, so she did not see his start of surprise at sight of her. But his half-whispered exclamation, "*Amanthis!*" told her why he failed to make the speech she expected to hear. With her hair done high, showing the beautiful curve of her head and throat as she stood half-turned toward him, he had caught another glimpse of her startling resemblance to the portrait. He could not regret losing his Little Colonel if that loss were to give him a living reminder of a beloved memory.

After breakfast, when an armful of birthday gifts had been duly admired and the donors thanked, and she had spent nearly an hour enjoying them, she strolled down the avenue, feeling very much grown up with the long dress trailing behind her. She wandered down to the entrance gate, hoping to meet Alec, who had gone for the mail. She was sure there would be a letter from Betty, for Betty never forgot people's birthdays. Then she trailed back again under the white arch of fragrant locust blooms. At the half-way seat she sat down and tucked a spray of the blossoms into her hair and fastened another at her belt. She had not long to wait there, enjoying the freshness of the sweet May morning, for in a few minutes Alec came up the avenue with a handful of letters and papers. She sorted out her own eagerly, six letters and a package.

She opened Betty's first. It was a long one, ending with a birthday greeting in rhyme, and enclosing a handkerchief which she had made herself, sheer and fine and daintily hemstitched, with her initials embroidered in one corner in the smallest letters possible.

The letters from Allison and Kitty were profusely illustrated all around the margins, and by the time Lloyd had read them, and Gay's ridiculous summary of school news, she felt as if she had been on a visit to Warwick Hall, and had seen all the girls. The next letter was from Joyce, a good thick one. But before she read it, curiosity impelled her to open the package, which was a flat one, bearing a foreign postmark and several Italian stamps. There were two photographs inside. She slipped the uppermost one from its envelope.

"Why, it is Eugenia Forbes!" she exclaimed aloud. "But how she has changed!"

The picture was not at all like the Eugenia whom Lloyd remembered, the thin slip of a girl who had raced up and down the avenue five years before at her house-party. She had blossomed into a beautiful young woman.

"A regulah Spanish beauty!" Lloyd thought, as she looked at the picture, long and admiringly,—the picture of a patrician face with great dark eyes and a wealth of dusky hair. The old self-conscious, dissatisfied expression was gone. It was a happy face that smiled back at her. It had been nearly a year since Lloyd had had a letter from Eugenia. She had written from the school near Paris that her father was on his way over from America to join her and take her home immediately after her graduation. Lloyd had sent a reply addressed to her cousin Carl's office, but had heard nothing more.

Thinking that the other photograph was her cousin Carl's, Lloyd unwrapped it, wondering if he had changed as much as Eugenia. To her surprise, it was not a middle-aged man she saw, with gray moustache and kindly tired eyes. It was the handsome boyish face of a stranger, yet so startlingly familiar that she looked at it with a puzzled frown.

"Why should Eugenia be sending me this?" she thought. "And where have I seen that man befoah?" Then, "Phil Tremont!" she exclaimed aloud the next instant. "That's who it reminds me of. It is almost exactly like him, only it is oldah-looking, and the nose isn't quite like his."

She turned the picture over. There on the back was written in Eugenia's hand the word Venice, and a date underneath the name, Stuart Tremont.

"Phil's brother!" gasped Lloyd, in astonishment. "How strange that she should know him!"

Tearing open the envelope lying on the bench beside her, Lloyd unfolded a twenty-page letter from Eugenia, written on thin blue foreign correspondence paper. Before her glance had travelled half-way down the second page, she gave another gasp, and sat staring at an underscored sentence in open-mouthed amazement. Then, never waiting to gather up the other letters which fluttered into the grass at her feet, as she sprang up, she rushed off toward the house as hard as she could go, waving Eugenia's letter in one hand and the photographs in the other.

"Mothah!" she called, as she reached the end of the avenue. She was tripping over her long skirt, and scattering hairpins at every step, as her reckless flight sent her hair tumbling down over her shoulders.

"Mothah!" she shrieked again, as she stumbled up the porch steps.

"Here in my room, dear," came the answer from an upper window. Falling all over herself in her undignified haste, Lloyd tore up the stairs. A final tangling of skirts sent her headlong into her mother's room, where she half-fell in a breathless, laughing heap, and sat at Mrs. Sherman's feet with her hair almost hiding her eager face.

"Guess what's happened!" she demanded, breathlessly. "*Eugenia is engaged! And to Phil Tremont's brother Stuart!*"

Then she sat enjoying her mother's surprise, which was almost as great as her own. "And she isn't much moah than eighteen," Lloyd exclaimed, rocking back and forth on the floor, with her arms clasped around her knees, while her mother examined the pictures.

"She looks twenty at least in this picture," answered Mrs. Sherman, "even more than that. Eugenia was always old for her years. If you remember, she was wearing long dresses when we left her the summer we were in Europe together."

"Yes, but it doesn't seem possible that Eugenia is old enough to be *married*," insisted Lloyd. "I can hardly believe it is true."

She sat staring dreamily out of the window until a slight breeze fluttering the sheets of paper still clutched in her fingers reminded her that she had read only two of the twenty pages.

"Heah is what she says about it," began Lloyd, reading slowly, for the closely written sheets were hard to decipher.

"'I know you are going to wonder how it all came about, so I'll begin at the beginning. Last summer papa came on to Paris in time for Commencement. He was so pleased because I took first honours, when he hadn't expected me to take any, that he said he would do as fathers sometimes did in fairy-tales,—grant me three wishes, anything in reason; for he had had an unusually successful year and could well afford it.

"'Well, I thought and thought, but I couldn't think of anything I really wanted, as I just had an entire new outfit in clothes, so I told him finally I'd like to stop in London long enough to have a tailor make me a riding-habit, and I'd think of the other two wishes sometime during the year. So we went to London. Papa is such an old darling, and we've grown to be real chums. After the tailor had taken my measure, we drove to our banker's for the mail, and who should papa meet there but Doctor Tremont, an American physician whom he knew years ago when they were young men. They belonged to the same college fraternity.

"'They forgot all about poor little me, sitting over in the corner of the office, and stood and talked about old times, and asked each other about Tom, Dick, and Harry, until I was thoroughly tired of waiting. But after awhile the handsomest young man came into the room, and Doctor Tremont introduced him to papa as his oldest son, Stuart. Then they remembered my humble existence, and papa brought them both over to me. In about two minutes we all felt as if we had known each other always.

"'Doctor Tremont said he had had a very hard winter in Berlin, making some study of microbes with a noted scientist,—I forget his name. He said Stuart had been closely confined also (he was taking a medical course), and they were off on a hard-earned holiday. They were going coaching up in the lake regions, first in England, then in Scotland, and maybe later would go over to the Isle of Skye.

"'Would you believe it, before we left the bank, Doctor Tremont had persuaded papa that he needed a vacation also, and almost in no time it was arranged that we should join them on their coaching trip. We had a perfectly ideal time, and Stuart and I got to be the best of friends. We corresponded all summer and fall after that. I didn't expect to see him again for two years, because he intended to stay abroad until he had finished his medical course. But along in the winter papa's health broke down, and the doctor told him he must keep away from business for a year, and ordered him to Baden-Baden for the water.

"'He was horribly ill after we got there, and I was so frightened and inexperienced that I thought he was going to die, and I telegraphed for Doctor Tremont. It isn't far from Berlin, you know, as we Americans count distances. But the doctor had gone to Paris for several weeks, and Stuart came at once in his place. Of course he wasn't an experienced physician like his father, but he was such a comfort, for he cheered papa up so much, and assured us that the doctor in charge was doing everything that his father could do. And he helped nurse papa, and boosted up my spirits mightily, and was so dear and thoughtful and considerate that, when he went away, I felt as if the bottom had dropped out of everything. You can't imagine how kind and lovely he was all that week. Papa fairly swore by him.

"'We wrote to each other every week after he went back to Berlin. Early this March papa and I went down into Italy. We shifted about from place to place,— Naples, Sorrento, Rome, Florence, and finally to Venice. I don't know why I never wrote to you those days. You were often in my thoughts, but you know how it is when one is constantly on the wing.

"'I used to wish daily that Stuart could be with us. He is the most satisfactory of travelling companions, but I didn't know how very much I wished it until one day in Venice. Papa was asleep at the hotel, and I was so lonely that I started out by myself to explore. I left a message with the clerk that I had gone to vespers at Saint Mark's Cathedral. There was a crowd of tourists in the square in front of the cathedral, feeding the pigeons. Hearing their English speech after so many months of nothing but foreign tongues made me homesick. In the whole plaza, no one but myself seemed to be alone. They were walking in groups or couples, and everybody seemed so gay and happy that I was glad to cross over to the cathedral to get out of sight.

"'The vesper service had just begun, and I stood inside the door listening to the chanting of the monks' voices, and getting more homesick every moment. Just as the tears were ready to brim over, I looked up, and there in the dim light beside me stood Stuart. I thought I must be dreaming, but it was a very happy dream, for I felt that I could never be homesick or unhappy again when he looked down and smiled.

"'I couldn't believe that I was awake and that he was really there, until we got outside the cathedral and he began to talk. Then he told me that he had gone to the hotel, and they had given him the message I had left for papa. It never occurred to me to wonder why he had come to Venice. It just seemed so natural and lovely that he should be there that I never even asked him why. He called a gondola, and we got in and went drifting down the canals under the bridges and past the old palaces, with the sunset turning everything around us to rose-colour and gold. Oh, I can't begin to tell you how perfectly heavenly it all was. There was a new moon in the sky when we turned back to the hotel, and, though Stuart *hadn't* proposed in the same way that Laurie did to Amy in "Little Women," he had told me why he came so far to find me, and I liked his way a great deal better than Laurie's.

"'Wasn't it all romantic? Papa was awfully surprised to see him, and nearly as glad as I, and I told him that now I'd claim the other wishes he had promised me at Commencement, and take the two in one. I wished that he would say yes to the question Stuart had come to ask him. Dear old dad, he always keeps his promises, so he said yes after awhile. After Stuart had explained that he didn't intend to ask him to give me up. When he finishes his medical course here next year, he has a position waiting for him near New York City. We're to have a little home on the Hudson, and papa is to live with us. So is Doctor Tremont, when he gets through with his microbe business. We are done with hotels for ever.

"'I cannot remember ever having had a home, Lloyd. I have always lived either in a hotel or at boarding-school. And Stuart says the only one he can remember distinctly was the one presided over by his great-aunt Patricia, and she never did understand boys. This summer I shall spend with papa in Switzerland. He is about well now. Then in the fall, when he goes back to New York, I am going to a delightful school near Berlin which I have just heard of. It is a school where none but the daughters of the German nobility are received, as a rule. They make an exception sometimes in the case of Americans like myself. There they are taught all the housewifely arts that delight a good frau's soul. Don't laugh at me, Lloyd. I'm going to learn how to broil and brew and conduct a well-regulated establishment from attic to cellar.

"'A year from this June, Cousin Jack and Cousin Elizabeth are to bring you and Betty on to New York to be my bridesmaids. I'd love to have Joyce, too, if it were possible for her to leave home. She has been so good to Stuart's brother Phil. Isn't it strange that we should all be so linked together? I'd like to have all of you girls that I met at your never-to-be-forgotten house-party. That was where I had my first taste of a real home, and found out that there is something to live for besides the things that money can buy.

"'I have looked so often lately at my little Tusitala ring. I have been a better girl because of that ring, Lloyd, and I intend it shall be the inspiration of all my married life,—to help me leave a road of the loving heart in the memory of every one around me.

"'I wish everybody in the world could be as happy as I am. I am sending Stuart's picture, so that you can see for yourself what a fine, splendid fellow you are to have for a cousin some day. Give my love to your father and mother and Betty, and do write soon and tell me that you are glad.

"'Your loving cousin,
"'Eugenia.'"

Lloyd looked up from the reading of the letter, wondering what sort of an expression she would find on her mother's face. To her surprise, it was one of approval, and there were tears in her eyes.

"Poor motherless child!" said Mrs. Sherman, softly. "I shall write to her to-day. I don't approve of early marriages, but Eugenia has always been more mature than most girls of her age, and she does need a home sadly. The care and pleasure of one will develop her character in a way that nothing else will. Let me see. She will be nearly twenty next June. Yes, I have no doubt but that, with this next year's training in housekeeping which she intends to take, she will be far better fitted for home-making than many an older woman."

"And may Betty and I be bridesmaids?" interrupted Lloyd, eagerly, a starlike expectancy shining in her eyes.

Mrs. Sherman considered a moment, then answered, slowly: "There is no reason why you should not be, so long as you are willing to go as little maids, and not young ladies. I am very jealous for your girlhood, Lloyd dear. I must guard against anything that would shorten it in the least. Mother's baby must not grow up too fast."

"I don't want to grow up fast, honestly!" cried Lloyd, scrambling to her feet and tripping over the long skirts again as she threw her arms around her mother's neck. "I'm not dignified enough yet to fit yoah dresses, and my hair simply won't stay up. Sweet sixteen doesn't seem half as old when you really get there as you think that it is going to. I'll do my hair down and weah short skirts as long as you want me to, but, oh, I'm so glad that I'm going to be a bridesmaid! It will be *such* fun. I must write to Betty this minute to tell her that you are willing."

That night Lloyd sat before her dressing-table again, this time with the new photographs propped up in front of her. Stuart's picture almost seemed to bring Phil before her eyes, and for a moment, instead of the familiar walls of her room, she saw the moonlighted desert, and smelled the orange-blossoms, and heard a strong young voice ringing out across the silence of the sandy cactus plains:

"Till the sun grows cold,
And the stars are old,
And the leaves of the Judgment
Book unfold."

"Wouldn't it be strange," she thought, "if he were really the one written for me in the stars, as Betty said in the beginning, and that we should meet at Eugenia's wedding again, and that some day, a long time after, I should find that he is the prince? But it couldn't be Phil," she said to herself after another glance. "He doesn't measuah up to Papa Jack's yardstick. Neithah does Malcolm now, for that mattah," she mused, with her chin in her hand. "Jack Ware might, or Rob, but they seem moah like brothahs than anything else, and would not fit my ideal of a prince at all."

"'NO MATTAH WHAT LIES AHEAD . . . I'LL NOT DISAPPOINT THEM'"

"'As the falcon's feathahs fit the falcon,'" she quoted, dreamily. "It would have to be some strangah that I've nevah yet seen, to do that. Or, maybe Mammy

Easter's grandmothah was right when she read my fortune in the teacups. Maybe I'll be an old maid. I wish I knew. I *wish* I knew!"

She peered wistfully into the mirror, as if she half-expected to see a shadowy hand stretch out of its dim background, and lift the veil of the future to her eager gaze. "The thoughts of youth are long, long thoughts." Lloyd's flew back to Eugenia's romance for an instant, then drifted far beyond the two in the gondola, with the Venetian sunset turning all their little world to rose-colour and gold.

One is a mariner at sixteen, sailing toward an undiscovered country, with seaweed and driftwood on the crest of every wave beginning to whisper, "Land ahead." Toward the dim outline of that untried shore, Lloyd drifted now in her reverie.

"I *wish* I could know what the next sixteen yeahs hold for me," she whimpered. "I hope it will be something bettah than I could choose for myself. Mothah and Papa Jack expect so much of me."

Then her glance fell on the unfinished rosary, and, picking up the string of tiny pearls, she looped it around her throat, and faced the girl in the mirror with resolute eyes.

"No mattah what lies ahead," she said, bravely, "I'll not disappoint them. I'll keep the tryst!"

THE END.

www.ingramcontent.com/pod-product-compliance
Lightning Source LLC
Chambersburg PA
CBHW061534050726
47593CB00002B/785